…abharlann Chontae Luimni
…CK COUNTY LIB…

Yaba Badoe is a Ghanian-British documentary film-maker and journalist. A graduate of King's College, Cambridge, she worked as a civil servant in Ghana before becoming a general trainee with the BBC. She has taught in Spain and Jamaica and is, at present, Visiting Scholar at the Institute of African Studies at the University of Ghana, where she is completing a documentary film – *The Witches of Gambaga*. Her short stories have been published in *Critical Quarterly* and in *African Love Stories*, an anthology edited by Ama Ata Aidoo.

YABA BADOE

True Murder

WITHDRAWN FROM STOCK

VINTAGE BOOKS
London

Published by Vintage 2009

2 4 6 8 10 9 7 5 3 1

Copyright © Yaba Badoe 2009

Yaba Badoe has asserted her right under the Copyright, Designs and Patents Act 1988 to be identified as the author of this work

This book is sold subject to the condition that it shall not, by way of trade or otherwise, be lent, resold, hired out, or otherwise circulated without the publisher's prior consent in any form of binding or cover other than that in which it is published and without a similar condition, including this condition, being imposed on the subsequent purchaser

First published in Great Britain in 2009 by Jonathan Cape

Vintage
Random House, 20 Vauxhall Bridge Road,
London SW1V 2SA

www.vintage-books.co.uk

Addresses for companies within The Random House Group Limited can be found at: www.randomhouse.co.uk/offices.htm

The Random House Group Limited Reg. No. 954009

A CIP catalogue record for this book is available from the British Library

ISBN 9780099523321

The Random House Group Limited supports The Forest Stewardship Council (FSC), the leading international forest certification organisation. All our titles that are printed on Greenpeace approved FSC certified paper carry the FSC logo. Our paper procurement policy can be found at: www.rbooks.co.uk/environment

Printed and bound in Great Britain by
CPI Bookmarque, Croydon CR0 4TD

To my mother, 'Ago' Fadoa:

1

Even now, after all these years, I can hardly bear to look in a mirror. If I had my way, I would shatter every mirror in the house rather than glimpse my reflection unawares. Yet it's not my looks that bother me. I have been told I am like my mother, beautiful some might say, with eyes as bright as a cat's, skin the colour of midnight. I have a long face, generous lips and folds around my neck, which suggest I was born gasping, adorned with the coiled necklaces of an African fertility doll.

I used to think that if I could only trust my instincts I would be able to catch the glint in my eyes and smile. But ever since Polly, I haven't been able to trust myself again. After all, if I'd behaved appropriately, saying the right words at the right time, keeping silent when necessary, the past would have turned out differently. I would never have gone to that school, I wouldn't have met Polly; I wouldn't have gone home with her; the trunks in the attic of the manor house where she lived might have remained sealed for ever, and the chain of events we unleashed by opening them might have been avoided. Perhaps if we had never met, Polly would still be alive.

I would like to believe I've recovered from the anger that almost engulfed me when she died; but until I can contain my rage it's safer for everyone if I live on my own in a room without mirrors. When I look into them, I am bruised by memories of Polly. She didn't see what I see, the ghosts eyeing my reflection. She didn't tap the hidden secrets of mirrors to contemplate the horror they reveal.

I'd like to put her behind me, once and for all, instead of dwelling on her day after day by hiding from my image. Perhaps if I can appease her by remembering the past, recounting the detail of what happened between us, I'll be able to look at myself. Then, instead of seeing Polly glaring at me, I'll see my own face again. If it were simply an effort of will, I might have done this years ago and the spell would have long been broken. As it is, those events I lived through have captured a part of me; to free myself I can no longer avoid them. Perhaps if I set them out in an orderly fashion I can begin to understand what happened and how events conspired to make me what I am. Perhaps then I will be able to relinquish this fear I carry with me everywhere. And through making this offering, like a libation, and asking my precursors to listen sympathetically as I piece together the past, perhaps I shall reclaim myself and be at ease once again.

2

Until recently, whenever I thought of Polly, I remembered the last time I saw her alive. She was leaning out of an upstairs window of Graylings, wearing a scarlet dressing-gown that set her unruly curls alight. Beside her, with a hand on her shoulder, was her mother, Isobel. It was Christmas Eve and I was with a group of carol singers from Sunday School. We were singing carols in aid of the World Wildlife Fund and when we had sung the final chorus of 'The Holly and the Ivy' I shook the box of donations I was carrying. Polly waved at me, shouting my name, inviting me in. Then she ran downstairs with her mother and opened the front door.

She led me into her house, the other singers trampling in behind. She took my arms and pulled me close. Her blanket of golden hair fell against my face; I felt the pulse of her breath as she warmed my body with hers. Even now, years later, whenever I am out in the cold over Christmas, my cheeks numb, my feet frozen; whenever I hear the melody of half-pagan English songs, I glimpse a flash of gold and scarlet waving at a window and, catching my breath, holding it as I remember how tightly she drew me to her, I try to grasp Polly once again.

*

We were not always good friends: 'Best friends. Friends for ever,' as she put it. We weren't always blood sisters, our lives flowing through each other's veins. To begin with I was wary of her, sniffing her out as a cat might an unfamiliar species.

Polly Venus arrived at school nine months after me. When I first met her she exuded the arrogance of a bird of prey and the seductive gaze of a gazelle. I didn't much like her and if Major Derby hadn't asked me to look after her, I would have avoided Polly, sticking by Beth, who was my closest friend at the time. But Major Derby, who with his wife owned and ran the prep school we attended, asked me to take care of Polly. He thought I should come out of myself more and get involved with my surroundings. To begin with, Beth had looked out for me, and knowing how strange it is being a new girl – like a snail that, having lost its shell, spends all its time looking for it, leaving a trail of tears everywhere – I didn't have much choice but to be civil to Polly.

The Derbys were my legal guardians. 'We're *in loco parentis,*' they used to say when they looked after me over the school holidays. I didn't mind for the most part, but I hated the start of a new term when I saw other children with their parents and was forced to bear witness to tender gestures of farewell. I avoided them by hiding in the school playroom: a long room with a radiator running down one side and a Victorian rocking-horse in the corner. I was sitting against the radiator, an open book on my lap, when Major Derby put his head round the door. He was a bear of a man with the long, loping stride of an Irish wolfhound. He smiled at me: 'The new girl's arrived, Ajuba.'

The expression on my face must have betrayed my reluctance to do what was required of me, for he added: 'She'll be needing you soon, and you remember what it was like, don't you, sweetie?'

I did. I slammed the book shut, aware that he was appealing to the part of me that struggled to overcome an ingrained shyness and attempted to laugh at other people's jokes.

Major Derby and his wife were ardent conservationists and often told us that they wanted to leave the world a better place for having passed through it. Nothing pleased them more, they said, than knowing that the children in their care shared the values they believed in: a respect for nature and all living things. I didn't much care for their love of what they termed 'outdoor activities', which entailed trudging through the countryside in inclement weather, but I knew instinctively that the Derbys' mission was also to conserve the good qualities they saw in each of us, nurturing us until we flourished at their school. His appeal to my better nature made me not want to let Major Derby down.

I ran upstairs to Exe, the dormitory where I slept with the other girls in Seniors. I rushed in, throwing the book on my bed, and saw Polly Venus for the first time.

She was standing beside her father, a tall, tousle-haired man who was deep in conversation with Maria Richardson's mother. According to Maria, another inmate of Exe, her mother was a famous journalist who campaigned on behalf of downtrodden people everywhere. From starving children in Africa to homeless vagrants in London, Emily Richardson waved a flag on their behalf, trumpeting good causes. From the way she wrapped herself in conversation with Polly's father, I couldn't help wondering if Emily Richardson had much time for anything other than herself.

Both adults seemed oblivious to Maria's clumsy attempt

at befriending the new girl by offering her a Mars bar. From the look on Polly's face, she was either bored or filled with such disdain for Maria that she could barely bring herself to glance at her. Evidently, Polly Venus didn't like chocolate.

'Hi,' I said. I told her my name, adding gloomily, 'I'm meant to look after you.'

The new girl was dazzling, with a sleek veneer of self-assurance that made it apparent that she was conscious of her long-limbed beauty and knew how to use it. Her eyes were a flash of kingfisher-blue and when she looked at me, sizing me up, it was as if a blaze of colour had woken me for the first time at school. Polly gazed at me, remarking in a dry, American accent: 'What makes you think I need looking after?'

New girls weren't supposed to be cocky. They were supposed to be downcast and despondent, as I had been.

'I don't have to look after you if you don't want me to but Major Derby says I should because you're new. Maria can do it if you'd rather.'

I hoped she would prefer Maria to show her around; but Polly sighed deeply and said: 'No, thanks. I guess you'll do.'

Her lack of enthusiasm reflected my own, yet I was determined to make an effort. 'Is that your dad?' I asked.

'Yeah. He's a foreign correspondent.'

'Are you foreign as well?'

'Kind of. We've been living in Washington for ever. I didn't want to come here. I don't think I'm the kind of kid that suits boarding school. But, hey, adults, huh? They have no idea how to handle pre-teenagers.'

I didn't have a clue what a pre-teenager was. But the fact that Polly saw herself as foreign, and didn't want to be at boarding school in England, helped me empathise: 'I know what you mean,' I mumbled.

Maria didn't, for she said very loudly, 'Don't take any notice of Ajuba, Polly. You're going to have a wonderful time. Josh and I simply love it here. That's why Mummy told Peter and Isobel about the school. Mummy knew we'd be the best of friends. Mummy, isn't that true?'

Josh was Maria's older brother. Vaguely aware of her daughter's intervention, Emily Richardson grunted in Maria's direction. Her eyes remained fixed on Peter Venus. They both had their diaries open and were jotting down numbers, suggesting possible dates to meet. The crackle of electricity between them, the intensity of her absorption in him, reminded me of the honey-eyed rabbits we sometimes watched on the top lawn at school: a doe thrusting her tail in a buck's face until she got his full attention. It was what Aunt Rose, my mother's sister, called Hanky-Panky: the activity my father indulged in with his girlfriends. 'Men are helpless creatures when it comes to women,' Aunt Rose said. 'A woman has to be her own watchdog, Ajuba. Never forget it.'

I hadn't forgotten. I recognised, even then, that the frequency with which Emily Richardson tossed back her hair, teasing the silver stud in her ear with nicotine-stained finger, was because she had allowed her watchdog to fall asleep.

Perhaps mindful of her father's charm, Polly responded with rigid indifference when it wasn't directed at her; she appeared contemptuous of her surroundings, staring blankly into space to avoid my eyes, but I sensed that she was listening to his every word.

Intrigued, I asked: 'What does a foreign correspondent do?'

Polly sniffed, 'He writes for a newspaper, silly.'

'Oh, like Maria's mother. Is he fond of victims as well?'

'No way! Politics is his thing. He gets to talk to powerful people.'

'Like who?'

She didn't have a chance to enlighten me, because the adults were preparing to leave. They promised to meet up in London and a hint of panic unsettled Polly's face as she clasped her father's hand, rubbing a cheek against his jacket. He stroked her hair and kissed her, reassuring her that all would be well; if she needed to talk she had his London numbers and Isobel was only a few miles away. For a moment Polly clung to her father, her arms draped around his waist. I thought she was going to cry and that when he had gone I would have to console a new girl who thought so little of me she'd dismissed me as silly. I needn't have worried. Polly didn't shrink into herself as I had done to keep body and soul together when my father left me with the Derbys in Devon. Instead, gathering strength from her father's caresses, his mention of his best friend Barnaby whom he'd met at school, Polly inhaled deeply and appeared to expand. She straightened her back and stepped away from her father, before escorting him out of Exe with as much dignity as Mrs Derby had had when seeing my own father off. When she returned with no trace of redness in her eyes, I was impressed. So much so, that I set aside my reservations and offered to help her unpack her trunk.

I soon realised that Polly Venus, meticulous in the ordering of her possessions, the placing of colour-coordinated knickers and clothes in the appropriate drawers and wardrobes, was much more organised than I ever would be. Moreover, she possessed a treasure trove of comics, which she stashed in the locker by her bed. I was flipping through one of them, beguiled and bewildered by its lurid contents, its glossy depiction of a subterranean world of which I had no knowledge, when Beth Bradshaw ran in with her dogs.

No animals were allowed in dormitories, not even Maria's hamster, which was kept in the school stables. But the Bradshaws went everywhere with Whiskey and Soda, their black labradors, and whenever Beth returned to school, for the first half-hour Bradshaw rules, which encouraged mayhem and excessive high spirits, prevailed. There was vigorous barking and the thumping of tails followed by imperious, futile commands of: 'Down, dog! Silly dog! Oh, how I love you!' Beth was passionate about animals. She seemed more distressed saying goodbye to her dogs than to her mother, a fat, rumbustious woman I rather liked.

'You'll come and see us again soon, won't you, Ajuba?' Mrs Bradshaw rarely spoke in a normal voice; she bellowed as if everyone around her was hard of hearing. They were a noisy family and I had learned how to shout and laugh very loudly when I stayed on their farm in the holidays.

Falling into the Bradshaw groove, chameleon-like, I yelled in my best British accent: 'Yes, please!'

'That's my girl!' Mrs Bradshaw waved goodbye, while Beth kneeled to kiss her dogs, their tongues washing her lips with saliva. Polly glanced at me, raising an eyebrow in disgust, a sentiment I shared.

As I was the only girl in Seniors not to have joined the Wildlife Rangers, it was well known among my peers that my feelings for animals were disengaged at best: a fatal aberration of character that occasionally led to discord with Beth. Dark-haired and green-eyed, she was wholeheartedly English in her capacity to be moved by the plight of animals. Her features constantly changed; she would be laughing one moment and then in despair the next over some injustice or other involving seals or whales. Indeed, she had once told me that if God existed she was convinced he was a whale.

The raising of the Venus eyebrow, a drawbridge retreating into a castle, warned me that a skirmish lay ahead.

Beth launched the opening salvo simply by being herself. Instead of family photographs on her locker, she arranged portraits of her pets: her ponies, Brillo and Flash, her dogs and her cat, Spider.

Polly remarked wryly: 'I see you like animals.'

We were sitting on Beth's bed with Maria sampling chunks of homemade fudge that Mrs Bradshaw had prepared for the start of the new term.

'Don't *you* like animals?' Beth retorted.

'I guess they are kind of cute.'

'Cute? Cute? Ajuba, she said animals are cute! Animals are magnificent!' Beth exclaimed. 'They're wonderful! They're much better than we are. They're superior to humans in every way imaginable.'

'Oh, yes, cockroaches and rattlesnakes and rats are much better,' Maria interjected.

'They're not animals,' retorted Beth.

'Rats are too,' said Maria.

'Rats are vermin. Like hamsters.'

'Godfrey isn't vermin. He's mine,' Maria wailed.

'Makes no difference. Vermin is vermin and that's that!'

Polly raised her eyebrow again. It was a facial tic I would see often in the coming weeks as, observing Beth's natural exuberance and then catching my eye, she would smile in gentle derision of my first friend at school. The inference was that Beth was childish.

Being party to the twitching eyebrow made me uncomfortable. In a way that I didn't then comprehend, my diffidence and sensibility as an outsider made me a useful ally in Polly's ascendancy in Exe and, once Exe had been conquered, its inmates subjugated, Seniors, our class. While Maria's eagerness to become the new girl's 'best friend' rendered her peripheral to Polly's campaign, Beth, through no fault of her own other than feeling more at home at school than the rest of us, became the target of Polly's opprobrium.

In those early days a glance from Polly, followed by scarcely audible put-downs such as 'Jeez', 'What a loser!', 'Is that girl *totally* insane?' underlined by the raised eyebrow, punctured Beth's enthusiasm, leaving a flicker of surprise on her face. She seemed unaware that the lightness of spirit and good humour which made her a force to be reckoned with in Seniors were the very qualities that Polly resented.

Embarrassed by my inadvertent collusion with the Venus eyebrow, yet half in thrall to the new girl already, I tried to find a way to accommodate Polly's presence in our lives. At the end of our first week of sardonic 'Hallos' and 'Is she on the same *planet* as us?' I begged Beth to talk about an incident that was part of Exe folklore.

Laughing the irrepressible Bradshaw laugh, Beth regaled us with our favourite tale. One Friday on a winter afternoon, when the Derbys were out, she'd responded to a dare from Joshua Richardson. Joshua and his friends had placed bets against her being able to climb the highest tree in the Washing Line Wood – an enormous beech nicknamed Methuselah. Tucking her skirt in her knickers and licking the palms of her hands for luck, Beth hauled herself up. After a climb of over half an hour, she reached the top and tossed her knickers down, shouting obscenities at the boys below. She won five pounds in total, a pound from every boy in Joshua's gang. Beth shared the money with me.

'Cool,' Polly murmured, genuinely impressed. 'Boys are such *suckers*.'

On this point at least all three of us agreed. We were of an age when boys left us indifferent; we thought them stupid, clumsy; a waste of time and space. So much so, that our antipathy forged a sense of solidarity between us: a shared knowledge of our innate superiority, which extended to Maria as well.

By the end of the second week of term, Polly's charisma, enhanced by an American glamour that set her apart, was drawing us into her private world. She possessed a macabre interest in murder. She talked about it incessantly, giving vivid descriptions of murder scenes: exactly how the crime had been committed. And when we were primed, desperate to know how a culprit had been punished and moral order restored, she would change tack. Instead of satisfying our lust for retribution, she'd start describing in detail the state of decomposition a corpse had reached by the time it was discovered.

In this, her abiding passion, her fascination with violent death, I was a helpless accomplice. The pile of comics I had rummaged through on her first day at school, and continued to mull over whenever the opportunity presented itself, were the source of Polly's hold over us, especially me. She was an enthusiastic subscriber to *True Murder*, an American monthly made up of features and comic strips of the world's most sensational killings. The magazines, thick and glossy, opened up a landscape of perversity depicted in primary colours. It was my willingness to enter this underground world, delving into the shadows of Polly's imagination, that changed our lives irrevocably.

One evening before Lights Out, when Polly was halfway through her daily ritual of brushing her hair one hundred times, I became so aroused by the salacious description of the *True Murder* case I was scrutinising that I began reading aloud. I knew the magazine was one the Derbys would describe as unsavoury, but I didn't care. Polly's fascination had rubbed off on me and I wanted to entice Maria and Beth into the terrifying terrain of the criminally insane. Sure enough, soon they were captivated as well.

'"He seemed an ordinary guy. He held down a regular job and he was liked. But Jeffrey Dahmer, the mass murderer of Milwaukee, killed at least seventeen people before he was caught."' I paused for dramatic effect; then, realising what Jeffrey Dahmer had done, I whispered in horror, 'And he ate them.'

I flung the magazine down, nauseated. *True Murder* was not always as ghoulish as the Brothers Grimm, but what gripped me, filling me with revulsion and secret pleasure, was that what I read had actually occurred. The stories weren't make-believe. They were devastatingly real. Beth and Maria lunged for the magazine and Beth, being taller, elbowed Maria out of the way. Beneath a photograph of an intelligent-looking young man, she found where I'd left off, and continued: '"The sixty-million-dollar question is: how did this regular guy become the Monster of Milwaukee?"'

Beth looked at Polly. The only audible answer was the steady counting of brushstrokes, so she examined Dahmer's portrait instead. 'He looks ordinary,' she said, astonished.

'That's the way the cookie crumbles.' A knowing smile played on Polly's lips as she came to the end of her pre-teen grooming and tied her hair up in a knot.

'What d'you mean?' Maria asked.

'You guys are something else. Do I have to explain everything to you?' Before anyone could protest, Polly went on: 'Listen, most murderers are people you know. You marry them, you eat with them. They're family. Right?'

We nodded, though why we didn't know: we had never thought along these lines before. Tiny beads of sweat started pricking my armpits as the wooden floorboards of Exe, the ground we had walked every day without mishap, began to shift, tilting us towards a precipice. Relishing our stunned silence, Polly slipped into bed. When she was settled, an elbow on her pillow, she continued our education: the facts of life as she understood them after a year's subscription to the magazine.

'Take those kids from California, the Menendez boys,' she began. 'They whack their parents and when they're caught, they say their pop abused them as kids. Neat, huh?'

'Couldn't they have called Childline?' asked Maria.

Polly raised an eyebrow. 'They were way too old for that.'

'You're never too old to ask for help.' Maria had learnt her mother's mantras well.

'Listen, people don't go for counselling when they want to whack someone. They do it. Period.'

'Is that what Americans always do?' I asked. 'Don't you people have any respect at all? How could they kill the people who brought them into the world?'

'Oh, yeah! And nobody gets murdered in Ghana, do they?' Polly's riposte silenced me. The more I thought about it, the more I realised that Polly's stay in Washington, DC, a city she claimed was the most violent in the world, made her and Americans very different to other humans.

'Anyone you know get whacked?' Polly asked the question of no one in particular.

Beth shook her head sadly, and then, remembering a great-aunt butchered by bandits in China, she revealed the little she knew. It had been during the Chinese Civil War and it had happened on a train. Her great-great-aunt Harriet had been a formidable Anglican missionary; but ignorant of the details of her demise, Beth stumbled at yet another fence Polly had placed before her.

'How about you, Aj?'

I remembered a distant relative, a military man my mother had once spoken of: 'A long time ago, my mother's cousin was murdered. The Army executed him when they seized power. But they couldn't kill him with ordinary bullets.'

Polly's eyes lit up. 'How come?'

'He'd done nothing wrong, you see, so God was on his side. The bullets bounced off his skin.' I looked at my roommates, preparing to change my story if they sneered. Their silence encouraged me to proceed. 'In the end they killed him with a special bullet. A bullet made from Ashanti gold.'

Polly's eyebrow went up again.

'It's possible. It could've happened that way.' Quixotic in temperament, Beth was always inclined to give me the benefit of the doubt.

'Oh, yeah? Don't tell me you believe in the tooth fairy as well?'

If Polly was unconvinced, Maria, whose father had been killed in Angola, wasn't so sure. 'Africa's a strange place,' she said. 'All sorts of weird things happen there.'

'And if you believe in God, anything's possible,' I added emphatically.

Polly gave a snort of derision. 'Get real,' she said. Gathering her knees to her chest, she was suddenly serious. It seemed that now the inadequacy of our shared experience had been fully exposed, she was ready to reveal what she'd wanted to all along. 'When I lived in Washington, my best friend Jacinth Ellberg got whacked. I saw her dead body.'

The horrified expression on our faces seemed to be what Polly had craved all along. She now had our undivided attention. Savouring her power, she told her story with the consummate control of a leading actress in a slowly unfolding melodrama.

'It was the Fourth of July and Jacinth was expecting me. When I got to her house, cops were everywhere. They wouldn't let me in, so I tell them I'm invited and I've got to see Jacinth. Then this big guy – a lieutenant, I guess – tries to tell me something, but he can't. He's crying and soon they're all crying. They say Jacinth's dead.'

'How did she die?' I asked.

'Mr Ellberg went nuts and murdered them all with a shotgun. Jacinth, and his wife. He even whacked the dog.'

'The dog as well?' Beth was horrified.

'Yeah. Frisbee, a red setter.'

'Hang on a minute,' said Maria. 'How did you get to see her body? They wouldn't let me see Daddy when he died.'

For a moment, Polly looked Maria straight in the eye. She looked at all three of us, and then, as if finding it impossible to disclose what she'd experienced, she closed her eyes, opening them again slowly. 'I went home, came round a back way, and slipped through a side door. Jacinth was in the den, a blanket over her. I lifted the cover . . .'

'What did she look like?' I whispered.

'Like a doll. She looked like a broken doll in a red dress. She was sticky with blood.'

'Did you cry?'

'Only babies cry,' said Polly, shaking her head. 'I wept.'

3

From the moment she told us about Jacinth Ellberg, we were under Polly's spell. She had had contact with death; she had touched Jacinth's body. We all believed her. But of the three of us in Exe, Maria, the daughter of a journalist, was the most sceptical. And Polly dealt with her later.

The day after she told us about Jacinth, Polly dragged us deeper into her world by taking us down to the Glory Hole, a cellar where the Derbys kept wood for the winter. It was a dank corner of the school filled with old chairs, desks and Mrs Derby's gardening tools. We were going to play True Murder, a game of Polly's invention.

She led us down the steps: Joshua and Maria Richardson, Beth and me. I was reluctant to play, but Maria said that if I didn't, she wouldn't play either, so Polly said I had to.

The cellar was pitch-black. Rather than turning on the light, Polly made us fumble our way onto the floor and sit in a circle. When we could hear nothing but the rise and fall of our shallow breathing, she ordered us to turn on our torches.

'Cards,' she said. I handed her a stack of homemade cards she'd given me earlier. Polly shuffled the pack, dealing them out face down. One card would determine the murderer, another the victim. Once this was established and a mode of death selected, the pair were to find a hiding place before the others hunted them down.

'Turn them over.'

We did as we were told. Everyone had blank cards except for Beth and me. My card was of a skull and crossbones, Beth's of a bleeding heart pierced by a dagger. According to Polly's rules, this meant that I was to be the murderer and Beth my victim. Beside me, Beth giggled nervously. I wanted no part of it.

'Can't Josh do it? Please, Polly?'

One look from her and I was quiescent. Polly wasn't someone to be crossed lightly. She dealt out three more cards, all of them for me. With trembling fingers, I turned over the middle card. It was a hangman's noose. Polly smiled.

'Death by hanging,' she murmured, and then, turning to Joshua on her left, she whispered: 'Rope.'

Joshua brought out a thick coil of rope from under his sweater. He gave it to Polly, who flung it at me.

'Please, Polly, I don't want to . . .'

'We're giving you twenty minutes, then we're coming after you. Josh, set the timer.'

Flashing his torch on his wristwatch, Josh obeyed. Beth got up from the floor, taking the rope. I couldn't move.

'Scram,' Polly hissed. 'I said *scram*!'

Dragging me by my jumper, Beth pulled me out of the Glory Hole. Outside it was getting dark and my first thought was to run away, to lock myself in a lavatory with a book and leave them to their game. Beth could guess what I was thinking.

'It's only a game,' she said.

'But Mrs Derby said we shouldn't go out when it's getting dark.'

'If you spoil this, Ajuba Benson, Polly won't speak to you again. Nobody will.'

I was eleven years old and scared. But the prospect of being ostracised by my friends was more frightening than playing True Murder; so, against my better judgement, I capitulated. With the arrival of Polly Venus at the school, I was discovering that in life there are those who lead and those who follow; those who dominate and those who are dominated. I was too unsure of myself to do as I pleased; I simply wanted to fit in. After all, it was only a game we were playing; there was no good reason for the stab of terror I felt in my chest. I followed Beth at a steady jog.

We ran alongside the classrooms, skirted the walled garden, then ran down a bridle path into the shelter of a beech wood. It was early evening and the last of the day's sunlight glinted through the leaves on the trees. The ground was damp underfoot and as I jumped over bracken and stumps of rotting wood, the thick warm smell of mulch hit my nostrils.

Ahead of me, Beth stumbled on a clump of ferns. The coil of rope slung over her shoulder fell to the ground. Brushing down her jeans she picked it up again. I was ahead of her now, so she followed me. We were heading for Bouncy Town.

On one side of the mile-long drive to the school, between the tennis courts and the beech wood, was a stretch of dense rhododendron bushes we called Bouncy Town. We had created a playground within the dark interior of branches through which we leapt, slipping and sliding, any sense of danger cushioned by a thick blanket of decomposing leaves.

Ploughing through the undergrowth on our bellies, I led Beth to a hiding place I had recently discovered during one of my solitary explorations of the school grounds, on a day when Mrs Derby had forced me outside, saying my blood would go thin if I stayed by the radiator any longer. I went exploring and found this secret place, a womb-like shelter between two bushes, roofed by intertwining tendrils in flower. Petals of dying rhododendron blooms littered the ground like tired balloons at the end of a party.

'Brilliant,' Beth said when she saw it. 'They'll never find us here.'

Her eyes settled on the branch of an old oak tree jutting through the rhododendron bushes. From under her jumper, Beth produced the coil of rope, tied it loosely around her neck and started climbing.

'We're supposed to stay together,' I said.

'Imagine their faces! They'll get the shock of their lives when they see me.'

Swinging her legs up, she climbed higher into the bushes. 'If I tie myself up there,' she pointed to the oak tree, 'they'll think you've really murdered me!' She heaved herself through a tangle of rhododendrons and inched closer to her destination.

'It's not safe, Beth! This isn't part of the game.'

She laughed, giving me a daredevil grin. As she turned, her foot slipped on the moist bough of the rhododendron. She struggled to maintain her balance, but with a leg curled around the trunk while the other dangled, blindly searching for a foot hold, her shoulders twisted to one side and she slid. The thick yellow coil around her neck caught in the cleft of a branch, binding itself to it like a malevolent serpent. Beth tried to shake it loose by jerking her head, but she was unable to see how it was trapped, and her movements tightened the rope, fastening its hold on her neck and the shrub.

'Hold still!' The panic I saw on her face was mirrored in my voice. Her legs thrashed the rhododendron branches, bringing down twigs and petals. At any moment the branch supporting her could break. Controlling my terror as best as I could, I positioned myself beneath her feet. If the branch broke, or if she slipped, I would try to catch her. I could hear her gasping for breath. Suddenly, I heard a scream as she lost her grip on the canopy. There was a crash of snapping branches as she fell, the rope around her throat.

I fell under her weight. I clawed my way out from under her and cleared the debris of broken branches and leaves covering her body. Her face was pale, her eyes closed. I tore the rope from her neck, exposing a purple weal where it had cut into her flesh.

'Beth! Beth! Wake up!' I sobbed. She didn't stir. At last, blinded by tears, I got up and ran. What I feared most in the world was happening again.

In my panic I didn't feel the leaves whipping my hands and cheeks, the twigs and stems catching my clothes. All I was aware of was having to find an adult quickly. At last I scrambled out on to the school drive. Out of breath, I bent double, clutching my stomach. Then, filling my lungs with air, I bellowed for help. Joshua and Polly appeared round a corner of the drive.

'She's dead!' I cried. 'Beth's killed herself.'

They followed me to where she was lying. Immediately, Joshua took charge. He sent Polly for help and knelt beside Beth. I explained what had happened.

'She was playing. She didn't mean to. It was an accident.'

He took Beth's wrist, fumbling for a pulse.

'Do something!' I urged.

Josh's face was drained of colour; even his freckles looked

LIMERICK
00629398
COUNTY LIBRARY

pale against a lock of hair darkened by sweat. I realised that this boy, whose bullying command of the English language made me stumble over my words and whose cocky self-confidence sapped me of mine, was as scared as I was. I watched him pull up Beth's jumper, his jagged nails catching in the wool. He was going to listen to her heart, he said. His fingers trembled, struggling with the buttons of her shirt.

'Give her the Kiss of Life,' I shouted.

Just then a whimper escaped Beth, and tears of relief flooded my eyes. I started stroking her face. Her eyes opened. The flicker of fear that passed through them reminded me of my mother's eyes when they had opened, her head on my lap, almost a year ago.

We had been living, just the two of us, in a bare London bed-sit. We'd run away from Ghana to Lewisham. For a month we had survived on next to nothing because my mother wasn't well enough to hold down a job. I stopped going to school in order to look after her. But no matter how hard I tried, I couldn't help her. I couldn't calm her. I couldn't distract her from faces she said she saw in the mirror.

She talked to them constantly. She said they were multiplying. And as their numbers grew, the faces stepped out of the mirror into the room and Mama became incomprehensible, cursing them as they followed her back and forth, pacing the floor. She wouldn't stop walking, and occasionally I fell asleep while she walked.

One morning, I awoke to find her in a deep sleep. When I tried to rouse her, her eyes wouldn't open. Her hands were cold. I rubbed them. I stroked her unkempt hair. I covered her with a blanket. I caressed her cheek, until, after what seemed a long time, her eyes opened at last. They registered fear.

Seeing that familiar look in Beth's eyes, I remembered my helplessness in the face of my mother's suffering, and my tears of relief turned into something else. I couldn't stop crying.

'She's going to be all right,' Joshua assured me, bewildered.

I jammed a hand in my mouth to stem my tears, biting hard until it bled.

4

Whenever I thought of home, I would see our house in Accra and imagine myself playing barefoot on the veranda, chasing lizards. I would smell the aroma of my mother's cooking. Then, forgetting my shame at undressing with strangers, who marvelled at the paleness of my palms and fingered the stubborn resilience of my hair, forgetting the chilblains on my fingers and toes, I would luxuriate in the warmth of home.

Our house on Kuku Hill was decorated with ferns and bougainvillaea. My mother loved plants, so the garden as well as the house was her domain. It was full of fruit trees: guava, avocado, lime, and to the left, equidistant between the compound walls, was a mango tree that Mama had planted on the day she discovered she was pregnant with me. It had grown from the seed of a mango she had eaten that day, so she called it Ajuba's tree.

My parents met as students in London when my father was becoming a lawyer. My mother was training to be a nurse at Lewisham General Hospital. They are both Akan, so even though my father is Nzema and my mother a Fanti, they have more similarities than differences. Nevertheless, my father told me when I was old enough to hear his account of their marriage, that had he known what he later discovered about my mother's 'people', as he calls them, he would never have married her. According to him, a taint of madness runs through her family. It touched Mama's younger brother first; a boy who by all accounts was a brilliant scholar; and then it touched my mother.

Aunt Lila, Mama's eldest sister, tells a different story. I'm inclined to believe her version because it coincides with what I remember. She says it would have been better for both my parents if they'd never married; they brought out the worst in each other.

'As for your uncle, our younger brother,' Aunt Lila said when I met her for the first time as an adult, 'he should have known better than to summon up a Mami-Water. The foolish boy wanted help in passing his exams. As if he wasn't clever enough already, he called up a sea goddess near the lagoon where we lived. The next thing we know, Kweku has lost his wits. Believe me, Ajuba, there was nothing the doctors could do to make him sane again. He should have known better than to mess with juju.'

Aunt Lila resembles Mama. Their voices are the same and they have that laugh: a laugh which makes you want to join in. But my aunt is altogether bigger and broader than Mama ever was. Lila has had seven children.

I met my aunt through a cousin who was at school with one of her children. I was in my early twenties by then and living alone in London; after what happened, Pa severed contact with my mother's family completely. We met at my instigation at Basil Street Hotel in Knightsbridge. I had heard she was passing through London and, thinking it prudent to meet on neutral ground where few, if any, Ghanaians would be present, I invited her for tea. We recognised each other instantly. She was wearing a glorious orange and maroon boubou with matching headdress, a black cashmere shawl slung over her shoulders, and dark glasses. She might have been an African diva taking London by storm.

I took to Aunt Lila immediately; despite our long separation, she was reassuringly familiar. She kept touching my arm when she spoke, and whenever she wanted me to pay particular attention to something she was saying, she would hold my fingers with her hands, looking me straight in the eye.

'Your parents returned home,' she said, 'with all sorts of new-fangled ideas about family life. I remember Grace telling me that for a modern marriage to succeed, a husband and wife must unite in everything and concentrate on their children. Husband. Wife. Children. That's all. They came home worshipping the nuclear family. With that sort of attitude in Ghana, Ajuba, they might as well have worshipped the nuclear bomb! Of course it exploded in their faces. By the time Grace was having trouble with her pregnancies she'd forgotten how to confide in us. Her own sisters! Either that or she refused to. So when she became ill, my dear, your father took his pleasure elsewhere.'

Yet there were happy times on Kuku Hill. Christmas parties on the veranda, my father serving drinks to family and friends, everyone going home with one of Mama's cakes. And Mama laughing, always laughing: teasing Pa with smiles until he would take her hand, telling the world he was the luckiest man alive. And there was Aunt Rose, trailing behind Aunt Lila and her children, bearing gifts.

After I was born, both my parents wanted more children. Mama would have planted an orchard of mango trees if she'd had her way, but unfortunately she kept miscarrying. She would be happy for what seemed like a long time, then suddenly she'd be silent, and the house would fall silent with her. The maid would carry her meals upstairs on a tray, Pa would eat alone, and I was told to keep out of their room so that Mama could rest. I walked the house on tiptoe, frightened that if I made a noise, I would never hear her laughter again.

When my mother gave birth to a stillborn child, the son my father wanted so badly, he was as distraught as she was. He explained that the brother I'd been looking forward to was in heaven, and my mother was ill. 'Will Mama die too?' I asked. He held me tightly. When I pulled away, demanding an answer, he had tears in his eyes. No, she wasn't going to die, he said, but we must be very patient because it was going to take a while for Mama to be well enough to leave hospital and get back to her old self. In the meantime, I was to be good because my Aunt Rose was coming to look after me.

An unmarried woman with a reputation for flightiness, Aunt Rose was a dressmaker by profession. According to Aunt Lila, Rose got into one scrape after another, always getting herself talked about for the same reason: men. She had a way with men that was uncanny. Whether it was the Wash Man, the Garden Boy, the House Boy, or my father for that matter, she'd have them eating out of her hand within half an hour. Her eyes sparkled in their company, and if she liked someone especially, she became dreamy-eyed, doe-eyed.

My father relaxed visibly in her company, and the house, which had long been quiet, became noisy with the clamour of her friends. I loved Aunt Rose because she was never silent. She had the radio on all the time: either the radio or the record player. She taught me how to dance the Highlife, a hand on my stomach, eyes closed, hips swaying. The more

I managed to make them sway, the louder she'd clap her hands. With Rose in the house, I never walked on tiptoe.

When Mama came back from hospital, the first thing she did was to turn off the radio. Taking the hint, my aunt tried to behave in a more subdued manner, and, sheltering behind her, I followed her example.

For a while Mama watched me. She watched my father with Rose and then all of us together. Then she began to woo me back, gently, carefully. She fed me fruit from her garden, a guava one day, a pawpaw the next. Cutting the pawpaw in half, she would scoop out its glutinous black seeds, and feed them to her chickens. To rid them of worms, she told me. Mama reclaimed me with fruit and stories her grandmother had taught her. By the time the mango tree was in season, I was hers again completely. It was then she struck.

It was Saturday morning and Aunt Rose was preparing to go to market. We were eating a late breakfast on the veranda when my aunt approached my mother for money. Taking a wad of notes from her handbag, Mama slapped it on the table. She looked Rose up and down. She looked at my father, then at me.

'This is *my* family,' Mama announced. 'No one will take it away from me. Certainly not you, Rose. Look at you! What sort of woman do you think you are, trying to steal my husband, my child?'

My aunt protested. My father protested, saying this wasn't the way to thank Rose for her kindness. Rose started crying. My mother was mistaken, she said; she loved me as an aunt, she respected my father as an in-law, nothing more. But Mama would have none of it.

'Can't you see what she's doing?' she shouted at Pa.

Pointing an accusing finger at Aunt Rose, she said, 'This woman here, this sister of mine, has had more men than a Krobo prostitute in Abidjan. Do you expect me to believe she left you alone, Michael?' Mama shook her head. 'How can you expect me to believe that?'

Aunt Lila says that Mama had a point. Rose was renowned for her affairs. But even Rose had her limits. 'Your father was not her sort at all. He's what I call an Englishman, Ajuba: stiff, aloof, rather formal. You know your father. Anyway, for all her faults, Rose wouldn't have done it. We were family. Your mother was ill.'

Under a torrent of abuse, Aunt Rose packed her bags and left within the hour, my father looking on helplessly. He tried to calm my mother, assuring her that nothing had happened between them, that Rose was innocent of her accusations; in fact she had been a godsend, a treasure. The more he defended her, the more convinced Mama was of their guilt.

Her suspicions didn't end with Aunt Rose. Before long, Pa's relatives gave up visiting us altogether. His friends, male and female, stopped dropping in at the house, and even Aunt Lila, the closest of Mama's siblings, was made unwelcome at Kuku Hill.

'Somehow, your mother got it into her head that we were all witches. All of us. Even me,' Aunt Lila told me when we met in London. 'Can you believe it, Ajuba? She thought we were feasting on her foetuses, that's how ill she was. Now, if she had said it was your father's people who were after her, I could have taken her seriously. Everyone knows what Nzema people are like: they mess around with witchcraft all the time. But when Grace accused me too, then I knew she was ill. What your father went through, Ajuba, I can't begin to tell you.'

I don't need anyone to tell me that part of my history, for I remember it clearly. It was after my little sister had died, a few hours after birth, a tiny, sickly child. It was the time when my parents talked to each other through me, a time of tears and tension, when a word out of place could shatter the brittle silence of the house. To keep the peace I was obliged to pass messages from one parent to the other.

My father must have realised that his marriage wasn't going to survive. He was biding his time, waiting for the right moment to leave. But there's never a good time to leave a grief-stricken wife. So, instead of abandoning us, Pa did the next best thing: he avoided my mother as much as possible, staying away for days on end. Dismissing her accusations of infidelity, he claimed she was imagining things; he was staying overnight with relatives. Since Mama wouldn't let them visit us, he was spending time with them for a change. Of course there wasn't another woman! Mama was being neurotic, overwrought. He made the situation worse by lying; he added to my mother's insecurity by avoiding her. He left her to me. And for that I can never forgive him.

Aunt Lila believes that if my little sister had lived, my parents might have stayed together. She's wrong. She didn't taste the slow poison of Pa's contempt for my mother. And Aunt Lila doesn't know what I know; she doesn't know about the mirrors.

Whenever there was a thunderstorm on Kuku Hill, the maid would rush around the house, covering every mirror with cloth. Mama used to laugh, teasing her. 'Tell me, Tawiah,' she asked, 'have you ever seen lightning strike a mirror?'

The answer would be no. But that wasn't the point, Tawiah

insisted. It was said in her village that the reflection of lightning in a mirror could kill you. What was even more terrifying were the ghosts in mirrors. Lightning could reveal them. Her people believed that during a thunderstorm, if you looked carefully, hovering behind your reflection you'd see the faces of your enemies.

One afternoon, soon after my sister had died, the sound of thunder woke me from a nap. I heard the first fat drops of rain hitting the roof. Tawiah was running from room to room, covering mirrors, shutting windows, protecting the house from elements physical and spiritual. The rain fell in torrents, lashing against walls, spilling down guttering.

At the first flash of lightning I ran to my parents' room. Pa had been away for several days and Mama was morose, yet because thunderstorms frightened me, I ran to the shelter of her arms. When I opened the door she didn't see me at first. She was staring at the mirror.

'Mama?'

She looked in my direction, a dazed expression clouding her face. 'Oh, it's you, Ajuba. Come here, darling. Come see what I see.'

I approached hesitantly, taking hold of her outstretched hand.

'Look,' she said, turning her face to the mirror. 'Can you see your father's whores? Look at them all. His sisters, my sisters, the women he calls his girlfriends. Look how they hate me, Ajuba!'

I could only see Mama's reflection and beside it, lower down, my own. 'There's no one there, Mama. Only you and me.'

'Look harder, Ajuba!'

I didn't want to see the ghosts in the mirror. I didn't want to witness the anguish on my mother's face. 'There's nothing there, Mama!'

Suddenly, my mother smiled. Then holding me close, she said: 'There's no need to be frightened. It's simply a matter of time, Ajuba. Your eyes aren't open yet, but when they are, you'll see what I see and you'll know what I know.'

'Come away from the mirror, Mama,' I pleaded. 'Cover it up!'

I tried to pull her away, but she wouldn't move. She was mesmerised by the faces she was seeing. Faces of fecund, nubile women. They were mocking her, she said, taunting her. Women who feasted on her babies, intent on stealing her womb, her husband, her child.

Should I have told someone? Should I have let someone know that before long she was talking to the faces in the mirror without the help of thunderstorms? If my father had been home, perhaps I would have been able to confide in him, but I believed what Mama told me: my eyes hadn't yet opened. It was simply a matter of time before I saw what she saw and understood. Anyway, Pa was away a week at a time, now. Two weeks. And Mama was waiting for him on the veranda. Watching and waiting.

I couldn't sleep the night of Beth's accident. After Major Derby had carried her back from Bouncy Town and Mrs Derby had shepherded us both into Tavy, a dormitory beyond the Derbys' bedroom that served as a sickbay, I refused to sleep. I wouldn't allow myself to in case something happened to Beth.

Mrs Derby had summoned the school doctor, Archie Whittaker, to make sure that we were all right. A thin, angular man with brusque, confident movements, he prodded Beth's neck and shoulders, before announcing that she had had a lucky escape. She was suffering from nothing more than a sore neck; and once I'd got over the shock of the accident, I'd be right as rain too. 'Children are resilient little buggers,' he said, cuffing me under the chin. 'You'll have forgotten what's happened in a day or two. You wait and see.'

I wasn't prepared to wait. I was taking no more chances. Polly had shifted the floorboards on which we walked every day, adjusting the rules of our lives, and Beth and I, tumbling into a yawning cavern underfoot, had entered a world where the certainties of school life no longer existed. A probing anxiety that I'd been trying to evade was encroaching. I didn't want to travel into my mother's nether landscape again. I didn't want to see what she had seen.

Sensing my anxiety, Mrs Derby, who combined the duties of Matron with Headmistress, spent the rest of the evening by my bed. While her husband interviewed the others involved in Polly's game, Mrs Derby held my hand.

She was tall, flat-chested and broad-hipped, her hair a light golden-brown with a tinge of red. Glasses shielded her hazel eyes and her features, accentuated by the severe styling of her short hair, were softened by the colours she wore, reassuring shades of green and brown, merging into chestnut and russet: warm, country colours. She usually smelt of lavender or lily of the valley. That night it was lavender. She dabbed some of her scent on my wrists and neck to calm me down.

'Are we in serious trouble?' I asked, struggling to inhale deeply. My breathing was rapid and shallow, my voice agitated, my mind wired to painful sensations that I tried, unsuccessfully, to suppress.

'You're not in any trouble at all, Ajuba. Everything's going to be fine. There, try to breathe in again.'

I did as I was told. For a moment my breathing eased,

but my lungs, wracked by prolonged sobbing, made me gulp for air as soon as I started talking. 'I tried to stop her, Mrs Derby, but she wouldn't listen. We didn't mean to hurt ourselves, honest we didn't.'

'I know, sweetie. It was an accident and accidents happen.'

She fell silent, trying to calm me with the balm of her presence, while I puckered the duvet as I wriggled beneath it, hitting my thighs to stop my legs shaking.

Folding my hands gently in hers, Mrs Derby said: 'Ajuba, you know you can talk to me about anything, anything at all.'

I nodded.

'Even if you think it's silly, I'm happy to listen.'

I didn't know how to transform what was racing through my mind into a language she would understand. I was preoccupied with Polly, my mother and Beth. I didn't want Beth to enter a deep sleep as my mother had done. I didn't want to have to wake her up the next morning.

'Are you thinking of your mother?' she asked.

I was always thinking of Mama, always perusing the image that I had locked away in my heart. Polly possessed a key to a reality that I sensed but wasn't yet able to understand. She held a clue to an aspect of my self I had misplaced and didn't want anyone else to find: a part of me steeped in my parents and their violent dislocation from each other.

One afternoon, when Pa hadn't been back to Kuku Hill for a month and a half, Aunt Lila came to visit with her two younger brothers, a family delegation sent to look after my mother's interests.

'We had to clarify the situation,' Aunt Lila told me over tea at the Basil Street Hotel. 'We had to let Grace know what was happening. You see, your father was no longer in the country by then. He'd found himself some lucrative job in Rome and he wanted a divorce. Can you believe it, Ajuba? He left the country without telling your mother. Grace thought we were lying at first, stirring up trouble, meddling in her affairs. But eventually she accepted what we said. He'd left her. However, she refused to contest the divorce. No matter what we said, she was adamant. She wasn't going to contest it, because she thought if she did, Michael wouldn't have her back!'

'I couldn't believe my ears,' Aunt Lila continued. 'So I told her the rumours I'd heard in town. The gossip put about by Michael's girlfriends. They were saying that Grace was unbalanced, and that your father had said that when he was settled abroad, he was going to get custody of you. That made her sit up. It drove your mother wild.'

The next day, Mama told me that she'd had a dream in which a colony of ravenous fruit bats attacked the mango tree in the garden. Their teeth glinting in the moonlight, they had devoured the tree's ripening fruit. It was an omen, Mama said, of what would happen if she left me in Ghana: for the bats had attacked my tree, Ajuba's tree. She must remove me from harm's way, far from Ghanaian eyes.

The dream galvanised her into action. Suitcases were brought out of wardrobes, clothes were washed and packed. She wrote letters to friends in London; she wrote to her old hospital. In the flurry of activity she seemed her old self. Mama said I was going to see snow. And if I was lucky I might see the Queen of England. Yet behind everything, behind the excitement and activity, the distribution of gifts and Tawiah's solemn vow of secrecy, I sensed Pa's presence casting a shadow over Kuku Hill.

For instance, Mama would be sorting out her jewellery,

humming to herself, when all of a sudden her face would cloud over and she'd touch me as if to steady herself.

'If your father should take you away,' she warned, 'don't believe everything he tells you, Ajuba. I know your father. He'll try to poison your mind against me. If he does, turn your back on him. And remember, I shall love you wherever you are.'

'But I'll always be with you, Mama. I'll always look after you.'

She sighed and then she kissed me.

Within two weeks of Aunt Lila's visit, my mother had taken me to London. Her plan was to gain employment as a nurse and to find me a school. Together we were going to start life afresh. We would be happy again. Unfortunately, her plans didn't work out. Four months later she had fallen into that deep sleep and been rushed to hospital, Pa had found me, and I was on my way to boarding school in Devon.

On the train, he tried to reassure me that it was for my own good; he tried to convince me that a British public-school education was the best in the world. I had a golden future ahead, he said. A girl of my intelligence could achieve anything she wanted.

'I want to be with Mama,' I mumbled.

He pretended not to hear me. We were on the journey from Waterloo to Axminster, sitting opposite one another at window seats. I was watching the high-rise buildings of London recede, when Pa said in a low, urgent voice that I'd never heard him use before: 'What your mother did was quite unforgivable. But you've got to forgive her. She wasn't herself, Ajuba.'

I nodded. I knew what he said was true. Mama hadn't been well for a long time.

'You must try to think kindly of her,' Pa went on. 'I know it will be difficult but you must accept what's happened. Anyway, it's all behind us now. She can't hurt us. We won't see her again.'

What Mama had foretold was coming true. At the time I was too frightened of the suffering on Pa's face, the tears he wiped from his eyes, to probe any deeper. But at the thought that I might never see my mother again a tremor of fear tingled through my body, and when I closed my eyes Mama surfaced behind my eyelids as vividly as the last time I had seen her. She was begging me not to believe my father's lies. The further we travelled from London, my life with Mama ebbing away, the more I tried to persuade myself that if Pa really had my best interest in mind he would come to realise that I needed Mama almost as much as she needed me. Of course I'd see her again. And until I did, nothing Pa said or did would stop me loving her.

This is what I told myself on the journey to Devon. Once we'd arrived and Major Derby had picked us up, driving us deep into the countryside to the school in its acres of forest; after Mrs Derby had shown us around the classrooms and dormitories and Pa was getting ready to say goodbye: only then did I realise that it was Pa's hand that I didn't want to let go of now. Forcing myself to be very small and still, so that when he walked away I would remain intact, I heard a desolate voice posing a question my mother had often asked: 'When am I going to see you again?'

'Very soon,' Pa replied.

Like my mother before me, I could tell from the relief in his eyes as he kissed me goodbye that he was lying.

*

So notwithstanding her concern for me that night, her hands warming my fingers in hers, I was incapable of expressing my feelings to Mrs Derby. I was mistrustful of discussing my parents with anyone. I simply wanted to be with my mother again, home in Ghana. 'There's nothing I want to talk about,' I told Mrs Derby eventually. 'I just want to go to sleep.' Escaping the headmistress's piercing gaze, her eyes magnified by steel-rimmed spectacles, I turned my face to the wall. 'You can go away now.'

She sat stroking my back for half an hour longer until, thinking I'd fallen asleep, Mrs Derby left me.

I stayed awake to hear the Derbys going to bed. I heard the reassuring murmur of their voices behind the closed door as they shared the stories of the day. My parents had often quarrelled at night thinking I wouldn't hear them, so to hear adults speaking softly to each other, occasionally laughing, eased my spirit. Polly's name was mentioned several times before they switched off their bedroom light. Beth's accident had brought my unease with Polly sharply into focus. But to keep out of Polly's way, I would have had to avoid myself. She was dangerous, she made things happen; yet I was mesmerised by her, a grasscutter dazzled in the glare of headlamps.

When I finally heard Major Derby snoring I got up to check that Beth was breathing. She had been sedated and was fast asleep. I shook her awake. Bleary-eyed, she shifted to the edge of her bed, allowing me to slip in beside her.

'I thought you'd died,' I whispered.

'I'm luckier than a cat with nine lives,' she purred, half asleep.

'What if you *had* died, Beth?'

'Well, I didn't, did I?'

'Beth, what if –'

'If you don't go to sleep, Aj, I'm going to shove you out of my bed.'

Unwilling to face the night's darkness alone, to endure the tremors beneath the floorboards without another body next to mine, I held my tongue. I listened to Beth's respiration; I felt the rise and fall of her breath, my chest against her back. I started counting each inhalation, every quiver and shudder she made until, realising that her grip on life was as keen as mine, I closed my eyes.

Polly once told us that she had travelled the world even as a foetus.

'What's a foetus?' Maria demanded, her grey eyes bright with curiosity. She ran her fingers through her raven hair in a gesture reminiscent of her mother, who had brought Maria up to believe that asking questions was a mark of intelligence. I didn't know what a foetus was either but was wary of exposing my ignorance.

We were in Exe, changing into our own clothes before going down to Seniors for Prep. It had been raining all day and the moisture in the air had seeped into the woollen jumper and the red pair of corduroy trousers I'd pulled on.

Polly sighed, raising an eyebrow: 'Foetuses are what parents make when they get it on, silly.'

'You mean making babies?'

'Sure! Women conceive to make men stick around. That's why they do it. It's what makes the world go around.'

'So that's why they get divorced when they can't have babies?' I queried.

'Not necessarily,' Maria replied. 'The Derbys don't have

children and they're still together. Not everyone can have babies, Aj, and not everyone wants them. Some people don't even *like* babies.'

'Really?' The idea that having children was not a pre-requisite of life was completely new to me.

Seizing an opportunity to share her insights with us, Beth leapt off her bed into the discussion: 'Listen, you guys, a foetus is a fertilised egg. Females carry them here in their wombs.' Beth patted below her stomach. 'Nowadays you don't need a man to have a baby. You can get one from a clinic. Or a vet can come to you.'

Living on a farm, though not quite as glamorous as being in the same class as Chelsea Clinton in Washington, DC, did at times have certain advantages. Beth knew more about the mechanics of sex than all of us. Once, when I'd stayed with her, she let me watch one of her mother's mares being inseminated. The mare didn't seem to mind much but it did look rather uncomfortable and sticky.

Polly went on to tell us that she was conceived in Rome, born in Paris, learnt how to walk in Madrid, and, before her stay in Washington, she had gone to school in Singapore. She declaimed before the whole dormitory that she was a true citizen of the world, cosmopolitan in every sense, at home wherever she pitched her tent – an expression of her father's, I imagine.

But although Polly boasted that she had more air miles than the rest of us put together, I was inclined to believe that she found the codes and habits of the English middle classes as bemusing as I did. She might have looked like them but their predilections and enthusiasms – their love of rambling, their obsession with tea at elevenses and teatime, their snacks of flapjacks and marmite on fried bread – puzzled her as much as they did me. The difference between us was that Polly never showed her bewilderment.

A few days after Beth had almost killed herself playing True Murder, I was still dazed by the collision of events: the memory of my mother's face over Beth's, the terror in both their eyes. Beth was in high spirits. Her close brush with death gave her a notoriety which, added to her popularity at school, made her irresistible. An American at heart, Polly decided to market her.

During break, she took us down to the bottom lawn, away from the Derbys' watchful eyes. A crowd of younger children followed. When we were out of sight, under instructions from Polly, Maria marshalled the children into a line. Beth and Polly stood at one end, while at the other end I collected money. It cost ten pence to look at the purple weal around Beth's neck, and fifteen pence to touch it. 'She almost died,' Polly said, urging potential spectators closer. 'She almost killed herself.'

A close encounter with death, I was learning, was a marketable commodity. We made over £6 that day, and spent it all on sherbet and blackjacks. In the evening I found myself reading *True Murder* again, like someone unable to resist picking at a scab.

I've read somewhere that children are fascinated by death. I don't think that's necessarily true. On walks together, I remember Beth used to examine every carcass she found on a track. Whether it was a sheep, a mouse or a bird, she would scrutinise it, picking it over with a stick. It wasn't that she was interested in death, as such, it was the opportunity its stillness afforded. She could study whatever she found at leisure. It couldn't run or fly away. In the aftermath of death she could do what she wanted: she could discover how bodies worked. Beth said she wanted to be a vet; either that or a jockey at Aintree.

Similarly we were interested in *True Murder* not only for its lurid details but for what it told us about life: the relationships within families that end in sudden explosions of violence. That night I had just finished the magazine's account of Ruth Ellis, the last woman in Britain to be hanged, and was reading a column by the magazine's resident detectives, Lieutenant Eugene Malone and his partner, a native of Louisiana called Beau Leboeuf, when I realised that Mrs Derby had just come in and was waiting to turn the lights out. Had I slipped the magazine away quickly, perhaps she would have left me alone. Unfortunately, I was engrossed in Malone and Leboeuf's ideas on the Basic Principles of Detection (Observation, Interrogation, Persistence and Intuition, give or take a Lucky Break or two) when I saw Mrs Derby. I must have looked guilty, for she walked over to my bed and picked up the magazine.

'Are you reading this, Ajuba?'

'Pardon?' I said, playing for time.

She flipped through the pages. 'Is this yours?'

She must have realised that the magazine wasn't mine. Major Derby had interrogated the True Murder brigade one by one: Joshua, Maria and Polly. According to reports, his interrogation method of dim lights, protracted silence and encouraging nods when the suspect started squealing would have made Malone and Leboeuf proud. It had come out that the game was Polly's idea. The props and cards Polly had given us were confiscated and everyone was made to promise that True Murder would never be played again.

Nevertheless, I didn't know how to respond to Mrs Derby's

question. After a moment's hesitation, it seemed to me easiest to nod assent. The magazine was mine.

'Are you sure?'

I nodded again.

'After what happened to Beth, Ajuba, I'm very disappointed in you.'

Lying in the bed beside mine, Polly sat up. 'It's my magazine, Mrs Derby.'

The headmistress looked from Polly to me, and then, adopting a stern expression, she thrust the full weight of her moral outrage on Polly. 'I'm going to say this once and only once, Polly. I don't want to see this magazine again. Or anything like it. Not in my school. Murder isn't a game and it isn't entertainment. The sooner you understand that, the better for us all. Do I make myself clear?'

Polly didn't flinch. 'Yes, ma'am. I'm sorry.'

Holding the magazine as if handling a dead mouse by the tail, Mrs Derby marched out of the room. She turned off the light without saying goodnight to anyone.

We fell asleep quickly that night, worn out by the events of the past couple of days. Later that night, Polly woke me from a deep sleep, the touch of her cold hand on my cheek. 'Move over,' she hissed.

I gathered my bedclothes around me. I didn't want her in my bed.

'Move over,' she repeated.

'No! You've got your own bed. Sleep in your own bed.'

Her own bed was wet, but I didn't know that then. Her hair fell about her face, a jumble of tangled curls. She appeared distressed.

'I keep thinking of Jacinth,' she said. 'Let me in. Please let me in.'

Apart from when she was saying goodbye to her father, I had never seen Polly about to cry before. It was so unusual that I eased myself over, making space for her. She climbed into my bed. I noticed now that she smelt faintly of urine.

'Do you miss Jacinth?' I asked.

'Do you miss your mom and dad?' She clearly thought my question stupid.

'I miss my mother.'

'I'll trade you mine any day.'

'I wouldn't swap my mother for anyone.'

'Hey, you haven't met Isobel yet.'

'Who's Isobel?'

'My mother.'

I was struck by the way she spoke about her parent as if she were a gem she wanted to give away. And she called her by her Christian name, a liberty I would never have taken with mine.

'You're welcome to come home and try her out, if you like. We're moving into our new house, Graylings, soon. It's a great big house in the country. Isobel says that in the end every family needs a home to go to. Want to come and try her out?'

'Polly, I've got my own mother.'

'I was kidding, OK?'

'You shouldn't joke about things like that. Mothers are special.'

'Lighten up, Aj.' Then in a voice devoid of sarcasm, she added: 'Aj, thanks for covering for me earlier.'

I was surprised she had bothered to express gratitude. Polly's superciliousness rarely succumbed to appreciation of others.

Settling deeper into my bed she asked: 'Do you really miss your mom?'

'Of course I do. Don't you miss yours?'

'I miss her not being on my case all the time, but apart from that, I guess not. I miss Peter most of all. Major Derby let me call him tonight.'

'Did you tell him what happened?'

'Sure. I prepared him for Isobel's wrath. She goes on and on at him whenever I'm in trouble. That's why I'm here. I knew it wouldn't work out.' Lying very still, her head cradled in her arm with her face turned towards mine, Polly appeared soft, almost malleable. 'I told them it wouldn't work out but they wouldn't listen. Adults never listen. At least not on Planet Earth they don't.'

'Do you think you're going to get expelled?' A part of me hoped she would.

'No such luck. Jeez, Aj, you just don't get it, do you? Adults like a challenge. They see a kid like me, they want to reform me. It makes them feel good about themselves.'

'Like Maria's mum and her victims?'

'You've got it. They have no idea what it's like being a pre-teenager.'

I wasn't sure I had any idea either, but the longing in her voice spoke to me. What was more, I had an inkling of Polly's frustration at being somewhere she didn't want to be, and, like a divining rod searching for water, I found myself drawn to every word she said.

'What did Peter say about the accident?'

'The usual. I shouldn't stir up trouble. I should try and "shape up" because if I put my mind to it I'm "game" for anything.'

'Sounds like the sort of stuff fathers say. They don't get it, do they? They don't get it at all,' I said, mimicking Polly's exasperation and experiencing my own. 'My father is impossible.'

'But you don't miss him, do you? Not like you miss your mom.'

I was silent and Polly, sensing my vulnerability, drew closer. Very gently, she whispered: 'What d'you miss about your mom, Aj?'

I wondered how best I could encapsulate the void left by my mother. I couldn't find English words for my sentiments, so I described my favourite food instead.

On her good days I associated my mother with food: the scent of ripe guava, the orange of mango and pawpaw. I remembered meals that she cooked for me: a plate of kenkey, pepper and fish; groundnut soup on a bed of rice; mashed plantain seasoned with ginger and chilli, then transformed at leisure, by frying in palm oil, into tatale.

I described all these meals to Polly, and, remembering familiar smells, I caught a glimpse of my mother's smile. She had a way of eating that invariably enticed me to the table. Watching her fingers shape a morsel of food for her mouth, I would want to eat whatever she held in her hand. Mama transformed the simple task of eating into an unsurpassed pleasure. I hadn't realised how ravenous I was to taste her food again.

'My mother's the best cook in the world,' I told Polly.

'Don't you have McDonald's in Ghana?'

I wasn't sure. 'We ate lots of McDonald's when we lived in London,' I replied. 'And Kentucky Fried Chicken. I don't like the food in London or the food here. It's not as nice as what we have in Ghana.'

Polly agreed that what passed for nourishment at school, Toad in the Hole in particular, was disgusting. But since she'd never tasted my mother's cooking, she didn't have a point of comparison. After some reflection she said: 'You know Isobel's supposed to be a good cook. At least Peter says she is and so does Theo, my brother. They can't get enough of her cooking. You'd like it too, if you tried it, Aj.'

'Do you like it?'

'Naaa. I'm *so* not into organic, wholegrain stuff. But Jacinth liked it and I reckon you would too.' Stretching out on her back, Polly yawned. 'Let's face it, Aj, just about everything on Planet Earth sucks, but at school it sucks a million times worse. Why not come home with me? Isobel might give you something to smile about.'

'You really think so?'

'I'm almost one hundred per cent sure,' she said, determined to convince me. Then, reacting to my puzzled silence, my inability to respond wholeheartedly to her invitation, Polly gave me a get-out clause. 'Look, if I'm wrong about Isobel, you can sue me. I mean, what have you got to lose? Just come for half term. I bet she'll make you feel better. She can't help herself, Aj.'

Her sales pitch had already persuaded me that I'd be a fool not to meet her mother. I said I'd think about it. But unbeknown to me what I thought was incidental, for Polly had already chosen me as her best buddy. And when Polly wanted something, she usually got it.

5

Over tea with Aunt Lila in London, my aunt said something that's stayed with me. I was telling her about my friendship with Polly and her family; our life together at Graylings, which I latched on to, absorbing the sensuality of the Venuses through my pores. Along with the nostalgia I expressed, Aunt Lila must have heard something else: a tremor of tenderness perhaps, a slight break in my voice that surfaces whenever I speak of Polly. Gathering my fingers in hers, clasping them to her breasts, my aunt sustained me through the most difficult part of our conversation. When I finished telling her everything, when I had shared the burden I have been carrying all these years, she helped me make sense of it by explaining her view of the world.

Aunt Lila believes that the emotional landscapes we inhabit and the houses we live in are the dwelling places of unseen entities: spirits from another world that permeate our own, influencing events. She believes that the realm of the senses is threaded with the breath of spirits, and that what is glimpsed with the human eye is merely a fragment of reality.

'Sometimes,' Aunt Lila said, 'reality is simply too bright, Ajuba. It's so bright that we have to blind ourselves to survive. What happened was not your fault. You were a child. You are your mother's daughter.'

From Aunt Lila's viewpoint, the events I am piecing together, the long libation I am pouring, reverberate with voices from my past and the house itself: faint echoes that grew louder, the more familiar I became with Polly's family and the place where she died.

At the time, Polly gave me a blow-by-blow account of her family's move to Graylings. It was only a week before the Whitsun break, when I was due to stay with them. I had decided to go home with Polly not merely to sample her mother's cooking, but because I liked her. And her willingness to palm her mother on to me, though confusing, intrigued me. Moreover, Polly's enthusiasm for her new home was contagious.

Graylings was a few miles from our school and the Venus family had been staying, up till then, in a rented cottage close by, Peter Venus returning home for the weekends from his houseboat in London, while his wife supervised the renovations needed to make their new home habitable. For the past fifty years the house had been the home of Miss Olivia Fielding and her companion, Miss Edith Butterworth; and for the past forty years, little had been done by way of home improvements. There was no central heating, the wiring had reached a dangerous state of decay, and what was left of the kitchen was dilapidated. Using a part of her considerable personal fortune, Isobel Venus set out to make her new residence worthy of her family.

I first met Mrs Venus when she came to collect Polly and me for half term. We were waiting for her in the school hall, a haven leading to the drawing-room, which the Derbys used as a study and a place for meeting parents. Isobel Venus arrived slightly late. She'd been summoned by Mrs Derby to discuss Polly's behaviour. She quickly kissed her daughter, said 'hallo' to me and then, standing to attention, she knocked on the drawing-room door, leaving a scent of bluebells behind her. Penhaligon's Bluebell, I later discovered: a blaze of indigo in spring sunshine.

She was an elegant woman, tall and fine-boned, with a luxurious sweep of hair the colour of ripe corn. When she glanced at me, her dark-brown eyes were unusually disarming in their frankness; it was this quality of hers, combined with her taste in clothes and perfume, that reminded me of a sleek saluki dog. She was wearing a white silk blouse and beige linen trousers, colours guaranteed to blend in no matter where she was. Unlike the other parents picking up children, Mrs Venus sported a suntan. She appeared calm when she entered the drawing-room, but when she emerged half an hour later, with a holdall containing Polly's confiscated magazines, she was seething.

Ever the tactician, Polly made me sit in the front of the family's black Mercedes for the journey home, while she sat in the back behind the driver's seat. She positioned herself so it was virtually impossible for Mrs Venus to make eye contact with her.

The grating irritation between Polly and her mother transformed what should have been a short drive into an arduous pilgrimage to an unknown destination. Polly stared nonchalantly out of the car window and Mrs Venus, her knuckles white, her hands clenched on the steering wheel, sparkled with anger. I shifted uncomfortably in my seat, rubbing the safety belt with my chin. I wondered when they would speak to each other and if what Polly had described as Isobel's 'wrath' was likely to erupt. Sensing tension mounting between them, sucking it in through the air I was breathing, I began counting the miles of our journey as they registered one after the other on the car meter. It wasn't until we'd passed through Axminster and travelled five miles into the countryside beyond that Mrs Venus spoke:

'Polly, please sit where I can see you.'

'I'm staying put.'

'Move!'

Grudgingly, Polly shifted a few inches. Adjusting the rear-view mirror, Isobel Venus glanced at her daughter. To my surprise, she began talking to Polly quietly, without fuss: a reprimand, followed by a stern warning never to take the magazines to school again.

'Give me a break, Isobel! I'm not totally dumb.'

'Cut it out, Polly. I'm not putting up with this, not this weekend or any other weekend. And I'm certainly not having you singled out as a troublemaker at school. Do you hear me?'

'There's no need to raise your voice, Mommy dearest. I'm receiving your signal loud and clear.'

'That's enough, Polly!'

But Polly had only just begun. 'I mean, why make such a big deal of something that wasn't even my fault? It was my idea, I admit. But did I put a rope around Beth's neck? I think not. The girl went crazy. It wasn't my fault, was it, Aj?'

I decided it was prudent to remain silent.

'I mean, why're you making such a big deal out of something Peter's cool about?'

At the mention of her husband, Mrs Venus bristled: 'Peter knows, does he?'

'I called him right away.'

Flipping back her hair, Mrs Venus retorted: 'I wish one of you would take the trouble to let me into your loop once in a while. Especially since I'm the one taking all the flak for you at school.'

'And who decided I should go there? Who decided we should live in this godforsaken country again? Was it me? Was it Peter? Hallo? I think not.'

Polly's mother glanced at me, acknowledging my presence in the car for the first time. She tried to smile but the expression that flitted over her face resembled a grimace. I was beginning to wonder if Polly had invited me home to distract her mother from being on her case all the time, when Mrs Venus, gathering her resolve with a sharp intake of breath, gave her daughter an ultimatum: 'If you know what's good for you, Polly, you're going to behave this weekend. We've finally found a home and we're going to be happy. Theo's arriving later with a friend and you've got Ajuba. So let's try and be kind to each other. Message received?'

Polly grunted. It was then, turning left into the drive, that a pair of dogs distracted us. Two huge boxers leapt at the car, barking furiously. They were with an old woman in a faded dress, a torn woollen cardigan flung over her shoulders.

'Candy! Fudge! Heel!' the woman bellowed.

Momentarily uncertain, the dogs slackened their pace as the Mercedes raced ahead.

'That's our resident bag lady,' Polly told me. 'She lives in the Gatehouse. You'd better believe it, those dogs are something else.'

It seemed to me, that first weekend, that Graylings was an Aladdin's cave of delights, and the Venuses an exotic variant of the human family. They shimmered and shone, and though unfinished, the work that had been done on their house complemented them, creating an illusion of light and warmth. Rooms had been gutted and an Aga installed in the new kitchen at the heart of the house, to create the dwelling of Mrs Venus's dreams: a place she could put down roots at last, gathering her family around her.

The colours on the walls were bright, the fabrics of curtains and upholstery luxurious, the carpets resplendent. The atmosphere was that of an eastern bazaar: a jumble of patterns that, like a complicated jigsaw, interlocked creating a sensation of harmony and sumptuous ease. Adorned with objects from the family's travels, the house contained exquisite porcelain from Singapore, metal-topped side tables from North Africa, and crockery from Andalusia.

Armed with ideas absorbed from *True Murder*, I used the Basic Principles of Detection as an anchor to prevent me surrendering, unreservedly, to a strangely alluring environment. Applying the first principle diligently – a detective is observant above all else; she keeps her eyes peeled and listens to every word that's said – I deployed Eugene Malone and Beau Leboeuf as I would a pair of sunglasses: to shield my eyes from the brilliance of the Venus sun.

I wanted to touch everything, to graze my fingers on every surface. But I didn't dare to, in case something broke. 'Am I allowed to?' I asked as Mrs Venus drew back the curtains in Polly's bedroom. They were Indian silk, pale as the ripening fruit of a dawa dawa tree: a flush of pink before it blushes crimson. I was tempted to embrace the colour, folding it against my cheek.

'You can do anything you want here,' Mrs Venus laughed. 'You're a guest in our home now, Ajuba. You're not at school.'

I stroked the curtains, and, feeling a ripple of excitement trickling through my fingers into my veins, I smiled at Mrs Venus. Her eyes softened, her delight in my pleasure brought the taste of molasses to my tongue: a taste that grew stronger as, the scent of bluebells enveloping me, she lifted up my chin, and planted a kiss on my mouth.

'I'm glad you've come home with Polly,' she whispered in my ear. 'I think we're going to be good friends.'

When her mother had left the room Polly shrugged dismissively. 'I told you,' she said. 'She can't help herself. Isobel does that to all my friends. Do you mind?'

I said I didn't mind. I rather liked it.

'Do you like my room? Do you like the colour?'

Overlooking the south-west slope of the garden, Polly's bedroom was a subtle shade of rose: a warm rose, which in the light of the setting sun became womb-like, a place for secrets and dreams.

'It's wonderful,' I exclaimed.

'Do you really like it?'

I said that I did.

'Isobel wanted to change the colour but I wouldn't let her. I like it the way it is. So does Peter. He says it sets my zebras off well.'

On a wall facing Polly's bed was a Serengeti landscape of zebras grazing in savannah; and beside a bookshelf was an elaborate collage made of zebras cut out of magazines. I might have supposed, had I not known better, that under Beth's influence Polly had succumbed to the wonders of wildlife in Africa. I was under no such illusion. Adjacent to the zebras was a garish poster, with an amputated hand in the foreground, of her favourite film, *The Addams Family.* Like me, Polly was given to unusual preoccupations. Her interest in zebras was purely aesthetic. Nevertheless, I told her that I liked them and my bed as well. It was beside Polly's, a simple wooden bed, a companion to the one beside it.

As soon as we were out of our school clothes Polly dragged me outside. I had confessed, during one of our late-night conversations in Exe, that at one time my most treasured possession at Kuku Hill had been a red bicycle. I had also confessed that I'd left Ghana before learning how to ride it properly, so Polly was determined to teach me, on a set of wheels she had brought over from America.

When I was able to maintain my balance, she fed me chunks of Toblerone; and when I could go a bit further, she ran behind me as I circled the building.

Graylings lay in a stretch of deciduous woodland. With part of its foundations dating from medieval days, previous owners had emphasised its ancient origins by adding a gabled entrance porch overlooked by oriel windows on either side. On the ground floor the yellow stone mansion peered at the world through mullioned windows. There was a fine cedar at the far end of the lawn, a monkey-puzzle tree a distance away and, between the top and bottom lawns, a crumbling stone balustrade.

Manoeuvring outside on Polly's bicycle, I saw Mrs Venus in the house wearing workman's overalls. She was arranging plates on the kitchen dresser: Moroccan plates, I later discovered. When I sped past a second time, she opened a window, asking what we wanted for lunch. Polly answered for us both: salami sandwiches and sarsaparilla. We laughed, hearing together the musical chime of the words running into each other.

We were upstairs, cocooned under our beds reading *True Murder* out loud, when the rest of the family arrived. The moment Polly heard her father's car on the drive, she dropped the magazine and ran downstairs. I followed her, only to find at the bottom of the staircase that Polly and her father were nowhere to be seen. Unsure what to do, I hovered at the kitchen door while Isobel welcomed Theo and his friend.

At eighteen, Theo was a male version of his mother. They had the same corn-coloured hair, the same brown eyes. I thought him beautiful in a way that only someone of a completely different physical type can be beautiful. I stared at him in wonder, his face radiant as he hugged his mother.

'Isobel, you've done marvels,' he exclaimed, his arm around her waist. 'Your palate may be a little hot for my liking, but this room works. It really works.' Theo wanted to be an architect when he was older; either an architect or a designer of some sort.

Mrs Venus laughed. Then, seeing me stranded at the door, she drew me to her side, introducing me to her son. I shook hands with him and the girl at his side: a slim, voluptuous teenager with the dark eyes of a sphinx, Sylvie was the daughter of Parisian friends.

Emerging from her father's study, Polly stared at Sylvie, raising an eyebrow. The French girl was dressed in what looked like the remnants of a jumble sale: a white cotton petticoat edged with elaborate flounces and a silk camise, at least a size too small, that exaggerated her cleavage. On her feet were black combat boots. Drawing me aside, Polly hissed in my ear: 'Theo likes girls with tits. Big tits.' I giggled as Polly gesticulated, making mountains of her breasts, while Mrs Venus and Theo, speaking occasionally in French, planned an itinerary for the afternoon.

Sylvie wanted to visit the seaside. She kept asking what colour the sea was in Britain: green, blue or grey? In the Caribbean, she said, her eyes half-shut in reverie, in the Caribbean at Christmas, the water had been a translucent turquoise. Perfect, quite perfect. And the Aegean in the spring was wine-dark. Now that she was in Devon, she wanted to see the Atlantic, to breathe in great gusts of iodine.

Mrs Venus suggested Branscombe. Theo said the houses on the Lyme Regis seafront were architecturally interesting.

Sighing dramatically, Polly said to her brother: 'She wants to look at the sea, stupid!'

'I know she wants to look at the sea. There's sea at Lyme Regis.'

'But the water at Branscombe is far nicer,' Mrs Venus remarked. 'If it's architecture you're after, nothing compares to Brighton.'

'Isobel dearest, we're *miles* away from Brighton!'

'I was only making a point, Theo.'

'Well, there's the Cobb at Lyme Regis, and the promenade, and its jam-packed with culture: Jane Austen, John Fowles. I'll run you down to Lyme, Sylvie, if Isobel will lend us the car.'

'You can borrow your father's car, darling. And while you're about it, you might as well take the children with you. It's time they went out instead of reading under their beds all day.'

Glaring at her mother, Polly replied with perfectly modulated condescension: 'What makes you think we'd even consider going to Lyme, Mommy dearest?'

'Everyone needs fresh air once in a while, Polly. I'm sure Ajuba would like a stroll by the sea, even if you don't.'

'Hallo? Did anyone ask us what we wanted to do? You might want to cramp Theo's style, Isobel, but we don't. Anyway, no one *strolls* any more. We want to hang out here. Don't we, Aj?'

'What colour is the sea at Lyme?' Sylvie asked dreamily. 'I want to stare at the sea.'

That afternoon, having won the battle to stay home, we did imitations of the French girl upstairs. We were at that transitional stage before the hormonal riot of puberty when passion, turning in on itself, becomes enamoured with its own kind.

'Sylvie has colossal breasts,' Polly began, augmenting her chest with a pillow.

Adjusting a cushion beneath my T-shirt I moaned, 'She has enormous tits.'

'Gorgeous boobs as vast as Vesuvius!'

'What's Vesuvius?'

'Some volcano in Italy.'

'Does it erupt?'

'Constantly.'

'Do people die?'

'They're always dying in Italy, Aj. If it's not volcanoes, it's the Mafia. They can't get enough of dying over there. They think it's so cool they sing about it all the time.'

'Do they?'

'Sure! In operas.'

Relieved that my father had sent me to boarding school in England, I continued our game: 'Sylvie's bosoms are as big as Brighton?'

'They're much bigger. They're so big her knockers are bursting with . . .'

'Milk? Yuk! Polly, do you think Theo touches them?'

'I'm sure he does. That's what boys do. That's why he took her to Lyme Regis, stupid!'

I screamed while Polly laughed at me. 'Touching tits is

no big deal, Aj. He can't help himself. It's his hormones. That's what Peter says. Would you like to grow big bosoms when you're older?'

'Not as big as Sylvie's perhaps, but I'd like them to get bigger eventually. Wouldn't you?'

'Maybe.'

Just as the afternoon was beginning to sag and we were tiring of enhancing our breasts with underwear and bedding, Mr Venus came out of his study. I knew because Polly stopped what she was saying. She seemed to have a sixth sense where her father was concerned, anticipating his movements as if his mere being could shift the mood in the house. He had spent the whole afternoon locked away. No one was allowed to disturb him. Yet even before his door opened Polly, sensing that he was available, ran to him.

The first thing Mr Venus did when he was out in the open was to put on a record, a family favourite: Van Morrison singing 'Brown-eyed Girl'. The English are not all the same, I decided, watching the intoxicating effect Mr Venus had on his family. He took Mrs Venus in his arms and they began dancing, hip to hip.

He was a handsome man in early middle age, tawny hair flecked with grey. His eyes were of the same intensity as Polly's, the result of some Irish pedigree in his blood, I believe; whenever he ate seafood, or drank excessively, his eyes took on a turquoise hue. Seeing him dancing, I immediately thought of Aunt Rose. Theo had grabbed hold of Sylvie and they were dancing as well. And Polly, suddenly gleeful, started leaping up and down. I tried to slip away, but she caught hold of my arm. I was to dance as well.

Embarrassed, I made the movements my aunt had taught me, swaying in time to the music. And when the chorus came, a deep gravelly voice rasping, 'Do you remember when we used to sing?' I joined in the '*shalalas*'. The Venuses shouted them, dancing around the kitchen table. Peter kissed Isobel, Theo kissed Sylvie, then we all changed partners.

Peter put the record on again. His brown-eyed girl was Isobel, he told me, but Polly was his heart's delight. He danced with her the second time, while Theo danced with me. His hand caressing my arm, Theo said that I reminded him of a Benin bronze. I thanked him – although I didn't know what he was talking about, I was aware that he was paying me a compliment. Then I shook his hand away.

I quickly realised that Mr Venus liked music from the Olden Days. He orchestrated the family's impromptu party, choosing songs from an extensive collection of vinyl in his study. He had all of Bob Dylan's LPs, Roy Orbison, old Chess records, Elvis Presley's Sun collection and shelves upon shelves of classical music and jazz CDs. After Van Morrison, he put on a record that I recognised immediately. It was one of the songs that Aunt Rose used to 'release the spirit', as she called it. 'To dance, Ajuba,' she would say, dragging me onto the veranda at Kuku Hill, 'you must connect with the spirit between your legs and hips. Dance is sacred joy and this song of all the songs I know will teach you every move necessary to party well. Now shake!'

The man singing told me to shake as well, and copying Aunt Rose's movements, following the singer's instructions on how to slither like soup, shoulders and hips swirling, a whip in motion, I learnt how to move, arms unfolding as my body looped and rolled.

The moment the opening chord struck in the house and Sam Cooke tickled the soles of my feet, inciting me to shake, Aunt Rose appeared, yelling encouragement. I trembled in anticipation of my aunt's sacred joy; my shyness evaporated and I was dancing. 'Roll those hips,' Aunt Rose called out. 'Faster. Put your hands on your hips, make your body slip. Yeah, you're looking good, Mama! The spirit's with you at last! You're flying, Ajuba!'

So when Polly, slipping into Aunt Rose's shoes, shouted: 'Go girl!' I laughed loudly with the spirit inside me. 'Aj, where on this planet did you learn those moves? You must teach me, kiddo. I want to move like that.'

Aunt Rose used to say that *obronie* – white people – couldn't dance to save their lives. But she hadn't seen Mr and Mrs Venus dancing. They moved with the practised grace of old adversaries locked in motion. 'Bodies never lie,' I heard Aunt Rose say. 'You must listen to your own, Ajuba. And watch those of the people around you.'

And then as if to prove that it wasn't just at school that the English were strange, even as Sam Cooke's song was binding us together, beads of panting expectation hanging in the air, the family suddenly stopped dancing and trooped upstairs.

They were going to change for dinner, Polly told me as I followed: not into formal clothes, but into clothes that marked the transition of day to night. If Peter was at home, it was part of their daily ritual to celebrate Mrs Venus's culinary efforts by candlelight, when, like a high priestess officiating at a shrine, she administered to family and friends.

The English learn how to cook from books, I explained later to my cousin Esi, Aunt Lila's daughter in Ghana. I was writing her a letter in my head to help me make sense of the Venuses. I had noticed, looking at the collection of books in the kitchen, that Mrs Venus was an admirer of Elizabeth David. When I got to know her better, she told me she swore by Jane Grigson for anything to do with fish.

And Polly hadn't lied to me. Isobel cooked well, from the books or adapting recipes she'd discovered on her travels. Nothing was too much trouble. The ratatouille we ate at dinner that night had taken over three hours to cook, thickening slowly on the Aga. And when her offering was laid out (as much care was spent on the colour and presentation of her food as on the objects in her home) Mrs Venus relaxed, allowing her husband to come into his own.

After a second glass of wine, Peter Venus's interest in people revived. He became voluble, extracting with ease the amusing events of everyone's day. While his wife sat back, he gossiped with Sylvie and Theo, demanding details of their expedition to Lyme Regis. He asked me how my cycling was coming along. And was I getting the hang of rollerblading? Polly replied on my behalf, while I listened and watched.

Aunt Rose used to say that you can tell what sort of man you're dealing with by the way he eats a mango. If he sucks it slowly, tenderly squeezing out all the juice before he devours the skin, then he's a man who likes women, and he'll treat you well and will satisfy you. But if he tears at the skin, hungry for the pulp inside, then he should be avoided. We didn't eat any mangoes that evening, but watching the care with which Peter Venus sliced a pear, savouring its scent before he slipped one piece after the other into his mouth, I decided Aunt Rose would approve of him. I liked his hands best of all: they were firm and dry, the fingers long, the moon of his nails large. I noticed them then, and later on when he played with Polly's hair. At the end of the meal, chocolate wrappers and half-eaten pieces of fruit and cheese littering the table, he cleared it for coffee. Later, with one hand warming a brandy, he slipped the other into his wife's open palm, gently kissing the tips of her fingers.

In England, I wrote in my letter to Esi, children are allowed to be rude to their parents and adults serve their children.

Mrs Venus was loading the dishwasher. I got up to help. She stacked the plates while Theo and Sylvie whispered to each other over coffee, and Polly, on her father's lap, nuzzled against him.

I handed plates to Mrs Venus, and then I passed cutlery, bowls and glasses. When the last utensil was in place, she smiled at me, touching my cheek. 'You're a sweetheart. Thank you, pet,' she said, stooping to kiss my forehead.

Polly's people are always touching each other, I told Esi. They're nice but they're not like us. Struggling to suppress my misgivings, I watched the Venuses lavish affection on one another: Theo embracing his mother after berating her (he claimed she was too much of a perfectionist), Peter kissing Polly and then, a moment later, tweaking his wife's ears. The Venuses were tactile. Fondling came easily to them, to kiss and be kissed.

I don't know which frightened me more: their sensuality or my aching desire, stirred by seeing them together, to have my own family around me again. Starved of affection as I was – despite their love of nature, the Derbys were not life-affirming huggers of trees or people – I found myself succumbing to the Venuses' charm.

My initiation began that evening. The meal over, Polly kissed her parents goodnight. To my dismay, they expected me to kiss them as well. I complied awkwardly. But with Isobel's third kiss and Peter's first, my enchantment with them ignited. The next evening, performing the same ritual, I discovered that I wanted to be kissed; indeed, I craved it. Like a kitten brought in from the cold, thawing out before a fire, I warmed myself against the Venuses. Without realising what was happening, I began to relax, to lower my guard.

As if by mutual consent they held back from asking too many questions. They left me alone until, seduced by affection, I was ready to talk. When the time came, it was Mr Venus who encouraged me: gently, carefully. I remember it clearly, for I was drinking my first glass of diluted red wine, poured for me by Theo. We were eating Chicken Veronique, a meal Polly picked her way through, eating the grapes and discarding the chicken, while Peter asked me questions. He already knew that my father was a lawyer working with an international organisation in Rome, yet he still asked me: where my father lived, what work he did. When I answered, he asked more questions.

'Is your mother in Rome as well, Ajuba?'

My mouth was full, so he turned to Polly, chiding her for playing with her food. Irritated, Polly turned on her mother.

'Why don't you cook regular food, Isobel? Like –'

'Like pizza and hot dogs and french fries?' Isobel replied.

'Because junk food isn't good for you, Polly!' Imitating her mother, Polly pushed her plate away in frustration.

My mouth empty at last, I answered Mr Venus. 'My mother's in Ghana staying with my aunt Lila. She's not very well.'

'Nothing serious I hope.'

I replied without thinking, speaking out of a need to share a side of myself I had long kept concealed. 'She's quite ill, I think. She's ill because I'm her only child. You see, my father wants more children, and she does too, but his family said they had to divorce. Then he took me away.'

'Your poor mother. She must miss you terribly.'

At that moment, Theo caressed my forearm. Whether he

touched me out of sympathy or because he liked the texture of my skin, I don't know. He startled me, and I withdrew my arm quickly, knocking my glass over. The wine spilled over the lace tablecloth, spreading to the centrepiece of lilac and bluebells that I had picked for Isobel that afternoon.

Afraid that the Venuses would not want me to visit again, I mumbled: 'Please forgive me. I'm terribly sorry.'

Peter Venus chuckled. 'There's nothing to forgive, little one,' he said. 'Spilling wine is a form of baptism in this family. You're one of us now, Ajuba. Welcome home!' He raised his glass and everyone started laughing. 'Here's to our new daughter!' he said. And they all drank to my health.

In six days the Venuses had extracted more information from me than anyone else had managed in a year.

6

Every other Thursday, at around seven o' clock in the evening, my father called me from Rome. He telephoned from his office at an hour when he knew I had finished Prep and eaten supper. Pa was punctilious in reaching me during the lull between the end of school and Lights Out – if only for a few minutes – before he dashed out to dinner. Our conversations were stilted, punctuated by long, gaping pauses while I struggled to think of what to say to captivate him a little longer. When Polly and I became friends, I found talking to Pa less daunting. I now had someone, apart from Beth, to tell him about: another family to interest him in. Prompted by Mrs Derby, I asked my father's permission to visit the Venuses regularly. 'Of course!' he replied, delighted I was finally settling down.

After half term, I became a frequent visitor to Graylings. I went home whenever Polly went home, which was almost every weekend. I was always made to feel welcome, yet my primary concern was how to get around calling Polly's mother by her Christian name.

Isobel insisted that was what she wanted. My suggestion of prefixing Auntie to her name she found anathema; the first time I tried calling her Auntie Isobel, she fell about laughing. I found it easier to use her Christian name after that, although it went against everything my mother had taught me about the deference a child owes an adult, to respect the gulf between us.

One weekend, when Theo and Peter had come home for the first time in ages, I sensed that Isobel was tense. She couldn't keep still. She went from room to room rearranging the position of lamps and ornaments, her hands fluttering over a spray of lilies which dusted her fingertips with pollen.

It was a hot day in June and I put her restlessness down to the weather. We were in the middle of a heatwave and I was aware that the English were inclined to find too much sun unbearable. Unloading the dishwasher, Isobel appeared tired. She seemed to want us out of her way; 'Out from under her feet'. 'You two had better hurry up,' she said. 'Beth Bradshaw will be here soon.'

Polly and I were loitering in the kitchen, downing milk-shakes. Beth? We hadn't been expecting Beth. Despite her notion of equality between adults and children, it was typical of Isobel to make plans without consulting us.

'Don't you want help clearing out the trunks in the attic?' Isobel asked. This was a job she had asked us to do over the weekend and one we had avoided.

'Not today . . .'

'Today!' she insisted.

Within the hour, Beth was at the house, ferried over by her mother, who stayed for coffee. Polly, Beth and I ran up the two flights of stairs to the attic, which was to the left of the top landing, under the south-west slope of the roof. Polly pushed the door open and switched on the light.

Wooden beams ran across a low, cobwebbed ceiling, giving the space the closed, inward feel of a room for discarded objects. In a far corner was a pile of dusty old lamps, packing cases and broken furniture, which Isobel had already sorted. She was thinking of transforming the attic into a studio for herself, to open it up by putting in skylights, painting it white, clearing out the rubbish. To help her achieve her aim, she wanted us to unpack two trunks of clothes left by the previous owner of the house. We were to sort them out into two piles, one for a bonfire, one for charity shops. Isobel had made her plans without considering the mayhem three pre-teenagers can cause with a treasure trove of clothes.

The large rectangular trunks were made of wood covered in varnished brown material, protected by strips of rusting plate metal. The lids were held in place by bronze-coloured lever catches. Polly tugged at the levers of the first trunk, and, after wrenching them apart, she flung the lid open and then pulled out an embroidered shawl that had been spread over the top. She sniffed it, wrinkling up her nose before throwing the shawl at me. I draped it around my shoulders, inspired by the rich tapestry of its colours: gold and red roses writhing against a black background, green leaves and stems twisting beneath the flowers. And tassels, tassels everywhere. I started dancing, curling the shawl around my arms, while Polly threw out three large blouses and a faded riding jacket.

'Whose are they?' Beth asked, donning the jacket.

'Miss Olivia Fielding's, I guess. She used to live here with the Bag Lady down the road.'

'Doesn't Miss Fielding want these things?' I wanted the shawl for myself.

'Not where she's at,' Polly said.

'Where's that?'

Polly pulled a face, slitting her throat with a forefinger. 'She's six feet under, kiddo.'

Then, in a frenzy, she tossed garment after garment over

her shoulders: jodhpurs, nightdresses, evening dresses, skirts. Beth and I dived into them like a pair of bargain-seekers at the January sales, wanting to try on everything.

We were playing at being mannequins in a matching set of striped cotton pyjamas as Polly tried to force open the second trunk. The clasps of its lid were stiff, so she hammered them loose, prising them open with a combination of strength and determination.

I saw her pull out a heavy astrakhan coat, marvelling at the softness of its texture and its silk lining. Polly seemed about to try it on; she unbuttoned it, gliding her fingers over the lining. I saw her pause to feel something between the lining and the lambskin. Carefully she teased out a small bundle wrapped in black cloth.

'Weird,' she said.

Beth and I stopped playing. Polly was opening the bundle, her deft fingers unpicking well-tied knots. She spread the contents out.

'What is it?' Beth asked.

I turned away. I had seen it and I didn't want to see it again, for I knew without a shadow of a doubt that it meant trouble. According to Malone and Leboeuf, the Fourth Principle of Detection was intuition: 'Whatever happens, trust your gut instinct because it's handing you clues you can't yet untangle.' My instinct taking hold of my body, made me turn my back on the contents on Polly's lap while she stared, bewildered.

'What is it?' Beth asked again.

'I don't know.' Then, wrapping the contents back up and scrambling to her feet, Polly ran downstairs, Beth and me running behind her.

Theo was home that weekend, so we ran to his room first.

He was practising tai chi, his right hand travelling slowly through the air as his knees dipped. He froze when he saw us.

'Look, Theo!' Polly thrust the bundle into his face.

Maintaining his position, he stared coldly at his sister.

'Look!'

He kept staring at us, the iciness of his silence forcing Polly to take a backward step. 'Can't you see I'm busy?' he said.

'But we've found something, Theo!'

'Shove off, will you?' He dismissed us by closing his eyelids. Opening them with a deep outward breath, he added, 'And for God's sake don't go disturbing the parents, Polly. They're wading through their shit again.'

At the mention of her parents, Polly bridled: 'Why not try and tell me something new for a change? Like something interesting? But, hey, you don't know how to, Theo, because you are so totally uncool, you suck!'

'Don't say I didn't warn you, Polly.'

We ran down to the kitchen. Peter was in the chair Mrs Bradshaw had sat in earlier. He was sitting opposite Isobel, and from the expression on their faces I knew something unpleasant was happening. Isobel was laughing unnaturally with short, furious barks of contempt that defied the despair on her face. Her eyes, glittering with tears, seemed unable to contain her anger. She was bolt upright, her palms flat on the table, the altar she worshipped at whenever her husband was at home. Peter was slouching, his body half-turned away from her, disengaged from whatever was being said. It appeared that Isobel, itching to move her hands closer to Peter, simply wanted to touch him again. Polly dumped the bundle between her parents.

'Open it, Peter.'

Peter covered his face with his hands.

'It's not that gross. We found it in the attic.'

Polly was trying to sit on her father's lap, but he stood, shepherding us out of the room. Ducking from his grasp, she grabbed the bundle from the table. 'Please, Daddy. Please look. This is really important.'

'Later, kitten. Not now.' Despite Polly's protests, he shut the door in our faces.

We retreated to the silence of Peter's study; a sanctuary lined with music and books from floor to ceiling. It had a calm, cloistered atmosphere, very different to the rest of the house, which was unashamedly luxurious in colour and texture. On the desk was a chunky grey *PowerBook* computer, on a shelf a cumbersome fax machine. The study was the one room that was truly Peter's; its wealth of books and music and a single painting on the wall its only decorations. On the lower shelves were long, leather-bound manuscripts, antique maps Peter had bought in the countries he had lived in. They looked unappealing until their rough pages opened to reveal glorious new worlds.

Polly had told me that the painting, the only one Peter possessed, was a Paul Nash landscape. On the few occasions Peter returned home, I remember watching him, his attention poised mournfully on the canvas's dark splashes of colour. He would stare as if realigning himself to a hidden constellation of stars that could take him back to a happier time. He appeared distracted, a traveller who had misplaced an inner compass and lost his bearings completely.

I gazed at the picture, wondering what Theo had meant when he'd warned us against disturbing Peter and Isobel. Immersing myself in purple and black brushstrokes, I delved deeper, intrigued by the source of Peter's sadness, until I found myself in a barren place without sun, the trees' dark silhouettes hobbled by wind and rain. As Polly spread out the bundle on Peter's desk, revealing its contents again, I was alone and frightened, submerged in the desolation of the painting. I didn't want to look at what was on the desk. I preferred the emptiness of the landscape in front of me, yet eventually I felt compelled to turn around for the same reason that I had played True Murder, and why I came home with Polly week after week. I was irrevocably drawn to her, and whatever interested her eventually held my attention as well.

The parcel contained the remains of what seemed to be small animals. There was little left of them apart from fragile bones and tiny fragments of skulls. Tears came to my eyes, yet my uppermost feeling was a thin thread of fear tugging at my heart. Emanating from the parcel, strong and corrosive as the touch of acid, was the suffocating stench of a grave disturbed.

'I think we should bury them,' I said.

'The poor kittens,' said Beth, her face flushed with sympathy. 'Whoever did this was disgusting.'

'I think we should bury them.'

Putting down the pencil with which she was prodding the bones, Polly looked at me dumbfounded. 'Bury the evidence and let the perpetrator escape? No way!'

'But Polly, they won't rest till we bury them. They want to be at peace again.'

I believed in omens and portents, in a golden bullet killing an Ashanti general. I believed in the blood-soaked dress of a child's broken body, in the faces of witches in my mother's mirror. And Malone and Leboeuf were whispering in my inner ear, telling me to go with my gut, to trust the shiver of revulsion making me recoil from whatever it was in front of me. A gash was appearing on the Venus veneer and I wanted to cover it quickly. Polly, however, had other ideas.

'Hallo? Am I hearing things? Did she say what I think she said? Wise up, Aj. We've got to find out who hid them. They could have been buried alive, for all we know. Right, Beth?'

'Poor little kittens.'

'They're only animals,' I said, desperate to suppress the implications of our discovery. 'Who cares?'

I was caught in a vice of terror and desire; desire to protect myself from an unspecified threat that was inching towards us and terror at stepping deeper into Polly's clandestine world. 'Whoever did this must have done it a long time ago. It makes no difference now. We should let it rest.'

'That's where you're wrong, Aj.'

'If something happened to you,' I persisted, 'would you want someone poking about with your bones? Bones should be laid to rest, it says so in the Bible.'

'Jeez, Aj, give me a break! If anything happened to me, I'd want you to investigate and find out what happened, like we're going to do with these bones. Right, Beth?'

Beth nodded half-heartedly, torn between Polly's instinct to solve the mystery we had uncovered – in a quest for knowledge I was drawn to as well – and my need to preserve the status quo. In the end, her choice came as no surprise: 'Whoever hid these kittens is despicable. They're wicked and should be punished. The least we can do is stop it happening again. I think we should call the RSPCA, Aj. Polly's right.'

'Yes! Gimme the phone book, the yellow one,' Polly instructed, indicating a pile of multicoloured books under her father's desk. Beth brought the yellow one over. Flipping though the pages, Polly found the section she wanted. She reached for Peter's phone and punched in the number for the RSPCA.

I spent the afternoon hoping they wouldn't come, hoping they'd think the call a hoax and disregard it. In an attempt to sound like an adult, Polly had tried to make her voice deeper. Giving the address of Graylings, she claimed to be her mother. She wouldn't have fooled me, so I thought it unlikely that they'd be fooled either.

By mid-afternoon, I could see she was growing tired of waiting. I imagined her burying the bundle in the garden, as I'd suggested, believing that if I imagined it, it might happen. The strand of fear around my heart slackened momentarily, only for it to tighten again when I heard Peter shouting: 'Why can't you leave me alone, woman! I've said all I want to say.'

From Polly's room, we could hear Isobel's voice begging, 'Let me in, Peter. Please let me in.'

As the afternoon progressed, Isobel became increasingly agitated. I heard her roaming the house with the restless rage of a caged lioness, opening and shutting doors; pushing windows ajar, only to close them again before pacing back to Peter's door.

While we were upstairs, I heard Isobel's muffled knocking. It was the fourth time she had made the journey to Peter's lair and on each occasion he compelled her to leave. He had barricaded himself in his study in response to a campaign she was waging to re-establish contact with him. I knew this was what she wanted for after knocking, she pleaded: 'Peter, we've got to talk. We've got to thrash this out.'

This time, however, Peter bellowed: 'Isobel, if you disturb me again, I promise you, I'm going back to London.'

Beth and I glanced nervously at one another.

'Don't take any notice,' Polly reassured us. 'They're always fighting. Parents, huh?'

Polly's phlegmatic attitude was in direct contrast to mine. I associated the contagion of melancholy permeating the house and infecting her parents with the bones we'd uncovered in the attic. After all, the Venuses' distress and our discovery had occurred on the same day, so in my mind the two events were inextricably linked. It was more than mere coincidence. Something vital pertaining to all our lives was beginning to unfold and I desperately wanted to rearrange events, turn back the clock. Indeed, I prayed that the RSPCA would ignore Polly's call and that by nightfall, when the bones had been buried, the listlessness oppressing the house would lift and Isobel and Peter would be happy again.

As I breathed deeply, my anxiety began to ease. When I smelt the aroma of baking bread seeping from the kitchen through the house, I almost believed that all would be well. Isobel was cooking again: a sign I had learnt to associate with recovery. But at four that afternoon, just as Polly's anticipation of the RSPCA was waning, and Beth, having exhausted the pleasures of whacking Mexicans in one of Polly's video games, was bored, I heard a van travelling up the drive.

'They're here!' Polly cried.

We ran downstairs. The doorbell rang just before Polly threw the door open.

'Hi! Come on in,' she cried, grinning at a burly, balding man in navy blue.

He said, 'Good afternoon, I'm Mr Burroughs, RSPCA.' Then he seemed unsure what to do next. He looked at us through tired eyes. I could see that he wanted to talk to an adult.

Luckily, Peter, having heard the doorbell, came out of his study. 'What's going on?'

Mr Burroughs replied: 'We received an emergency phone call, sir.'

'I'm sorry, there must be some mistake.'

'This is Graylings house, isn't it?'

'Yes, but no one called from here.'

'I called you,' Polly admitted.

Peter glared at her.

'Well, you wouldn't listen,' she protested. 'I found these upstairs.' She handed the bundle of animal remains to the RSPCA man, who began examining them closely.

'They're bones, Daddy. Dead bones.'

Peter looked embarrassed. 'I'm afraid you've been called out on a wild goose chase. I'm terribly sorry.'

'It's no trouble, sir. If you don't mind, I'd like to see where these were found.'

Yes! Polly mouthed, punching the air.

We took the man up to the attic, to the astrakhan from the second trunk. The garment was lying on the floor, a handsome stray wantonly discarded. Polly showed Mr Burroughs where the bundle had been hidden: between the lining and the coat's soft brown fur.

'I knew in my gut something was wrong,' she said.

Peter smiled. 'You've made my daughter's day, Mr Burroughs. But there's bound to be a simple explanation.'

'What would you suggest, Mr Venus?' Unlike Peter, Mr Burroughs wasn't taking the matter lightly.

'Perhaps it was someone's idea of a practical joke?'

'Some joke!' Beth muttered.

'Peter, only a pervert would do something like this. It's not funny in the slightest. In fact it's totally, totally sick, Daddy.'

'I think we should take a closer look at these remains,' said Mr Burroughs, placing the bones in a plastic container, the frayed black cloth in another.

'Is this really necessary?' There was a note of impatience in Peter's voice, as if he thought the man overzealous. 'Miss Fielding died years ago, and her estate has been trying to sell the house for four years at least.'

I think he wanted the matter dropped; like me, he wanted the bones left alone. Mr Burroughs disagreed.

'With respect, sir,' he said firmly, 'we have to make sure these are what we think they are.'

Of course, Polly was delighted. And in the evening her pleasure at what she had accomplished, the discovery of the bones and their removal, prevented her from seeing what was obvious to Theo and me: Isobel's misery.

Isobel had cooked roast lamb and haricot beans for dinner, taking extra care with her roast potatoes, which she had parboiled and coated in salt and flour, so that when she removed them from the Aga they were battered crisp and crusty, the way Peter liked them. I remember that she smelt of bluebells that evening. Bluebells and something else: her unhappiness added a layer of decaying, crushed violets, so that she exuded the strong, sweet smell of fear. Glancing at her, I saw the image of my mother on her face.

'Go and fetch your father,' she asked Polly, when we were at table.

At her mother's request, Polly's delight at the day's events melted away. 'Why don't you get him yourself, Isobel? I'm not going to talk to him for you. I'm not going to pass messages again.'

'Polly, this is not what I need from you right now. Please ask your father to come to the table.'

'I'll go,' Theo volunteered.

'No, I want Polly to do what I asked her.'

Staring above Isobel's head at a celestial audience she was performing for, Polly sighed, exasperated: 'Jeez, I wonder why you want Polly to do your dirty work for you, Mommy dearest? Is it because Polly gets better results? You see, folks, Peter listens to her cos Polly's his pearl; his little girl. Sorry, Isobel,' she said, eyeing her mother. 'I'm not going to do it again. This is your headache. You deal with it.'

'Please, Polly.'

I couldn't bear to hear her pleading with my friend. My mother had never begged me to do her bidding; I had interceded willingly between my parents. Getting down from the table, I went to Peter's study.

'Will you come and eat with us?' I asked him.

He was staring at that picture again and it took him a few seconds to register who was talking to him. When he saw that it was me, he smiled.

'Of course, little one. Have you had a good day?'

'I didn't like the bones,' I confessed. Peter was always easy to talk to, always sympathetically inclined to me.

'Well, that makes two of us. They're best forgotten, I think. Let's pretend they never existed, OK, Ajuba?'

'I'll try,' I said.

Peter ate dinner with us as Isobel had wanted, though it was evident to everyone but her that it would have been better if he hadn't been there. He ignored her comments, drinking steadily until his eyes, a sodden turquoise, appeared amused, puzzled by his surroundings. He kept looking around as if he couldn't see the point of Isobel's possessions cluttered about him, couldn't quite understand where they'd all come from. As soon as he finished eating, downing Isobel's lemon sorbet in a single, wolfish gulp, he returned to his study.

The awkwardness of the meal and the speed of Peter's departure made me realise that unless something changed quickly there would be no more music or dancing around the kitchen table. There would be no more singing of Van Morrison's song, and Sam Cooke would fall silent. I couldn't understand how, in less than a month, Aunt Rose's sacred joy had evaporated. What had Isobel done? I wanted the family to return to what they'd been. I wanted to be kissed by them again and again.

That night, Isobel's unhappiness seeped into my sleep and, catching sight of my mother again, I woke up from a nightmare to hear the house whispering to me. My mother was calling me, pleading with me to come home. I'd seen Mama in my dreams before, but this time the dress she was wearing made me recoil. She was in a flowing full-length indigo boubou embroidered with rows of eyes. The eyes blinked shut. When they opened again, they glistened with the brightness of Peter's eyes. She wanted me home again, so I would see what she had seen.

I woke up, my head throbbing. I had to stop the bad thing happening again. I had to prevent a deep sleep of dejection descending on Isobel as it had done on my mother. At the mere thought of Isobel, the pain of my headache intensified, and the house, sighing, carried Isobel's sobs to my ears.

She was crying in the bathroom opposite, her lungs heaving with the pain of a traumatised child. Propelled out of bed by an overwhelming fear of the past repeating itself,

I ran to the bathroom. In the gap between the floor and the door, I saw a flicker of candlelight. Seeping from the bath itself was the sharp tang of Bromley's Herbal Essence: a scent guaranteed to soothe, relaxing the limbs. When I'd heard what I needed to, when I'd confirmed that Isobel's tears were real and not tears streaming through my dream, I bolted to Peter's room.

Over the weekend, he had taken to sleeping in his dressing-room, leaving Isobel alone in the marital bed. I ran into his room without knocking. He was still awake, reading in bed, a pair of half-moon glasses on his nose.

'Help me, Peter,' I cried. 'My head's hurting me and I don't want it to happen again. I don't want to remember. Please give me medicine for my head.'

Gathering me in his arms, he held me close, calming me with the warmth of his body and his words. I was going to be all right. I had nothing to worry about, he said. My headache would get better. It had been a difficult day for us all.

He smelt of cedar and cinnamon and a deep musky scent that men exude from their pores. I breathed it in, clinging to his neck, and as he lifted me in his arms, my headache evaporated.

'I need medicine,' I pleaded, determined to achieve my goal. 'My head's hurting.'

The medicine cupboard was in Isobel's bathroom. Leaving me in his room, Peter went to fetch me an aspirin. He returned with Isobel and a glass of water. I swallowed the pill and he led me to bed, kissed me goodnight, then returned to his room and Isobel.

I heard them talking late into the night. They spoke of the house and Polly. They spoke without shouting at each other. And when their talking ceased, I heard them laughing shyly, conspiratorially, apparently content to be together again.

I fell asleep, delighted with what I had engineered. I sincerely believed they would bc happy; and that with their happiness would come satisfaction for me, blessed relief from my mother's eyes. I was a child, so I knew no better. I didn't know that what consenting adults choose to do is their business and theirs alone; and that as a child, a friend of their daughter's, my actions were peripheral to the drama unfolding in our lives. This is what I've been told time and time again. I am not to blame. What happened did not occur because I engineered it. But if I hadn't brought them together, if I had adopted Polly's sophisticated attitude of never meddling in matters pertaining to the adult heart, a decision she had reached at some cost to herself, would events have turned out differently? I shall never know.

7

To say that our lives changed significantly after our discovery of the bones in the attic is not an exaggeration. At the outset, the three of us, Polly, Beth and I, savoured our first taste of tabloid publicity; and with that came a degree of notoriety we welcomed. We became local heroines, a trio of innocents dragging a deed that had been done in darkness into daylight. Alexander James, Crime Correspondent of the *Devon Gazette*, came to see us and our photograph was in the newspaper.

I'm told that the Derbys tried to stop him. It wasn't the sort of publicity they wanted for the school. So when the reporter called Mrs Derby asking permission for an interview, she refused. But there wasn't much they or anyone else could do to prevent the story appearing because Belinda Bradshaw alerted the *Gazette* to our adventure. Then, with the backing of Isobel Venus, she invited Alexander James to Graylings. He came on a Saturday morning with a photographer, and after he'd jotted down our names and ages, we had our photograph taken. Instant fame. Our fifteen minutes.

I have the clipping in front of me now; when the story came out, Polly decided we should keep a record of our exploits, a scrapbook of our *True Murders*. Under a bold front-page headline: BABIES' BODIES PUZZLE – WORLD

EXCLUSIVE, there is a photograph of Polly, Beth and me and an article written by Alexander James. In his usual, breathless style he described the events at Graylings a few weeks previously: our discovery of what we believed at the time were animal remains, which Mr Burroughs, finding no evidence of fur, had taken to the police. They in turn sent the remains to a Home Office pathologist for post-mortem examination. They were confirmed as human. The police took photographs of the trunk in the attic, then, they interviewed the three of us in the presence of Peter and Isobel. There was going to be an inquest.

I can't say that I didn't enjoy the attention. I did. We all did. And despite my initial inclination to suppress the evidence by burying it, in the aftermath of the story surfacing, I was glad that Polly got her way.

She was in her element, a diminutive Agent Starling on the trail of her very own *Silence of the Lambs*. After all, she had uncovered the parcel, and the babies had been hidden in her attic, so she gave us our name. We became 'Crimebusters', junior sleuths determined to track down whoever was responsible for the heinous crime. Though there was no proof, we were convinced the babies had been murdered. Polly was in earnest, but to begin with for Beth and me, Crimebusters was a game: a continuation of the game of mannequins we'd been playing when the bundle was first discovered. But for Maria, who hadn't been with us, pretending to be detectives was a waste of time.

Our constant refrain was 'Who did it?', 'Who did it?' Who had hidden the babies in Miss Fielding's trunk? I must have asked the question at least ten times as I cut the clipping out of the newspaper and started gluing it into the scrapbook.

It was evening, the curtains were drawn and we were in Exe getting ready for bed. As usual, Polly was in front of the mirror, brushing her hair.

'Who do you think did it?' I asked again.

Beth answered: 'Miss Fielding? Miss Edith? Anyone could have.'

'Naa,' said Polly, turning around. 'Your mom said Miss Fielding was nice. Miss Edith's kind of weird, I guess, but she's too ordinary.'

'But you said murderers are often nice,' Maria recalled. She was reading a book in bed. She put it down. 'Don't you remember, Polly? You said that it's often the nicest people who end up being murderers.'

'Maria, honey, you have no idea what it takes.'

'What it takes to do what? To get my face in the paper?'

'To pull a trigger. To put your hands around someone's neck and . . .'

As she was speaking, Polly walked to where I sat on the floor. She placed her hands around my neck. 'To put your hands around someone's neck,' she repeated, 'and *squeeze.*'

I felt her fingers tightening. She closed her eyes. I began gasping for air. The bottle of glue tumbled from my fingers. I wanted to push her away; but for some reason, I didn't. I must have trusted her. I must have known that she had no intention of hurting me. I was aware of Beth and Maria looking on, mesmerised by something they saw in Polly's face. My eyes were beginning to shut and my body was drifting away when suddenly Polly relaxed her grip. I began to cough, breathing in great gusts of air.

'You've got to hate someone to kill them,' she said.

For a moment there was silence while we stared at her. Then Maria, irritated no doubt by what she saw as Polly's attention-seeking exploits, blurted out: 'You said that sometimes people kill just for the thrill of it.'

'Put a sock in it, Maria!' Beth shouted.

'Shut up yourself, Bradshaw!' Maria was livid. A flush of anger rose from her neck covering her face and the tip of her ears, clouding her pale grey eyes. 'And while you're at it, stop crowing about those bones. They're pathetic! Utterly pathetic! It's only Alexander James who says they're babies' bones. And what does he know? Mummy's never even heard of him. He's pathetic and so are you!'

'As if!' Beth scoffed.

Polly raised an eyebrow. 'Is this kid for real?' she asked, pulling a face at Maria.

I could see that Maria was close to tears. I'm sure she would have liked to have discovered the bones with us; I know she would have liked her photograph in the papers. But as chance would have it, after half term she'd spent most of her weekends with her mother in London. Anyway, Polly didn't like her.

Beth started giggling, so did Polly. I remember Maria choking back her tears. She seemed to be weighing something up, deciding whether to inflict maximum pain, or beat a hasty retreat. I think it was when I started giggling as well that she made up her mind.

'You think you know everything, don't you, Polly Venus?' she sneered, hoping to wipe the smile from Polly's face. 'You think you know everything, but you don't. You're as pathetic as your stupid father. He wants to marry my Mummy, that's how *pathetic* he is.'

Maria's raw hatred crushed the tears out of her. She wept in fury while Beth and I watched, waiting to see what Polly would do next. To our surprise she continued smiling: a world-weary smile imbued with wisdom beyond her years.

'Wise up, Maria,' she said. 'Balling someone means zit nowadays. Fucking is no big deal at all. This is the *nineties*, kiddo.'

Polly tucked a strand of hair behind an ear and began laughing again. Beth and I followed her example, though we had no idea what we were laughing about. I felt a sudden release of tension that made me laugh louder. Clutching her stomach, Beth rolled onto her bed, shaking her legs in the air. Polly grabbed hold of me and we collapsed on the floor together. We laughed, while Maria, crying, ran from the room to find her brother.

Following Polly's lead, we chose to ignore Maria's revelation that her mother was having an affair with Peter Venus. Uppermost in our minds was what we should do as Crimebusters to solve the mystery of the bones in Miss Fielding's trunk. The sexual antics of adults were insipid in comparison to our obsession with how the dead babies had ended up at Graylings. Walking arm in arm along the Bottom Lawn, as confident in our notoriety as the Three Musketeers, we discussed our next move. It was break time and some children in Juniors, spilling out of a classroom, careered across the lawn, chasing one another. Ordinarily, they would have bumped into us, sidling up to Beth to glean scraps of information. But that afternoon, an air of cocky invincibility shielded us and they kept their distance. Perhaps they were in awe of Polly, who was in favour of conducting a full-blown investigation into our discovery. She wanted action.

'The Bag Lady down the road's got to know something,' she said.

'Such as?'

'I don't know. I haven't talked to her yet.'

I noted the 'yet' with a tremor of apprehension. 'The police are investigating, Polly. Let's see what they find out.'

'Crimebusters don't wait,' she retorted, sucking hard on a blackjack before passing it on to Beth. 'Crimebusters do things. They solve crimes, they stop murders from happening.'

'A bit like *Crimewatch* on television,' Beth added enthusiastically. 'Do you think they'll invite us on *Crimewatch*?'

'I hope not!' Having my photograph in the paper was quite enough for me, yet I had an inkling of the direction Polly was heading. Miss Edith Butterworth had lived for years with Miss Fielding. She had been her companion. She might give us some answers.

'Know what we got to do?' Polly said.

'You're not going to get us into trouble again?'

'Naa . . .' she assured me. 'If we want to find out what happened, we've got to pay the Bag Lady a visit.'

'OK,' I replied tentatively. 'But if we're going to do it, we've got to do it properly. We've got to follow the Basic Principles.'

'What are you on about, Aj?' Beth, temperamentally light of spirit, was always taken aback by my seriousness.

'Malone and Leboeuf's Basic Principles of Detection: observation, interrogation, persistence and intuition – give or take a lucky break or two. You know, Eugene Malone and Beau Leboeuf, the detectives in *True Murder*? The ones who work for the NYPD?'

'Jeez, Aj, they're not real. They're made up.'

'They're real, Polly! They've solved more homicides than anyone in New York. They're world famous,' I added. Indeed, Malone and Leboeuf had become so real to me that they sometimes walked either side of me, reaffirming my feelings by whispering in my ear.

'She may have a point.' Removing a wafer-thin slab of the blackjack from the tip of her tongue, Beth returned it to Polly, who was staring into the middle distance, gazing dreamily at a pair of children rolling on the grass without a care in the world.

'Yeah, Venus, Benson and Bradshaw! We should make diamanté Crimebuster badges with our initials on them. Aj, I think you're on to something. If we use the principles, we'll crack the case wide open. Good thinking, kiddo!'

Before I could reply, Polly had slipped what was left of the blackjack into my open mouth and I was sucking it.

Our first visit to Miss Edith Butterworth was on a warm Saturday afternoon towards the end of term. With the sun bright in a sailor-blue sky, we arrived at the Gatehouse as Venus, Benson and Bradshaw of Crimebusters Incorporated: the most successful detective agency in Devon. Polly, our leader, knocked vigorously on the door.

After what seemed an eternity of barking and muffled, hesitant movement, the door opened a few inches. It was held in place by a chain. Our first close encounter with Miss Edith was with an anxious old woman, half-hidden by a door, wielding an umbrella. She was taking no chances.

'What do you want?'

Polly gave the old woman her most winning smile, holding up a carrier bag. 'My mom asked me to give you this.'

The three of us had decided to arrive bearing gifts of strawberries and peaches to ensure easy entry into the house. Miss Edith appeared puzzled. Perhaps she imagined at first that we were trick-or-treating out of season. We were wearing what might have looked to anyone else like fancy dress. Polly had started lending me her clothes and I was in a pair of turquoise pantaloons from Thailand and a fuchsia pink puffa jacket. Polly was going through a lime-green phase and everything she had on sparkled an acidic, brilliant green, while Beth, in faded jeans, was wearing Miss Fielding's own riding jacket. Adding to our unusual appearance were our Crimebuster badges pinned to our chests: our initials in glitter glued to cardboard.

Miss Edith opened the door wider to receive the parcel. It was then that she must have recognised us from our photograph in the paper and her daily walks around the Gatehouse.

'I suppose you'd better come in,' she said.

Polly stepped inside, followed by Beth and me. I was nervous of dogs and clung on to Beth's jacket.

'There's no need to worry, dear,' said Miss Edith, holding a boxer by the collar as I sidled down the corridor. 'They won't hurt you, you know. They've eaten already.'

She led us along the narrow corridor into a cluttered kitchen. There were unwashed pots soaking in a stone sink, and on the floor two bowls spattered with minced meat and biscuits. Unwrapping the contents of the carrier bag, Miss Edith lifted a peach to her nose, inhaling its scent with almost mystical glee. 'Ah,' she sighed. 'Nothing gives me greater satisfaction than a whiff of the Mediterranean. The Promenade des Anglais, a piazza in Florence, figs and Greek yoghurt. Please thank your mother. It's very kind of her to think of me.'

For such a small woman she had a strong, melodious voice. She was untidy: her clothes, a faded summer dress and a bedraggled cardigan, were thrown together in a haphazard manner. Petite, with cropped iron-grey hair pulled away from her face with a large grip, she made bird-like, almost flighty movements. Her face was weather-beaten and covered in a mass of fine wrinkles. Her eyes were a light hazel colour, and when Miss Edith smiled, as she did when talking of her adventures abroad, they suggested a lively sense of humour and warmth. As we discovered later, she had needed both qualities during her years with Olivia Fielding.

Quickly making us a jug of lemonade, Miss Edith ushered us into her sitting-room, a salon with french windows that opened out to a patio. I noticed a pack of cards spread on a table wedged between pots of geraniums and stock. Even though the french windows were wide open, letting in the sun and a light summer breeze, a heavy odour of dank musk hovered in the room: an unsettling clammy scent masked by a sprinkling of vetivert.

The plan we had agreed on before entering the Gatehouse was that Polly would lead the interrogation. I was to ask follow-up questions and Beth and I would observe the suspect's habitat for potential clues.

The room was crowded with memorabilia: photographs and furnishings accumulated over fifty years at Graylings. Against one wall was a bookcase crammed with poetry as yet unfamiliar to me: the complete works of Elizabeth Barrett Browning and her husband, Hardy's love poems, Shakespeare. Beside the bookcase was a Regency writing-desk with a matching chair.

At either end of the mantelpiece were portraits of a woman I assumed was Miss Fielding. On the left was a studio photograph of a young woman in a lace blouse, a cascade of pearls around her neck. Her black hair was swept up in a dark crown. Her eyes, equally dark, appeared intense, and her straight nose gave a regal aspect to her bearing. Sipping lemonade, I looked from the portrait on the left to the one on the right. It was of the same woman many years later, striking a pose in a loose velvet dress, a Spanish shawl around her shoulders. I recognised the shawl as the one I had played with in the attic. It was now mine, spread on my bed at the house. The woman's hair was still swept up from her face, but her expression had changed: the friendliness had disappeared, replaced by a commanding stare, although her mouth was still soft, still tender.

While Beth fondled the dozing dogs, Polly gazed at the photographs, overcome by curiosity. 'Is that Miss Fielding?' she asked, nodding at the portraits.

'Yes, it is.'

'Kind of grand, ain't she?'

The old woman chuckled. 'That's one way of putting it.'

Miss Edith was sitting very still on the edge of the sofa, her eyes on us. She seemed to realise what we were after. Her expression made me uncomfortable. It was as if she was looking straight through us, examining our thoughts with the ease of a photographer sifting through negatives. She was flattered by our interest none the less.

'She's sort of like a duchess, ain't she?' Polly remarked.

'A queen, more like it!' And then throwing us completely off track, Miss Edith slowly recited a nursery rhyme:

> The Queen of Hearts, she baked some tarts,
> All on a summer's day;
> The Knave of Hearts, he stole those tarts
> And took them clean away!

We stared at her bewildered.

She laughed. 'Curiosity killed the cat!' she cried. Beth burrowed her face into the neck of a dog, trying to suppress giggles.

Polly knew when she was being fobbed off, so she retaliated with another question. 'You mean Miss Fielding was a knave? I thought she was your best friend.'

'I was her companion,' came the indignant reply.

'You mean she played with you?'

Miss Edith gave a sly chuckle. She was obviously enjoying playing cat-and-mouse with us. Yet the game she was playing was dangerous. She was leading us on, whetting our appetites at the same time as obstructing our hunger for information. We didn't yet appreciate that women of her generation reveal themselves slowly, grudgingly, having established trust over a period of time. They weren't the sort of women who would appear willingly on the Oprah Winfrey show, or sell their story to a newspaper as Isobel and Belinda had orchestrated for us. I didn't yet know this, so I asked the first question that entered my head.

'Did you love her?'

The directness of my approach must have made her reply without thinking. 'Love!' she exclaimed. 'I gave her everything.'

Then, unwilling to say anything else, she dismissed us abruptly.

'Can't we stay longer?' Polly pleaded.

When she said that this was impossible, Beth asked if we could at least take the dogs out for her once in a while.

'Are you Brownies?' Miss Edith asked suspiciously. We assured her we were not and, gratified, Miss Edith accepted our offer of help. Once in a while, we could visit her at the Gatehouse and take her dogs out for a walk.

8

Our first encounter with Edith Butterworth stimulated our desire to know more about Graylings while Miss Fielding was its owner. We weren't alone in our interest. Everyone was talking about the house, even the teachers at school; and apparently lots of the younger children were spending the weekends trawling through their own attics in the hope of uncovering equally ghoulish traces from the past. After publicising our find, Belinda Bradshaw and Isobel took to having long, rambling conversations over coffee, which would end abruptly when we crept up on them. Once I overheard Belinda, determined to finish a train of thought, whisper, 'I'm telling you, Isobel, my mother used to hunt with Olivia Fielding and she was not all that she seemed. She had a will of iron, that woman.' The Derbys expressed their disapproval by watching over me with particular concern now that Polly and I were bosom friends. Following our attic discovery, I suspect their reservations about Polly were reinforced.

Beth was besotted by Miss Edith's boxers, deciding that anyone with dogs as wonderful as Candy and Fudge couldn't possibly have had anything to do with the babies in the attic. In any case, she believed that Miss Edith was gaga, completely off her rocker, her lights were on but there was nobody inside. On this point Polly was inclined to agree, although back at school, we considered the possibility that Miss Edith was leading us on, that perhaps she was trying to make us think she was mad.

'That's what witches do,' I explained.

We were in the Glory Hole, away from Maria's interference, discussing our first visit to the Gatehouse. We were sitting cross-legged in the dark, our faces illuminated by torches held beneath our chins. We were half-hidden by a barrier of broken desks and chairs, and the moist earthy smell of Mrs Derby's gardening tools crept into our nostrils. It was Polly's idea, another of her inspired ventures.

'This isn't a game,' Polly said, turning on me in exasperation. 'This is for real, Aj, like Jacinth was real.'

'But it's true, Polly. Witches make you think they're mad, and then when you're asleep, they suck out your soul.'

'Real detectives don't believe in witches.'

'They do in Ghana,' I muttered. 'And Malone and Leboeuf visit clairvoyants when they can't crack a case. They believe in ghosts and witches too.'

'Well, we're in Devon! And they don't have witches here. Do they, Beth?'

'They do on Dartmoor,' Beth replied. 'At least they used to, and who knows where the Bag Lady comes from?'

It wasn't that I thought Miss Edith was a witch. Although I was aware that she was an unusual old woman who fitted the stereotype, my mother's experience had taught me that it was women you least suspected of dabbling in the dark arts who used them. Attractive, nubile women who steal husbands, women such as Emily Richardson, were the worst offenders. They were the ones you had to watch out for, along with family members who might wish you harm: beautiful women, women close to you.

Polly had brought us down to the Glory Hole in order to delve into the mind of whoever had hidden the babies in Miss Fielding's trunk. She was using us as guinea pigs. Beth and I had to pretend to be the culprit, while Polly asked us questions.

Beth decided to go first. My prime suspect was Mr Furzey, the gardener at Graylings; he had worked there when Miss Fielding was alive and had been kept on by the Venuses. But Beth had had the same idea, thus depriving me of my role. I stuck out my tongue at her.

'How did you whack the babies?' Polly asked.

'I throttled them,' said Beth. 'You see I'm married and I didn't want my wife to find out. And . . . well . . . I was having an affair with one of Miss Fielding's maids and she had twins.'

'Why didn't she say something?'

Beth pondered for a moment. Then she said: 'She was really stupid, you see. Thick as two planks. She didn't even know she was having babies. What happened was that one day she went to the loo and they both dropped out of her. And the babies drowned.'

We laughed as Beth continued: 'So I didn't throttle them really. They died accidentally and I hid them. Then I gave the woman a hundred pounds to go away.'

Believing she had exhausted Beth's insights, Polly turned to me. 'How about you? Who are you?'

I said the first thing that came into my head. 'I'm the mother of the children.'

'Yeah? What sort of mother murders her kids?'

'I didn't murder them.'

'As if!' Beth exclaimed.

I felt a spider crawling over my knee. I swept it aside. 'I didn't murder them,' I replied.

'How come?'

'I didn't murder them,' I repeated firmly. 'I gave birth to them and they were dead when they came out. I kept having dead babies. Eventually I didn't want anyone to bury them. They belonged to me, didn't they? So I kept them. I hid them in the trunk.'

My fellow Crimebusters were silent. Eventually, Polly asked: 'Why did your babies keep dying?'

'They cursed me. His women cursed me.'

'Whose women?' Beth demanded.

'My husband's girlfriends. So my babies came out dead. Only one lived. The first one. But I kept the others. I hid them in the trunk.'

Beth and Polly glanced at each other, then looked at me. 'Aj, you're weird,' Polly exclaimed.

I believe she intended to pay me a compliment. She went on to take the floor herself, determined to arrive at another explanation, a rival to mine. She took on the role of Miss Fielding, and, unsure how the spinster – a pillar of the village community and a local JP – had come to have babies, she vacillated between a tall dark stranger from overseas or the possibility that Miss Fielding and Miss Edith had been Satanists. The latter idea won our approval, and, embellishing her theory with details that any tabloid journalist would be proud of, Polly described midnight masses at which the diabolical pair drank the blood of new-born babies.

I listened with only half an ear. I was thinking of my mother. Alluding to her experiences had brought back memories I had tried to forget. Dead babies and miscarriages: nature's aberrations which caused my mother such distress. Had I seen my sister before she died? I hadn't. My mother's ordeals had taken place in the safety of well-equipped hospitals. So where did the memory of my sister come from?

It was the trace of a dream, perhaps: Mama calling me to her bedroom and in a small white coffin on the bed, my sister, her body covered in a kente stole. She is dead and Mama says, 'I want you to see this and remember, Ajuba. As God is my witness, this is the work of your father's sisters. They are witches. They kill my babies so your father will leave me. This is the work of your father's people.'

I remembered. But was it a dream, or had it happened? The atmosphere in the Glory Hole was thick with our fantasies that evening, so for a few minutes my ability to distinguish what was real from what was imagined blurred. I recalled my mother's tears after my sister's funeral. But then I saw a child being taken away and Mama wanting to keep her, to hold her a day longer, two days; and then to go to the grave with her. 'But, Mama, you still have me,' I say. And she takes my hand, allowing my sister to go. What happened? Why didn't my mother write to me? I wanted to hear her voice again in words scrawled in her round, sloping hand. I prayed, when Mrs Derby was handing out letters, that one day she would give me a letter from Mama. As yet that day hadn't arrived.

I put down my torch, allowing my tears to fall unseen.

I believe it was at this point that the door of the Glory Hole opened. Someone turned on the light, and for an instant we were blinded.

'Piss off, Maria,' Beth shouted from our hiding place behind desks and chairs.

Polly thought it was Maria as well. She started yelling 'Sucker! Sucker! Sucker!' I joined in, and so did Beth, until we realised that the legs standing in the doorway didn't belong to Maria Richardson. They didn't belong to Joshua either. It was Major Derby in a pair of long, baggy shorts.

'What on earth are you doing, girls? I've been looking everywhere for you, Ajuba. Come out. All of you. I hope I never hear you using that sort of language again. To anyone. Am I making myself clear?'

We apologised. Nevertheless, he confiscated our torches and, as we were walking away, he summoned me back. 'You've just had a call from your father,' he explained as I looked up at him. 'He's in London. He'll be coming down to take you out on Saturday.'

I'd seen my father twice since I'd been at school, when I'd travelled to Rome for a few days over Christmas and Easter. On both occasions, in spite of our conversations on the phone, we hadn't been able to find the right words to talk to each other, and I hadn't known how to broach the questions that were uppermost in my mind. Why hadn't he told Mama where I was so that she could write to me? I wasn't brave enough to ask him. Instead, I told him what he wanted to hear. I was doing well at school; I was very happy; I'd made lots of friends.

Before I knew what was happening, I was crying in the corridor. I didn't want to see my father. I wanted my mother. At the very least, I wanted her to write to me. Philip Derby, a flush of concern passing over his face, gently patted my head.

'There's no need for tears, Ajuba. You'll have the whole

day together.' Anxious to calm my distress, he came down to my level and gripped my shoulder. 'You're going to have a wonderful time, sweetie. You wait and see.'

He didn't understand and I couldn't explain myself to him. I didn't want to see my father. My father was the last person in the world I wanted to be with.

9

Polly was kneeling on my bed, trying to pull a comb through my hair. We were preparing to go out with my father. She had agreed to come with me on condition that I considered spending the summer holidays at Graylings. I wasn't sure if that was really what I wanted, but all the same, I appreciated her willingness to meet my father, taking it as another sign of our friendship. Tugging her comb through my tight curls, Polly yanked at my hair. The comb snagged, breaking several teeth.

'Where's your comb?' she asked

'I lost it.'

'Where'd you lose it?'

'Don't know.'

Disentangling the comb, Polly wrenched it through my hair again. More teeth fell out. Despite the torture I was subjecting myself to, having someone concerned about my hair, someone willing to struggle with it on my behalf, reminded me of happier times. Times when my father was my friend.

'No wonder Michael changed his hair. You should change yours, Aj.'

She was referring to Michael Jackson, of course, not Michael Benson, my father.

'Sometimes it helps sprinkling water on it. It makes it easier to comb.'

She ran out of Exe to get some water. While she was out of the room, I tried combing my hair myself. I'd left it unkempt for such a long time that it had become unmanageable. I'd decided not to do anything about it when my comb had disappeared. Now my hair was thick and impenetrable, a dark jungle of matted curls.

Disconsolate, I spat on my hands, attempting to change the colour of my shins by gliding my damp palms over them. I never used to look like this, I reflected, recalling my earlier incarnation in Ghana when I had felt differently about myself: when I was tidy and at ease with my father. Mama used to smooth my skin with cocoa butter, moisturising my hair with oils of coconut and shea nut. Once upon a time, I remembered, I'd shone like polished, black coral.

I was beginning to wonder if I should run and hide from the disappointment I was sure to see in my father's eyes, when Polly returned with a beaker of water. I dabbed some of it into my hair. She sprinkled a bit more, and then, wielding the comb once again, she forced it through. I screamed. Mercifully, the comb broke in two.

'I wish I had one of my mother's wigs,' I mumbled.

'Me too. Perhaps he won't notice.'

'He notices everything.'

'I'm glad he's not my father.'

'I wish he wasn't mine as well.'

Polly folded her arms, stood back, looked me up and down and said: 'I guess putting on a hat would help.'

'If I wear one, will you wear yours? And will you put on school uniform as well, so I don't look weird?' My own clothes no longer fitted me properly, and, unless I was with Polly at Graylings wearing her clothes, I preferred to remain in school uniform.

Polly appeared doubtful.

'Please, Polly. I'll ask him to take us to McDonald's.'

'Followed by cream tea at Ford Abbey?'

I nodded.

'It's a deal!' she said.

Rummaging through her bottom drawer, Polly extracted the straw hat that we were required to wear for church on Sundays. She put it on. Out of the same drawer she retrieved another. Polly and I had recently pooled our resources, to prevent me losing things. It seemed to help. Like her mother, Polly was careful with her possessions; meticulous.

She placed the hat on my head, stepping back to examine her handiwork. While she fussed over the angle of the brim, pushing it one way and then the other, I remembered my mother. I used to believe that I looked after Mama, yet it was she who'd taken care of my hair: plaiting it, nurturing it as tenderly as a nursery of orchids. She knew what to do. I couldn't help wishing that I did as well.

Satisfied at last, Polly stood to one side: 'Yeah, it helps. It makes you look snappier somehow.'

I wasn't convinced. Once we'd changed into uniform, I followed her downstairs to wait for my father. Together, we clambered on to the windowsill of the school pantry, where the silver and crockery were kept in glass cabinets. We positioned ourselves so we could watch cars arriving down the school drive. I was determined to catch sight of my father before he saw me.

It was Saturday afternoon and the school was silent; expectant. All the boarders were out shopping. Beth was at home, Maria in London. Isobel was in London as well, for a weekend with Peter on his houseboat. According to Polly they were going to thrash things out. 'I don't know why they bother,' Polly had said, swearing me to secrecy.

Once we were settled on the windowsill, I followed Polly's example, pulling my blue candy-striped dress down over my knees. Trying to emulate her pre-teen grooming skills, I struggled to imitate her composure but was unable to do so. I began nibbling the elastic of my hat while Polly stared vacantly out of the pantry window, her hands clasped around her knees.

Her hands reminded me of Peter's: she had the same long fingers with large moons. Looking out onto the front lawn, she appeared as distant as only Peter could be: lost in a desolate canvas of her own creation. Even though she often shared my bed at night and took as much care of my possessions as she did her own, I was perplexed by her apparent indifference to Maria's revelation about Peter. To the child I was back then, her lack of concern seemed even more bizarre than her defiant separation from Isobel. I remember wondering, as I sat watching her, why she couldn't admit that her father's adultery hurt her.

'Why do you pretend you don't care when Peter has girlfriends?' I asked eventually.

Surveying a cluster of flowers coming into bloom, Polly said nothing before slowly turning her head towards me: 'Because his girlfriends don't matter. He always comes back because of me. That's why they had me.'

I didn't understand what she meant, so she said very deliberately, as if explaining the alphabet to a simpleton: 'They wanted to make things better between them, so they had me.'

'How do you know?'

'Theo told me. Isobel tells him things.'

'Then why does Peter still have girlfriends?'

She gave a worldly shrug, raising an eyebrow. 'Some guys are like that, Aj.'

I realised that what she was saying was true. 'My Aunt Rose says that some of them are like that even in the Bible. She doesn't understand why people make such a fuss about it. But then Aunt Rose is a bit unusual. She likes men a lot,' I confessed.

'And Peter likes women. Adultery hurts, Aj. It hurts Isobel.'

I had believed until then that Polly didn't appreciate her mother's unhappiness. She did. Yet her acceptance of her father's behaviour shocked me. Despite the wealth of my aunt's biblical anecdotes, proving that even God's favourites indulged in sin, at heart I was my mother's daughter, imbued with Mama's outrage at Pa's infidelities. The idea that such behaviour could be taken for granted was disturbing. Yet, in itself, the behaviour was familiar.

'Yes, some fathers are like that,' I acknowledged. 'It drives my mother crazy. Does Isobel go crazy as well?'

Polly nodded: 'Yeah. She doesn't understand Peter like I do.'

'Just like my mother.'

'Yeah?'

'She hates it when Pa has girlfriends. She says some men can't help themselves. Then she cries, and when she stops crying, she says they're weak – like children.'

'Isobel can't understand why he loves me best. That makes her mad, real mad.' Polly's eyes settled on mine, disarming me with their frankness, until I remembered the time she told me about Isobel. It was the first time she came to my bed at night, and she'd talked about her mother as if she were a jewel she wanted to lose somewhere. I now understood how she could turn her back on her mother. They were rivals.

Polly smiled at me. – 'Jeez, Aj, they're so blatant. Emily started hitting on Peter the moment she saw him. The woman's a dog, believe me!' Just then a white Fiesta drove through the school entrance. A man I recognised switched off the ignition. Beside him, in the passenger seat, was a woman.

When she got out, for one glorious moment I thought she was Mama. She was doe-eyed and pretty and she had that laugh: the laugh, which made me want to laugh out loud as well. When I looked again, I realised my error. She looked like my mother, and the quality of their laughter was similar, but this woman was younger, plump, her braided hair threaded in luscious gold strands. And when she looked at my father, he took her by the hand.

'Wow!' Polly exclaimed. 'Your mom looks awesome, Aj! She's totally cool.'

'That is not my mother,' I screamed, jumping down from the windowsill. I fumbled for a word to describe the woman. When it came to me, I spat it out with the same venom my mother had used at her angriest. 'That's not my mother. That's one of my father's whores.'

'Holy shit!' The expression on Polly's face made it a word worth remembering. I wouldn't forget it again.

Thanks to Polly I survived the ordeal of meeting my father and his new girlfriend: Nina, the woman who transformed his life, bringing the lightness of love to his eyes again. He hadn't prepared me for her existence; he hadn't warned me that he'd be arriving with her. I don't think he set out deliberately to hurt me; few adults are consciously insensitive to children. It's just that most of them are willing to sideline children's needs to follow their own trajectory in the pursuit of happiness. Of course, most adults will say that they want nothing but the best for their children; they'd be willing to die for them, if it were necessary. That's what they say at any rate. Yet seeing Pa with Nina, witnessing the intimacy they shared walking up the school steps in their matching flowing robes of embroidered red linen, I felt myself shrinking. It was like when Pa first left me at school. Only this time it was worse. I wanted to scream and cry at the same time. I wanted to howl in rage. But if I did, I knew I would break into irretrievable pieces. To stop myself fragmenting, I made myself so small that I shrunk into the heels of my outdoor shoes.

Malone and Leboeuf, taking hold of my fingers, whispered, 'Shit happens, kid. It's tough, but just remember, keep your eyes peeled.' Polly, grabbing hold of my shoulders, looked me straight in the eyes: 'The show must go on, kiddo! We're in this together.'

Bolstered by Polly's theatrical bent and Malone and Leboeuf, my ego rose to the occasion. I played the role Pa had designated for me: that of his clever daughter, confident, independent. Taking him by the hand, I showed him around the school. I took him to see the bed I slept on in Exe. And when I introduced him to Polly, insisting that she spend the day with us, I could see that he approved of her. I suspect he hoped that some of her poise and assurance would rub off on me.

I wasn't especially friendly to Nina. I remember I kept asking her to remind me what she was called (as if I would ever forget her name) and even though she told me again and again, I still managed to forget. At least I pretended to, until Pa, suggesting that I call her 'Auntie', forced me to come to a decision. I wasn't going to call her anything at all.

To begin with, I think Pa must have felt proud of me. He seemed to relish my kiss of welcome and enjoy my new-found ability to hold his hand and hug him whenever I could. He didn't seem to realise that I was doing everything possible to stop Nina drooling over him. I had been brought up to believe that Africans were undemonstrative in public, and that what was important was affection and respect expressed behind closed doors. I thought, at the time, that the change in Pa's behaviour was because Nina was Senegalese, an 'executive administrator' with his organisation in Rome. The Senegalese must behave badly, I decided. Either it was the fault of the Senegalese or those wretched Italians again, with their grand operatic gestures and their love of death. Unfortunately, no matter how hard I tried, I couldn't stop them touching each other.

After lunch at McDonald's, followed by a walk along the Cobb at Lyme Regis, I persuaded Pa to take us for tea at Ford Abbey. I don't think he was used to dealing with two children at once. Whenever I made a request, Polly seconded me; whenever I made a statement, Polly confirmed what I'd said. But in the end, we were as unsuccessful as King Canute in holding back the waves of adult infatuation. King Canute, however, knew what he was up against. I did not.

They couldn't stop touching each other, sharing smiles and tender asides. I understand now that after years of a difficult marriage, my father, having found a companionable woman to share his life with, was supremely happy. Finding Nina, Pa told me not so long ago, was like bathing in the warm light of a Sahelian winter's day. After the harshness of a protracted dry season, the glare of the sun had softened, become dappled, luminous. 'It was the difference between famine and rain, Ajuba. Night and day. For the first time for many years I was finally content with a woman who loved me. What more could a man want?'

To the child that I was back then, Pa's joy was palpable, and Nina's pleasure in his company intense. Their excitement with each other generated a force field that repelled me, no matter how hard I struggled to find a path through it. Despite all my attempts, the numerous times I omitted calling Nina by name, my efforts to drag Pa away from her along the pebbled beach of Lyme Regis, I was unable to find an opening into their new-found love.

'Later, Nina,' Pa murmured as Nina, stroking the hairs of his arm, began tickling them with her forefinger. 'Stop it!' he whispered.

Half-smiling at him, half-laughing, Nina kissed Pa's nose. He picked a wisp of dandelion fluff from her braided hair, flicking it into the air. It floated down, landing on a burnished copper arm that glowed in the shade of a beech tree overhead.

We must have made an incongruous party sitting under the tree at Ford Abbey: Pa and Nina flamboyant in red while Polly and I, strait-laced in candy-striped dresses and straw hats, stared at them between mouthfuls of scones and clotted cream.

'Michael!' Attempting to look annoyed, yet apparently incapable of denying my father anything he wanted, Nina laughed again and kissed my father on the mouth.

'Disgusting,' I whispered to Polly.

'Gross,' she affirmed.

'Vile toad.'

'Adults, huh?'

'I want some more lemonade,' I said loudly.

'Me too.'

Pa ordered a second jug of lemonade and a few more scones and cream. When the tray arrived, Nina stirred the juice, pouring it out into clean glasses for us. Her movements were fluid, graceful; and though she was younger than Pa by fifteen years – to my father's embarrassment, I'd asked her how old she was – I could see she was trying to please him by ministering to me. Even though she wasn't particularly interested in me, she wasn't as averse to me as I was to her.

It was a hot afternoon and, relaxing back in her seat, Nina removed a fan from her handbag. She whirled it in front of her face. 'You two must be hot in those hats,' she said languorously.

Polly and I ignored her. We must have given them the impression that we hadn't eaten properly for days. As I was splitting the last scone in half to share with Polly, Pa said: 'You've eaten enough to sink the *Titanic*.'

'The who?'

'The *Titanic* was the most famous liner of its day. It sank on its maiden voyage. Aren't they teaching you general knowledge at school? Now when I was at Achimota . . .' Pa continued in a tone of voice he used whenever he was intent on improving my mind.

'I know all about Nelson Mandela and his long walk to freedom,' I retorted.

'I should hope so too. Do you remember your African capitals?'

'Of course I do!'

'OK, what's the capital of Cote d'Ivoire?'

'Abidjan.'

'Burkina Faso.'

'Ouagadougou.'

The questions and answers went back and forth across the table with the speed of machine-gun fire. We had covered most of West Africa and a part of southern Africa, when Nina prodded Pa's arm with the fan.

'Michael, she's a child,' she reminded him.

He had asked for the capital of Mauritania, knowing full well that by returning to West Africa, he'd interrupt my flow. His strategy proved correct. I couldn't remember. Pa turned to Nina: 'Do you know the capital of Mauritania?'

'What do you take me for?' she giggled, tickling his palm. 'I didn't learn what I know at school, did I?'

Pa grinned. He was about to start groping her again, when I slapped him on his thigh. 'Pa, Pa,' I cried. I tugged at his leg, pushing Nina away. His linen outfit felt harsh and stiff when I touched him. 'Pa, why don't you talk about Mama any more? Is she happy? Will I ever see her again?'

'Ajuba, this isn't the time or place to discuss your mother. We can talk about her later; tomorrow.'

'But you're going tomorrow.'

'Ajuba, what's past is past. It's over. Finished.'

'But I miss her. I miss her.'

In a rare gesture of affection, my father lifted me onto his knee, patting my arm in sympathy. 'I miss her too,' he said. 'But I want you to be patient. We're going to find you a new mother.'

I glanced at Nina with open hostility. 'Do we need a new wife?' I demanded.

Pa trailed a finger down my cheek. I believe he saw my

mother in my eyes: her anger, her venom. A trace of exasperation entered his. 'Yes, we do need a new wife,' he admitted. 'You want me to be happy, don't you, Ajuba?'

I laid my head against his shoulder, struggling to answer his question. Of course I wanted him to be happy but my well-being depended on Mama's return. I knew my parents were ill-matched – indeed, they made each other miserable – and yet, faced with the impossible choice of putting my father's happiness before my own, I couldn't find the words to say what he wanted to hear. In my dilemma I rubbed my head against the abrasive fabric covering his shoulder. I felt my hat slipping off, but I didn't care. I wanted to be my father's friend again; to be thrown up in the air and held by him, like when we'd lived at Kuku Hill. For the life of me, I couldn't say the words. I couldn't say, Yes, I want you to be happy Pa, I'll take Nina for my new mother.

Then I remembered. Pulling away from him, I screamed, 'Nouakchott! The capital of Mauritania is Nouakchott!'

Pa embraced me. 'That's my girl!'

My straw hat fell to the ground, exposing my tough, matted curls. Nina touched them gently. '*Mon dieu*! These people have no idea how to do our hair. You poor baby.' Tapping Pa's arm, she said, 'Darling, let's go back to the hotel. I've got to do her hair.'

In a flurry of activity, Nina broke the first moment of intimacy that I'd shared with my father for years. She slung her bag over a shoulder, hurrying to the car as Pa paid the bill. As I watched her rolling down the windows before sliding inside, I came to a decision.

'Are you going to ask him or shall I?' I asked Polly.

'Ask him what?'

'If I can spend the summer holidays with you?'

'You want to? You really want to, Aj?'

Adopting a pose I'd seen Polly assume many times before, I shrugged nonchalantly: 'Well, they're going to get married, aren't they? They're not going to want me around. I'm not stupid.'

'I guess not. They won't want you for a while, anyways. Hey, I'll ask him if you like.'

Walking arm in arm, Polly and I wandered back to the car.

She cut my hair. She cut my hair short, and with every snip of the scissors I found myself hating her more. My father's whore, my soon-to-be stepmother: Nina. She cut my hair so short that if she had seen me, my cousin Esi would have shouted '*Sakola*! *Sakola*! Bald-head! Bald-head!' Who would think me beautiful now?

When she finished, Nina brought out a looking-glass for me to see myself. I refused to touch it, I wouldn't look at it. Instead, I turned my back on her. I believed that her face, kind though it seemed, was one of the many my mother had seen in her mirror. She was one of my father's whores.

What surprised me was my relief. I couldn't understand why I was pleased my hair was gone, when my mother had spent so much time nurturing it. I felt unencumbered with cropped hair. And when Nina gave me a proper comb for African hair, a jar of blue pomade for my scalp and some moisturising cream for my skin, I remember saying 'Thank you'. Yet I pulled away when she tried to pat me on the head. It was then that Polly asked about the summer holidays.

Before he replied, my father looked over at Nina. She nodded, yet Pa hesitated. Eventually he said he wanted to meet Polly's parents to discuss the holiday with them.

'But they're in London!' I cried.

'Then I shall meet them in London on our way back to Rome,' he insisted, taking Peter's numbers from Polly. Once he'd met the Venuses, Pa explained patiently, he would let me know his decision.

I'd like to think that if I hadn't seen Nina nod I would have given her more of a chance. After all, she was trying to be kind to me; yet when I saw Pa turn to her for advice, the course of our future relationship was determined. First of all, I knew with certainty that they were going to get married. I had witnessed the signs that afternoon; but in that single gesture, the almost involuntary turn of his head, I saw my father's need for Nina. And her nod of acquiescence I took as rejection of me. I hated her with the silent ferocity of a frightened child. I blamed my mother's absence and my father's equivocation on her. So when her head came down, I swore in that instant that one day I would pay her back. One day, I would have my revenge.

I can only wonder at myself. Can a child make such a decision? And having made it, act on it? The answer is yes. I know because I did it. I've been picked over by enough specialists to know the jargon. I can talk about my ambivalence towards my stepmother and my father's ambivalence towards me. I can talk about the symbolism of having my hair cropped, my stepmother shredding me of femininity. And then there's my mother's part in this story: her tremendous anger towards Pa and his women, which I swallowed whole through being her child. I loved my mother, so I'd learnt her lessons well.

I can discuss all these things until the burden of responsibility shifts, as is the fashion nowadays, away from myself onto those around me: my father especially. I was only a child, and how can a child be held responsible? Wasn't I the principal victim in their pursuit of happiness?

Of course I was a child. Of course it wasn't going to be easy becoming Nina's stepchild. But my hatred of her propelled me into an act of devastating violence that I deeply regret.

10

For the rest of term we returned, time and time again, to our favourite topic: the babies in Miss Fielding's trunk. It was like revisiting a place where the most hideous of crimes had been committed, revisiting it because it held a clue which, if unravelled, would enable us to understand everything we would ever experience. We discussed the babies incessantly, we played games involving them, we kept a scrapbook about them. When, eventually, we were banished from the Glory Hole and it was locked up and made Out of Bounds, we brought our obsession into the open air.

It was a bright July evening and the sun was still warm in a cloudless sky as we searched for wild strawberries at the edge of the front lawn of the school. Mrs Derby had sent us outside, saying the weather was too fine for us to remain huddled in Exe. She didn't know it, but we were discussing the opening of the inquest for the babies.

The proceedings had begun a week previously and Alexander James had written about it in the *Devon Gazette.* The *Guardian* newspaper had picked up the story, and in both accounts we were mentioned. I had already put the clippings in our scrapbook and hidden it under my pillow when Mrs Derby came in and hustled us outside.

It was Polly's opinion that now the parameters of the

police case had been laid out, we could accelerate our own investigation. According to Alexander James, the police were launching a full-scale inquiry to establish the provenance of the babies. The Home Office pathologist who had examined the corpses explained that they were so decomposed it had been impossible to establish any relationship between them without testing their DNA, which in due course would be done. Furthermore, from the fragmentary evidence available, there was no way of determining whether the babies had been born fit and healthy or not. 'We shall never know the answer to these questions,' the pathologist was quoted as saying; though he then went on to suggest that it seemed probable that one of the infants was stillborn.

Detective Inspector Roberts, the officer in charge of the case, stated categorically to the *Gazette* that he intended to leave no stone unturned in pursuit of the truth. 'We owe it to these unnamed, forgotten children to find out where they came from and who they belonged to.' There was talk of testing the DNA of everyone alive who had lived and worked at Graylings in the past thirty years; and even Mr Furzey, the mildest, gentlest of men, was now a potential suspect. As was Miss Edith.

Apparently she had attended the proceedings. In an interview with Alexander James afterwards, she claimed she knew nothing about the contents of Miss Fielding's trunk. She could offer no explanation either. Out on the lawn hunting for strawberries, I was inclined to believe her, though Polly was not.

'If anyone knows something, she does,' Polly insisted. 'She lived there for years. She's got to be hiding something.'

'Like what?' Beth and I enjoyed our visits to the Gatehouse

and were both averse to thinking ill of Miss Edith. I was even beginning to like her dogs.

'She knows what happened. I can feel it in my gut.' Then, taking us through what the police had discovered thus far, Polly said: 'Let's start from the beginning. What've we got?'

Picking a strawberry from a pile we'd collected, Beth put it in her mouth: 'We've got two mouldering babies in a trunk. They might be related, but the pathologist couldn't tell.'

I continued: 'One was stillborn. The other was . . . was . . .'

'*Murdered*,' Polly said emphatically. She fell down on the grass, her hair spilling over daisies. I sat down cross-legged with Beth beside me.

'The pathologist wasn't sure about that either,' I remembered.

Beth agreed. 'He said it could have been stillborn as well.'

'So why hide 'em? Someone is guilty as hell.'

'But who? And how can we find out?'

'Seems to me we've got to stay on the same page as Malone and Leboeuf and keep on with what we've been doing,' Polly said, answering my question. 'We've got to keep on pestering the Bag Lady until she spills the beans.'

'And how long is that going to take?'

'All summer,' Polly replied with a smile. 'We're going to visit her every day until she tells us everything.'

It wasn't the sort of summer I'd envisaged when I received permission from my father to spend the holidays at Graylings. But whichever way I looked at it, getting the truth out of Miss Edith was going to be much more interesting than spending time with Nina in Rome.

*

On the first day of the holidays the summer seemed to stretch up to the sky like a tall mango tree laden with fruit. I intended to pluck one every day, savour it for a few minutes, suck it slowly dry, till there was nothing left but the stone and strands of orange hair stiffening in the wind.

Downstairs, Mrs Venus's small sitting-room had recently been painted a soothing yellow, and upstairs the main bathroom had been refurbished, with a shower and Moorish tiles around the new bath and basin. The floor was covered in a brick-red carpet.

To the left of the house, a tennis court was in place, and the gardener, Mr Furzey, was working steadily to fulfil Mrs Venus's requirements. A herb garden was being planted by the back door and a new herbaceous border created; and on the far east slope of the grounds, over a stretch of land that had been left idle by Miss Fielding, there were plans to create a woodland copse. If Mr Furzey held strong opinions about the changes taking place, or harboured thoughts about the babies in the trunk, he mostly kept them to himself. His conscience was clear; or so Belinda Bradshaw claimed he had said to her cleaner. 'Just as well,' Isobel replied serenely to Belinda, who had taken to trailing morsels of gossip to Graylings like a cat does captured mice. 'I'd hate to let the poor man go.'

Methodical and diligent, Mr Furzey did everything he was asked to on the estate as quickly as he was able. But when Mrs Venus suggested that she hire a young man to help him, he agreed, visibly relieved.

The house and its grounds were in a state of transition, bending to Isobel's will. On the first day of the holiday, I trotted obediently at her side as she described her plans for restoring the property to its former glory. Polly had refused to come with us, adopting an attitude of lofty disapproval. She didn't care about the house or the garden; and when Isobel tried to interest her, her eyes turned heavenward. 'Do what you got to do,' she drawled. 'You always do in the end, Isobel.'

As I followed her to the garden, Isobel told me that when the balustrade and steps linking the two lawns were mended, a pergola would be built across the bottom lawn; and coming out from the back of the house, a brick terrace with steps in three places. She told me many things: things I didn't fully comprehend but listened to, conscious that no one within the family seemed to listen to the mistress of the manor.

Yet for all her talk of things – how they would change, how they would look, the colours of the plants that would clamber the pergola, the way they would blend with the terrace and its steps, merging landscape and house into one – there was one thing I knew with certainty: Isobel was depressed. She was gaunt, and her inability to sit still, to take stock of what was happening, was because she was frightened. She was tumbling into an abyss, but she wasn't ready to acknowledge it yet. She couldn't smell the odour of fear exuding from her own pores, the stench of crushed violets on her skin.

I sensed it as acutely as I'd perceived my mother's distress. Recognising it for what it was, I tried to comfort Isobel. Even though I couldn't fathom the implications of the angry assertions she made repeatedly, I did my best to listen. She said that I should never trust a cheating man; and under no circumstances was I to listen to his confession, for his guilt would consume me and in the end, taking me for granted, he'd up and leave. I expressed wonder at everything she said.

I used every expression available to me, every expletive I knew in a bid to make Isobel feel better.

And while I listened, walking the garden beside her, I tried to imagine what everything would look like in the end. Not in the house and garden especially, but with the Venuses. My one wish was that Isobel would be happy again, that Peter would come down from London instead of staying away all the time. And if he couldn't come back straight away, I wanted Theo to come home quickly. Theo would make his mother better.

I scarcely slept that first night. I stayed awake listening to the house talking to me. I heard Isobel getting up, the bath water running. I heard her weeping and then the tap turned on again, loudly. While Polly slept, I prayed to God to make Isobel better.

Theo's arrival at the end of the week was not the success I had hoped it would be. He was full of himself and his exams. Unlike Polly, he was affectionate to his mother, though he too refused to participate in her plans for the house. Creating the perfect home didn't appeal to his minimalist taste.

'You're too *Home and Garden*,' he said to Isobel. 'You've too much clutter about the place. If I were you I'd throw most of it out and start all over again.'

'And end up looking like Conran?'

'You know what I mean, Ma. I'm not into this.' Theo looked around him as if he were a vegetarian standing in the middle of an abattoir, though in fact he was in Isobel's new sitting-room.

'Maybe it's all right for someone of your generation,' he conceded, 'but I prefer something simpler. Don't you, Polly?'

Of course, Polly agreed.

'I like it,' I said.

Polly made a slurping noise. 'Ajuba, you always like what Isobel likes.'

'I'm not sucking up,' I protested.

'You are too!'

'Well, at least somebody likes what I'm doing.' Pushing Theo out of the room, Isobel escorted him on a tour of her renovations.

I couldn't understand why, when I woke the next morning, a nervous tremor passed through me, coiling in my abdomen. As the day wore on, the coil tightened until, in the middle of the afternoon, I plucked up the courage to ask Theo a question I had wanted to ask for some time. Where was Peter? And when was he coming home again?

Theo explained that his father was in Paris covering a G7 meeting, and he would be back in London within the week. Theo was going to join him on his houseboat, before going to the Dordogne to spend the summer with Sylvie and her family. I noticed that when Theo mentioned Peter's name, Isobel turned away.

If they were aware of their mother's unhappiness, Polly and Theo made no concessions to it whatsoever. Incapable of adopting their detachment, I followed my instincts; I felt like a seal-cub searching for its mother, swimming blindly towards an expanse of stormy sea.

One afternoon, when I'd observed that Isobel was no longer eating proper food, grazing instead on sunflower and pumpkin seeds, cashews and walnuts, thin, cool slices of melon, she reciprocated my concern for her with an ashen smile. Her eyes were dark moons in her face, her collar bones protruded, and the mood of the house, brewing with desolation, propelled Polly and me outside. If I'm honest, I was as relieved as Polly was to leave Isobel for the Gatehouse.

We claimed we were interrogating Miss Edith. But interrogation is perhaps too grand a word for our visits with Beth, which we combined with sustained stalking of the old woman, tracking her commando style as she exercised the dogs and went shopping. Our excuse was that we were trying to get a sense of the 'big picture', as Malone and Leboeuf called it. We believed that if we developed a clear idea of life at Graylings in the olden days, if we could imagine what it had looked like with its furnishings, appreciating the geography of where Miss Edith and Miss Fielding slept, then we would begin to know its inhabitants and the people who worked for them: Mr Furzey included.

Observation, Malone and Leboeuf explained in *True Murder*, only begins to make sense when it is written down. A true detective spends much of her time writing, recording all the evidence she's uncovered and scenes she's witnessed, in order to fully appreciate them. 'Writing is the key to analysing a case and solving it.' And so it was that under instructions from Polly, Beth borrowed her mother's Polaroid camera to photograph the old woman and the Gatehouse as documentary evidence for our scrapbook, while in the evening I noted everything down.

That afternoon, following at a safe distance, we tailed Miss Edith to the Co-op at the end of the road. She had the dogs with her. They kept looking back at us and barking as she brought them to heel. Beth took a photograph of Miss Edith entering the shop, then waited outside for a snapshot of her leaving. After a suitable interval, Polly and I shadowed the old woman inside.

She usually bought her provisions on Mondays and Thursdays, surviving on a meagre diet of Quaker porridge oats, milk, bananas, peanut butter, bread and varieties of cake. But that Thursday she bought nothing but a large bottle of Tio Pepe sherry. I was noting down the drink and the brand name as Polly read the label out loud, when, doubling back on her tracks, Miss Edith accosted us.

'What the hell are you children doing following me around everywhere?' she yelled. 'What the blazes have I ever done to you?'

Polly, who had obviously thought of such an eventuality, simulated embarrassment before saying ruefully: 'I'm sorry. I guess we should have asked your permission, but we've been visiting you for research, Miss Edith. You see, we're studying you for a history project at school.'

'Yes, history,' I concurred, surprised by the old woman's language. I had never heard her curse before. She was angry, and anxious to placate her, I added: 'You see other people in Seniors are talking to their grandmothers.'

'And we don't have grandmothers,' Polly lamented. 'And poor old Beth's grandmother is six feet under as well.'

'So we've chosen you.'

She didn't believe us. Hugging the bottle of Tio Pepe like a talisman to her shrivelled chest, she shook her head violently: 'You're talking nonsense both of you. And you know it. Anyway, what makes you think I'd allow you to use me? I don't want you following me around any longer. Do you hear me?'

Polly glanced at me in a way that implied that perhaps I might be able to change Miss Edith's mind. After all, I was able to make the Derbys and the other teachers at school think kindly of me, while they bristled at what they took to

LIMERICK
COUNTY LIBRARY

be Polly's impertinence. So, allowing my face to crumple, I rearranged my features to elicit maximum sympathy. My eyes melting, my mouth trembling, I murmured: '*Please*, Miss Edith, we don't have any grannies of our own to talk to, and we desperately need you for history coursework. Mr Derby says we've got to find out what it was like living here in the Olden Days. Please help us.'

I must have seemed on the verge of tears. A pair of leather-clad teenagers stocking up on cider stopped what they were doing. A middle-aged man buying bottles of gin looked over; and Miss Edith, appearing distracted, began mumbling incoherently. She looked up and down the aisle, tugging at the sleeve of her dung-coloured cardigan. I suspect she was acutely sensitive to the rumours circulating about her and the impression she was giving, because she seemed to relent. At any rate, she didn't want to make a scene. And she certainly didn't want witnesses to me bursting into tears in front of her. Thrusting the bottle of sherry at Polly, she said gruffly: 'Well, if you're going to pester me, you might as well make yourselves useful. Hurry along now.'

Beth took a photograph of us leaving the Co-op, then bounded ahead with the dogs, while Polly and I walked either side of Miss Edith. She moved slowly, stepping cautiously and deliberately, so it was quite arduous maintaining her pace. It takes great patience to survive being ancient, I realised. As we escorted her home, Polly grumbling at the aggravation of doing coursework in the holidays when no one took a blind bit of notice of history anyway, at least not on Planet Earth, what struck me most about Miss Edith was how changeable her moods were. Having expressed irritation at us in the shop, she grunted at Polly's remarks, occasionally smiling. And when we returned to the

Gatehouse, instead of sending us away as I'd anticipated, she invited us in.

Beth fed the dogs, then, settling us in the salon and pushing open the french windows to let in some fresh air, Miss Edith announced: 'Fire away, girls. What is it you want to know?'

To our surprise it turned out that Miss Edith's old room at Graylings was now Polly's. 'Far out!' Polly shrieked, as Miss Edith talked of the rose room, its view of the garden, its gentle embrace of the cedar and the setting sun.

'Did you have horses?' Beth asked. For half an hour, Miss Edith narrated tales of Miss Fielding's love of animals: the horses and the dogs she had kept; how heartbroken Olivia had been when the old mare, Medea, had died.

'Poor Olivia,' Miss Edith sighed. 'She couldn't afford to replace her. We cut back on the heating and everything. No more port after dinner. No more pheasant or Turkish delight. We even had to let the Bramleys go and instead of investing in central heating, we were reduced to using the old ceramic hot-water bottles in our beds. 'If you're cold,' Olivia would say, 'you should put an extra eiderdown on the bed.' I froze, my dears, I simply froze in that house. So buying another mare was out of the question. We had to face facts.'

'Did you hunt?'

'I didn't hunt, but Miss Fielding did. Do you hunt?'

'Not yet,' Beth replied. 'My sister Dinah does, and soon I'm going to as well.'

Miss Edith shuddered.

'Don't you like hunting?' I asked.

She refused to respond, turning her head away: the first inkling I had that Miss Edith was not wholly supportive of Miss Fielding's hobbies.

'What was Miss Fielding like?' Polly asked in her most beguiling voice.

'I don't think I can answer that question.'

'Why not?'

Miss Edith hesitated. She started to say something and stopped, a nerve at the side of her mouth contracting. She lifted up a glass of lemonade, taking a sip. The glass in her hand shook. I know, because I was sitting beside her. I stared at her, absorbing her anxiety like a piece of blotting paper sucking up ink.

Now it was my turn: 'Did Miss Fielding like children?'

'She adored them. She simply adored them.'

She had responded too quickly, her bottom lip twitching. It was then, I believe, that our investigation turned a corner, in the words of Malone and Leboeuf, and we realised that behind Miss Edith's eccentric facade was a woman with a wealth of secrets to tell. And there was something else, something I spent the next eight years trying to understand. In Miss Edith's wary hazel eyes, I saw a flash of fear. Not to the same extent as Isobel, perhaps, but by linking the two women in my conscious mind, I began to wonder if our probing about the house – with questions ranging from the geography to the relationships of the people within it – hadn't aroused it, quickening it with our breath. I didn't know if such a thing was possible, so I wondered out loud:

'Is there something wrong with the house, Miss Edith? Doesn't it like us? Is it making Isobel ill?'

'Fiddlesticks!' Miss Edith laughed. 'Olivia adored children. Every year, we used to throw a party for the village. A summer party with cakes and trifle. You'd have enjoyed yourself, Ajuba.'

'Are you sure?'

'As sure as I am of anything, my dear. You'd have loved it. That house and its grounds have had more children running through it than you can begin to imagine.'

According to Malone and Leboeuf, 'An aspiring detective should never leave a stone unturned. The good detective,' they wrote in their column, 'always checks and double-checks every aspect of a suspect's story.'

Consequently, as soon we left the Gatehouse that afternoon, we tracked down Mr Furzey in the garden. Polly said, and I agreed with her, that we had to verify Miss Edith's account of the good old days: when pheasant and Turkish Delight were consumed for dinner, and a couple called the Bramleys cooked for Miss Fielding and drove her and Miss Edith around. We had decided, between us, that Mr Furzey was our best source of secondary information; another route to establishing the truth.

He was busy finishing the new herbaceous border for Isobel's grand design: a border of purple delphiniums and hollyhocks opposite the rose bushes in the walled garden. He was spreading compost into the soil with the help of a red-haired, freckle-faced young man, his new assistant, when Polly, adopting the rather grand tone her mother often used with the gardener, said, 'Mr Furzey, please may we have a word with you?'

'I'm working, Miss.'

'But this is important.'

'That may be so, but unless I'm mistaken, according to your mother, this is mighty important as well.'

Attempting to coax him into co-operation by playing good cop to Polly's aggressive one, I said in a wheedling voice: 'Mr Furzey, would you like a nice cup of tea?'

'Now that's what I call a sensible idea.'

Beth and I hurried inside to make a pot, carrying it out with two mugs and a selection of Isobel's chocolate biscuits. As he was drinking the tea, we bombarded him with questions: all in aid of our history project, of course, though why no one seemed to believe that we were serious students of the past we couldn't quite understand. All the same, I scribbled down notes of Mr Furzey's answers.

He remembered the old days clearly, nostalgia warming his voice as he spoke. I recall him rubbing the knees of his corduroy trousers, brushing a wisp of white hair from his face. He quickly confirmed Miss Edith's story of a gradual decline in Miss Fielding's fortune, demarcating his time working at Graylings into two parts: pre-Medea days when Miss Fielding kept a stable of horses, and post-Medea days, when eventually the Bramleys, Nancy the maid, and everyone else working on the estate was dismissed. Everyone, that is, except for Miss Edith, who had remained, managing the house on her own.

'It couldn't have been easy for her,' Mr Furzey remarked. 'Miss Fielding wasn't what I would call an easy woman.'

'Do you reckon she was criminally insane?' Polly enquired.

Mr Furzey laughed. 'It depends what you mean by criminal, Miss.'

'Was she psychotic and murderous and did she tell lies all the time?'

'Did she look you in the eye when she talked to you?' I added.

'Or was she cruel to animals. Did you ever see her torturing them in secret?'

'Well, she liked her animals, that's for sure. And what with her being a Justice of the Peace, I wouldn't call her a criminal as such. Though some would say that people of her ilk are always up to something, one way or another. If you catch my meaning.'

We didn't catch his meaning. We stared at him mystified, until Polly, invariably emboldened by adult prevarication, asked irritably: 'What exactly do you mean, Mr Furzey?'

'No offence meant, Miss. But some things are best left unsaid. That's what I mean.'

Unsure how best to proceed with our line of questioning, the image of the babies sealed in Miss Fielding's trunk prompted me to exclaim: 'But did she like children, Mr Furzey? And did you have summer parties for them here, like Miss Edith said?'

Taking a final sip of tea, Mr Furzey appeared to reflect deeply before nodding. 'Yes, we did have parties for kiddies in the old days. But if you really want to know, I would say that Miss Fielding was more of a one for animals than kiddies. You see, she treated her dogs better than she did the rest of us; even Miss Edith.'

Immediately sympathetic to the type of person he was describing, Beth smiled. Then, as if to hide her embarrassment at Mr Furzey's disapproval of women who prioritised dogs and horses over children, she blurted out a question we all wanted answered: 'Have they come for you yet, Mr Furzey? Have they taken you away and DNAed you?'

To our astonishment, he answered without hesitation: 'Indeed they have. Like I said before, I've got nothing to hide; nothing to be ashamed of. And they've tracked down the Bramleys too. Seems they were up in Northumberland somewhere. And there's Nancy Spurrell in Exeter, they've found. Miss Butterworth will be next for the DNA business, and there's talk of them digging up Miss Fielding herself. Digging her up from her grave. That's what they're saying.'

'Jeez,' Polly marvelled, wide-eyed. 'That policeman guy is seriously kicking ass. I guess he'll be swabbing everyone who ever set foot here next. Do you think they'll want to talk to us, Mr Furzey?'

'Well, if Inspector Roberts says he's going to get to the bottom of it, he will, you mark my words. Even if it means prising Miss Fielding out of that walnut coffin of hers. If that's what it takes to get to the bottom of this terrible business, I reckon he'll do it.'

11

Mr Furzey's revelation that Miss Edith would soon have her DNA tested precipitated a change of tack on our part. Instead of daily visits to Miss Edith, Polly decided to further our enquiries by making Beth and I stake out the Gatehouse during daylight hours. Her idea was that we should photograph Detective Inspector Roberts entering the house with his team, and then carrying Miss Edith away, screaming and kicking, in handcuffs.

The next day, Beth and I spent the whole afternoon hiding behind the yew trees in front of the Gatehouse, the Bradshaw Polaroid at the ready. Nobody came and Beth, bored by hours of prolonged inactivity, decided that being a detective was crap if it meant hanging around doing nothing. I tried to explain that persistence, the Third Principle of Detection, requires discipline and patience, and that good detective work always takes time. But when she said that she thought that Malone and Leboeuf were crap as well, I suggested that she go home. Nevertheless, I appreciated her unhappiness at us doing all the spade work in our joint endeavour, while Polly stayed at home thinking and planning what we should do next. I decided that I wasn't going to do any more stake-outs unless Polly was with us as well. I needn't have worried, because a few days after Theo had gone, Peter returned and Polly wanted to be with him.

Peter's visit began inauspiciously. He spent the morning holed up in his study while Polly ran to and fro, lavishing attention on him. She made him cups of tea and toast, she offered him a golden apple, a mint; her endless concern for his well-being was in marked contrast to her indifference towards her mother. Polly seemed to believe that whatever was happening between her parents was her mother's fault. I suspect Peter enjoyed being the favoured parent, for instead of having to talk to Isobel, Polly gave him someone to hide behind.

While Polly ran in and out, pampering Peter, I helped her mother in the kitchen. I remember my confusion that morning, the sense of foreboding I struggled to define. I didn't have the words to explain what was happening, but I remember the feelings and the atmosphere. The air bristled with static and I found that whenever I touched Isobel, a jolt of electricity ran through my fingers. So I stopped touching her.

Isobel was as tense as a leopard stalking its prey in her hunger for Peter. Every nerve in her body seemed alert to him: to the sounds coming from his study, the food and drinks being taken in and out. She was cooking an elaborate meal for the evening, which would culminate with his favourite pudding of chocolate mousse flavoured with orange peel. Her movements were quick and skilful, and as she beat eggs into a stiff white froth then stirred it into a pool of chocolate, I sensed her stealth, her patience, her willingness to suppress her anger to achieve her aim.

I was nervous; although Isobel seemed in control, the atmosphere in the house weighed down on me. I remember my growing apprehension as I set the table for lunch. Unwittingly, we were being dragged towards the eye of a whirlpool. I didn't understand what was going on, but I could feel its current, strong and menacing.

Lunch was a humble affair: bread, goat's cheese and fruit. Isobel had made a green salad and served some to her husband. They weren't speaking. Peter helped himself to some wine. Unlike other occasions, when we had sat down to similar lunches of bread and cheese with salami and olives, the atmosphere that afternoon was so oppressive that I had difficulty swallowing. Polly, caressing Peter, was leaning against him while she toyed with her food.

Isobel chose to ignore her, instead asking me: 'More cheese?'

'She doesn't like it,' Polly retorted. 'Nobody likes goat's cheese but you, Isobel.'

'Ajuba can speak for herself,' her mother replied. But Polly, indignant, refused to be silenced.

'I don't like it, Theo doesn't like it, and he's swimming in cheese in France. So why do you buy it, Isobel?'

To Polly's fury, her mother pushed the cheese platter towards me, even though I still had some left on my plate.

'Isobel, she doesn't want it!'

Her mother stared at her coldly. 'Either you sit up properly, young lady, or you leave the table.'

Cutting a slab of chevre, she put it on my plate. 'Don't let her bully you, pet.'

'Look who's talking! Aj, don't eat it. You don't have to eat it,' Polly yelled.

Peter took a sip of wine. He appeared bored by the fracas, but addressing his daughter in a quiet voice, he said: 'There's really no need to shout, you know, Polly.'

I didn't know what to do; whatever I did, I would displease one of them. It seems odd that I didn't ask to leave the table, which was what I wanted. Instead, I allowed Polly to speak for me, in a manner I found offensive. I fumbled with the food on my plate. Isobel urged me to eat.

'Leave her alone!' Polly screamed. By now she was trembling.

I nibbled at the bread and cheese. I felt my mouth go dry, my throat tighten. I put the food down again. 'I'm not hungry any more.'

'Happy now?' Polly asked her mother. Then, her eyes filling with tears, she bellowed: 'You make me want to puke!' In a gesture of utter frustration, she picked up the bread from her plate and flung it at Isobel, hitting her on the head. At last, Peter was stirred into action.

'Polly! Don't ever do that again!'

Unused to him raising his voice to anyone but Isobel, Polly froze, her tears falling silently. I'd never seen her crying before, and as she struggled to retain control, sitting upright in her chair, she seemed angrier at her own fragility than at Isobel. Under the table, I inched my hand toward Polly's, clasping her fingers.

'You know, when I was your age,' Peter said, his voice calm again, 'your grandfather told me something I've never forgotten. He caught me fighting with a friend over a comic. I had given the boy a bloody nose by the time he pulled us apart, so he tore the comic up and sent me to my room. That evening, he sat me down and said: always remember, Peter, it's people that matter in life, not things.'

'Sure,' Polly sobbed. 'It wasn't his comic, was it? He had no right to tear it up.'

'He was my father,' Peter stressed. 'He had every right to

stop me hurting myself and other people. You see, kitten, what you think about goat's cheese is irrelevant. What matters is that you listen to your mother and that Ajuba feels at home with us.'

At the mention of my name, Polly reciprocated my touch with a squeeze as Peter, warming to his theme, continued: 'And you should try and be kind to Isobel as well. To everybody, in fact. But to your mother especially.'

With a clarity that was unnerving, Polly replied: 'Why should I be kind to her, if you're not?'

'Well, she's your mother for a start. And she's going through a tough time. We both are.'

'So? What's new?'

'Don't be a smart-arse with me, Polly. I want you to behave yourself. I don't want you making a martyr of your mother when I'm gone. Promise me you won't?'

I wasn't aware that Peter was saying anything out of the ordinary. He was always going away; he was usually absent. Though I believed that I knew them well, I was an outsider in the Venus family, a favoured guest unable to decipher the secret code and signals family members sometimes use. Whether it was the severity of Peter's tone, or the words themselves which alerted Polly to a change in the family's circumstances, I shall never know. What I remember is my friend staring at Peter with a scrutiny that seemed to tear open his heart. After what seemed a long time, she whispered in a small voice untypical of her: 'Daddy, are you going to leave me?'

'No, kitten. I'm never going to leave you. I'm separating from your mother.'

'No!' Polly wailed, dropping my hand and any pretence of adult composure. 'No! You can't. I can't live here without you, Daddy. I can't stand her!' she screamed. 'It's your fault, Isobel! You've made him run away.'

'Now you see what happens when you're not around,' Isobel said icily. 'Now you see what I have to put up with. If it's not bed-wetting it's those bloody babies in the attic. We need you at home, Peter! Polly needs a full-time father.'

'Don't do this to me, Mommy! Please don't do this to me!'

As his women started yelling abuse at each other, Peter grabbed Polly by the arm and dragged her, kicking and screaming, from the room.

After clearing up the wreckage of lunch, I followed Isobel into the rose garden. I hadn't fully grasped the repercussions of all that had been said over lunch. As far as I could see, Isobel and Peter led separate lives already. Unaware that separation is often a precursor of divorce, I believed that even if they were living apart, they still might come together again.

The walled garden was a pleasant sanctuary on cool evenings, when the scent of roses filled the air. Polly and I sometimes played Scrabble on one of the benches after supper. But on a hot, humid afternoon with the sun beating down, it was not a place for the faint-hearted. I think that after the debacle of lunch, Isobel wanted to vent her anger on something, and, unlike her daughter, the plants couldn't talk back. Armed with a pair of secateurs and wearing a sun hat, she attacked the rose bushes with the ruthlessness of a house-frau gutting fish. I carried a basket for the cut flowers, their delicate heads bleeding over the edge.

Isobel struggled with a blossom, severed it and threw it on top of the others: 'She shouldn't take advantage of you,' she kept saying of her daughter. 'You ought to stand up to her more, Ajuba. We can't have her getting her way all the time, can we?'

I didn't reply, so she turned from the task in hand to me. The secateurs looked vicious. 'She's my best friend,' I explained.

'*Yes*,' she said, her impatience forcing her to stress the word, transforming what was meant to be acquiescence into a hiss of denial. 'I know Polly's your best friend, dear, but that doesn't make you her slave.'

'I'm not her slave. I'm her best friend.'

She decided to change tack, and, severing a rose the colour of her hair, she held it seductively beneath my chin. 'You're better than butter, you are,' she whispered. 'You deserve better than Polly.'

She held me with those brown eyes of hers in a lingering, complicit gaze. I was out of my depth, drowning in the sensuous warmth of her eyes, when a pebble landed at my feet. I tore myself free and saw Polly, half hidden behind a shrub, beckoning. I handed the basket of roses to Isobel. 'I'm sorry. I'm supposed to . . . we're . . .' Polly and I were meeting Beth to stake out the Gatehouse that afternoon. However, Isobel had left me dazed, tongue-tied. There was a maggot in my mango and I didn't like the taste of it. As if sensing my unease, Polly's mother smiled at me.

'You're on holiday, pet,' she murmured. 'You can do whatever you want.'

I took a backward step, then I ran to Polly. As soon as we were out of the walled garden and out of hearing range, Polly asked, 'What was she saying?' Red-eyed and deflated, she was holding a carrier bag.

'Are you all right?' I asked, as we walked past Peter's Renault.

'I'm waiting for you to tell me what Isobel was saying.'

'She wasn't saying anything.'

'She sure as hell was saying *something*.'

'It was nothing much.'

'Bullshit!'

'Bullshit to you!' I shouted.

Polly threw down the carrier bag and, grabbing me by the shoulders, shoved me against the garage door. In a single movement she had me pinned by the throat, depriving me of air.

'Out with it. Tell me what she said.' She slackened her arm to give me air enough to speak. 'Are you my best friend or not?' She was crying, and the absurdity of such a question when she was squeezing the breath out of me gave me the strength to kick her on the shins. Polly fell to the ground, weeping.

'What's the matter with you, Polly?'

'You've got to tell me what Isobel was saying. If you were my best friend, you'd tell me. I know you'd tell me.'

So I lied to her. My excuse is that I was trying to protect my friend. I was trying to placate both mother and daughter by lying to one about the other. 'She said . . . she said she's always thinking of you. And she said that she loves you. Then, she begged me to be your friend, for ever and ever. Amen.'

Polly, however, was still suspicious. Experience had taught her that Isobel was adept at manipulation and capable of making mincemeat of the gullible. 'Isobel said that?'

I crossed my heart, and, licking my forefinger, stuck it in the warm afternoon air. 'Cross my heart and hope to die,' I said, expecting to be struck dead in an instant. Nothing happened and although suspicion still lingered on Polly's face she didn't say anything. She couldn't, because just then Beth appeared on her bicycle, peddling furiously. When she was almost on top of us, she squeezed the hand brakes, dropping her legs to the side.

'I haven't missed anything have I?'

Polly and I shook our heads at the same time.

'Well,' she chuckled, unable to contain her glee, 'you've missed something absolutely stupendous! I was outside the Gatehouse waiting for you guys when Detective Inspector Roberts, of all people, turns up. He goes into the Gatehouse and – hey presto! – I take his photograph.'

Getting down from her bike, Beth opened the satchel in which she kept her mother's camera and brought out two photographs. The first was of a tall, lanky man in civilian clothes entering the Gatehouse with a uniformed policewoman beside him. The second was of the same pair leaving through the side door. Miss Edith was nowhere to be seen.

'Didn't they take her with them? You mean she's still there?' Polly protested.

'Of course. She's only a suspect at this stage,' I replied.

'Yeah,' Beth confirmed. 'And they won't get the results of her test for yonks. Mummy says the final inquest won't happen until around February at the earliest, and we're only in August, you know.'

Our instinct to investigate quickening, Polly and I followed Beth on her bicycle towards the Gatehouse and the Bag Lady.

Our absorption with Miss Edith was not entirely ghoulish. Even when Beth and I realised that Polly was right in supposing Miss Edith knew more about the contents of Miss Fielding's trunk than she was telling us, when I browse through the pages of our *True Murder* scrapbook, what stands out above everything else is what excellent friends we were back then. And in the end, Miss Edith became our friend as well. In addition to newspaper cuttings from the *Gazette* and the *Guardian*, a carefully drawn map of Graylings with the names of the rooms and where the staff and Miss Fielding slept; along with photographs of Miss Edith at the Co-Op, Mr Furzey in the garden, and Detective Inspector Roberts at the Gatehouse, the book contains more or less anything that caught our attention that summer: a crow's feather picked up on the drive, a leaf from the copper beech at Ford Abbey, a mass of dog hairs brushed off Candy and Fudge, and a series of portraits of ourselves. There are pictures of Polly dressed in fluorescent t-shirt and a tight black skirt, attempting to bump and grind to our favourite song that summer, Shaggy's 'O Carolina'. There's a photo of us wearing our Crimebuster badges and then the three of us draped in Miss Fielding's clothes. Beth is in her riding jacket, I am in her shawl and Polly, her face half-hidden by a pink silk hat, smiles coquettishly at the camera.

'It was your Summer of Love,' Belinda Bradshaw told me years later. 'While the Venuses were breaking up, you girls were completely absorbed in each other's lives. I'd never seen anything like it. You seemed oblivious to what was going on.'

To this day, I don't think Belinda is aware of how deeply involved we became with Miss Edith. She assumed, as did the other adults around us, that we were only interested in walking Candy and Fudge. They didn't realise what our interrogation was doing to Miss Edith and to what extent our persistent extraction of details of her past life, compounded by the police investigation, was beginning to upset her.

That afternoon we found Miss Edith still in her dressing-gown. She was outside, sitting in a garden chair, sorting boxes of photographs on a table. The day was humid, the air prickly with the promise of rain. The garden needed water, as did the potted plants on the patio, but Miss Edith, immersed in the past, seemed unaware of the weather.

'You're not ill, are you?' Beth asked. Miss Edith must have been still undressed when the police came to call, I thought. I noticed a half-eaten digestive biscuit and a glass of water beside a stack of photographs. Her face was flushed, and her deeply wrinkled skin looked like the skeleton of a leaf, the sun shining behind it.

'I'm fit as a fiddle,' she snarled.

I stared at her while Polly, dipping into the carrier bag, produced the remainder of the goat's cheese she'd fought over at lunch. 'Shall I put this in the kitchen?'

'You realise you don't have to keep on bringing me things, don't you? You can come visiting without bearing gifts, you know.'

'I know that.'

Avid to learn more about Miss Edith's former life from her photographs, Polly and I inched closer to her. We both thought, with the absurd optimism of the very young, that by the end of the afternoon, we'd have all our questions answered.

As if understanding our interest in her affairs, Miss Edith said: 'Come along, girls, I want to show you something.'

We clustered around her, Beth and I leaning over an arm of the rattan chair, Polly on the other arm, as Miss Edith turned the pages of her album.

She pointed out a photograph of Medea to Beth, who was immediately smitten: 'I'd die for a horse like that!'

Then she showed us Miss Fielding's photographs of summer parties at Graylings and holidays in Europe: Miss Fielding with her Brownie Pack, Miss Fielding dressed as Brown Owl, in the uniform of a Queen's Guide, in a bathing costume diving into a Norwegian fjord. There were snow-capped mountains in the background, so I asked Miss Edith if Norway was cold.

She shivered, remembering just how chilly it had been: 'The water was freezing, my dear, like a knife slicing my skin.'

She brought out photographs of a holiday in Orkney and then another taken in the Highlands of Scotland.

'Where's a whiff of the Mediterranean?' I wanted to know. 'The Promenade des Anglais and that piazza in Florence?'

Surprised that I had remembered our first conversation, Miss Edith smiled wistfully: a nursery-pudding smile, which darkened her eyes with a sprinkling of nutmeg. 'Olivia wasn't like you and me, Ajuba. She insisted on travelling north, never south, because she loathed the heat. She thought the Latin temperament vulgar; excessive. And, oh, how she hated garlic!'

'Mummy doesn't like garlic either,' said Beth. 'She says it makes your breath stink.'

'I wouldn't know,' said Miss Edith. 'We weren't allowed to have it in the house in case I was tempted to use it.'

'Weren't you allowed to use it to frighten off vampires and werewolves?' I asked.

'Not even for that, my dear.'

Rummaging through a cardboard box at Miss Edith's feet, Beth discovered a photograph in an envelope and brought it out. It was of a man leaning against a gate, an arm around a bashful Miss Edith. 'Who's he?' she asked.

'Yes, who is he?' Polly reiterated. 'He's kinda cute, ain't he?'

The man was of medium height and stocky build with black hair and a warm smile. Miss Edith gazed at him. 'The Lake District,' she said slowly. 'It must have been the Lake District. I can't remember when it was, but I remember we walked for miles that summer.'

'You mean you took him on holiday with you?'

'No, we met him up there.'

I stared at the old woman intently. 'What's his name?'

We were full of questions about the man's name and his age, where he came from and what he did. With our inquisitive eyes appraising her past life, our questions tumbling out one after the other, Miss Edith soon protested. She claimed she was exhausted.

'Look, if you girls want to be helpful, take the dogs out for me, will you? Candy, Fudge. Walkies!' The dogs started barking, eager to be running outside.

'But we want to help you with this.'

'You'll find their leashes in the hall,' Miss Edith called as Beth and I slipped back inside with the dogs. Polly, of course, hung back.

'I don't want to go. I want to help you sort out your photographs.'

'Well, I don't need your help! I'm old and decrepit and I need my afternoon zizz. So go on, off with you.'

Polly left the house with us.

Within the hour, the humidity in the air had swelled into a summer squall that brought us running back to the Gatehouse. We found Miss Edith still on the patio, crying in the rain, with several photographs at her feet. The silk-covered album, now sodden, had stained her fingers a putrid green.

We didn't know what to do. We had never seen her like this before. While the dogs whined, nuzzling against her knees, we glanced at one another, unsure of ourselves. Eventually, Beth took her by the hand. 'You can't cry in the rain,' she said firmly. 'You'll catch your death.'

Miss Edith moaned. She allowed us to help her out of the chair and into the house. I got her a towel. She told us to go; she didn't want us around; at least not for the time being.

'What's wrong?' Polly asked. 'What's bothering you?'

The tears started again. All the questions we'd been planning to ask about the man in the photograph were forgotten in the face of her distress. Suddenly Miss Edith looked very old: small and shrivelled up like a tiger nut someone had forgotten to eat.

'I'm going to run you a bath,' I told her, speaking louder than was necessary. Baths seemed to help Isobel, so perhaps a hot bath would help Miss Edith as well. We only called her the Bag Lady in our fantasies. She was strange, yet we liked her. And when she wasn't overly distracted, she seemed to enjoy our company. So why was she crying? Had we asked too many questions? Had the Inspector's visit unnerved her?

Polly recovered the last of the photographs from the patio and handed them to Miss Edith, who let them fall on her lap. She didn't want to look at them again. Beth had made a cup of sweet tea, and, sipping it, Miss Edith recovered somewhat. She had painted such an idyllic picture of life at Graylings during Miss Fielding's time that we assumed her tears were shed for the past: her life with Miss Fielding. The three of us believed that Miss Edith was simply missing her friend. We had no idea how wrong we were.

12

Two weeks later, Isobel's listlessness had crept through the beams of the house and dimmed the brightness of the walls, cracking the plaster beneath. Her mood created a cloud of cobwebs around her, so when I touched her, I felt compelled to shake spiders off my fingers, wiping my hands clean. What had seemed beautiful had lost its lustre. As her sadness deepened, I noticed she no longer ate solids, subsisting instead on a diet of yoghurt and liquidised fruit: soothing, baby foods for a woman unable to stomach what was happening. Peter, unwilling to taste the chocolate mousse she had made for him, had returned to London the day of his visit. It was no big deal, Polly insisted. Everyone divorced nowadays and if everyone else could handle it, she sure as hell knew that she could. Divorce was of no consequence whatsoever. I didn't believe her. My parents had taught me otherwise.

It was one of our rituals that every evening Polly and I took a bath together. It was our favourite time of day, a time of intimacy and complicity when, indulging our mutual passion, we read snippets of *True Murder* to each other and plotted the progress of our investigation. Polly had just finished running a bath and was dribbling some of Isobel's herbal essence in the tub, swirling it with her hand, when I heard the sound of Isobel weeping.

Even though the bath was full, Polly turned the tap on again. I turned it off. 'Can't you hear her?'

Isobel's muffled sobbing rose and fell like the lilt of a willow in a breeze. 'She's always crying,' Polly replied.

I suppose she had enough to contend with without being swept away by her mother's despair. None the less, Polly's behaviour seemed extraordinary, and I went into the corridor to listen. Hearing Isobel's sobs grow louder, I said: 'Go to her, Polly. That's what daughters are for.'

'And what are best friends for?' she asked, responding to my challenge with one of her own.

I took a step towards the bathroom, and it was then that Isobel's weeping ceased. I stood still, alert to danger. Experience had taught me that it is when mothers stop crying that harm befalls them. It is when there is silence that danger is imminent. Sensing my hesitation, and taking it as a sign of disloyalty, Polly slammed the bathroom door in my face.

Waiting outside Isobel's door, I strained to hear her voice inviting me in. I had knocked several times already and there had been no reply. I knocked once again and hearing nothing but an ominous silence, I gripped the door knob and turned it.

Isobel Venus was at her dressing-table staring at a reflection devoid of make-up. She looked wretched: her eyes sunken, her cheekbones prominent. I believed that what she glimpsed in the mirror was the face of a stranger; several strangers perhaps. As I entered the room, she swept a silk scarf over the glass.

She has been talking to her enemies, I decided, the scarf reminding me of another mirror: a scarf covered with prints of African parrots and turquoise cooking pots. She had been talking to Emily Richardson, and everyone who'd cheated her of her husband, forcing her to hear his confession. She saw them. She talked to them. They were in the mirror.

'I expect you to knock before you come in here,' Isobel said, clasping her towelling bathrobe around the neck.

'I'm sorry but I did knock. I thought I heard you crying.'

'It wasn't me, pet.'

I stood awkwardly in the middle of the room. I wanted to step closer, to insinuate myself between her legs, purring good luck and keeping her warm. Her lie confounded me. Isobel had been crying. I had heard her. I'd been listening to her tears for weeks.

Assuming the same nonchalance that I'd often seen in Polly, Isobel removed the scarf from the mirror, examining her reflection intently.

'Don't! Don't look in the mirror!' I screamed.

My terror must have resonated with something within her, unleashing her feelings once again. She covered her face with her hands and gave vent to her frustration and pain.

I crept closer. I had heard such crying before, and many a time I'd witnessed that same look of utter desolation. I'd suffered its vacillations, the cut of its scythe. Having endured it once, I welcomed it a second time.

Touching Isobel's cheek in the certainty that I'd found my way home at last, I murmured: 'Don't cry, Mama. Don't cry. Please don't cry,' as she clutched me to her shrunken breasts.

To Polly's annoyance, I spent the next morning looking after Isobel, feeding her a bowl of yoghurt and honey and cups of herbal tea. I would have spent the whole day fretting over her if I'd had my way, but in the afternoon when Belinda Bradshaw dropped by for a visit, I followed my fellow Crimebusters on to the kitchen lawn.

We were trying to decide how we should proceed with our case. We'd resolved, after witnessing Miss Edith's distress, to back off, giving our suspect space to recover before interrogating her again: a strategy that had often proved effective for Malone and Leboeuf. We were weighing up the advantages of a more subtle, nuanced approach, the benefits of tactical kindness as opposed to probing aggression. But our imaginations got the better of us and we started speculating again. The way we saw it, Miss Edith was responsible for the babies in the attic. The man in the photograph had most probably fallen in love with Miss Fielding, the more attractive of the friends.

'He could have fallen in love with Miss Edith,' Beth suggested.

I disagreed. 'She couldn't remember his name.'

'Aj, you should never believe what a suspect tells you.'

The three of us were sitting on the lawn making a daisy chain, while Polly, pretending to be more hard-nosed than Beth and me, added flesh to our theories.

'OK, the Queen of Hearts falls in love with him and they have a baby.' The Queen of Hearts was the name we had given Miss Fielding.

'They have twins,' I reminded her.

'Fine, they have twins. Then he wants to marry her. So the Bag Lady flips. First she poisons him, then she strangles the babies.' She looked at us for approval. I nodded while Beth shook her head.

We were grappling with events beyond our comprehension, attempting to make them safe by putting a shape to them and providing our characters with motives. It was like going over the details of a story day after day; one in which the innocent and vulnerable are consumed by a predatory adult. Even then, we made the culprit someone we liked, for somehow that made it safer. We knew Miss Edith would never intentionally hurt us, so we made her the villain of our piece. Beth, however, was too much of an animal lover to cast Miss Edith as a murderess.

'As if!' she exclaimed. 'She worships Candy and Fudge! Anyone who worships dogs couldn't hurt a fly. Could they, Aj?'

'I wouldn't be so sure. My pa says Hitler loved Alsatians.'

'As if!'

'He did too. And he was worse than a serial killer. He murdered tons and tons of people.'

'He couldn't have liked dogs then.'

'Oh, yeah?' Polly sneered.

'Look, if Miss Edith whacked him, where's the body?' Beth pointed out.

'Am I a clairvoyant? I'm a detective!' Polly exclaimed.

Beth laughed and, bringing us down to earth again, she said, 'Well, if you're a detective then I'm Mr Blobby and Malone and Leboeuf all rolled up together.'

But Polly wouldn't let the subject drop. In fact, having witnessed Miss Edith's tears, she was drawn to it with renewed fervour. And the babies hidden in the trunk led us to another macabre game: another version of True Murder in which one of us pretended to be a murderer or a victim of murder, assuming their stillness in death, while the others had to guess who we were.

I rather liked being Ruth Ellis while Beth relished playing the Yorkshire Ripper. Oddly enough, I can't remember the roles Polly opted for. But that afternoon our speculation about Miss Edith led me to ask a question to which I already knew the answer.

'She wouldn't hurt us, would she, Polly?'

She thought for a moment, looking from Beth to me. Then, because the purpose of our game was contradictory – it was as much to do with making us fearful as easing our fear – Polly opted to give us a frisson.

'With a sicko like that,' she whispered, 'you can never tell.'

Placing the daisies around Polly's neck, I noticed Isobel staring at us from the kitchen window. Belinda Bradshaw had gone and the look of unquenchable hopelessness that I had come to know well was stamped on Isobel's face again.

Curious about what had caught my attention, Polly and Beth turned to gaze at Mrs Venus. She was like a ghost at the window. A pale, voracious, keening ghost.

'It's Peter,' Polly announced. 'She wants him back. But he doesn't want her any more. He told me. She's trying to get used to it, but life sure as hell sucks when you're going through the menopause. And when it sucks as much as it does right now, it's not surprising she's miserable.'

'What's the menopause?' I asked.

'Hallo? Ever wonder why so many women over the hill are alone, Aj? It's called the menopause. It's when a woman can't have any more children. It's when her eggs shrivel up and die and no one wants her any more.'

Unwilling to believe that this would be Isobel's fate, despite my ignorance of a woman's reproductive cycle, I demanded: 'How do you know she's shrivelling up and dying? How do you know, Polly?'

'Because Theo told me. She's always telling him things that she'd never tell me. Like gruesome, grisly things I'd rather not know. Like things that make me want to puke and are so uncool that I swear I will *never* be like her. Not in a million, trillion years. Got it?'

13

Two days later, Peter Venus was back at Graylings again, and the day after that Polly and I were in London with him. Isobel wanted time to think. And to give herself the solitude she needed, she'd decided that Peter could have us for a change. It was time, she said, that he sampled the delights of being a full-time father.

Life had taught me that despondent women, women who gaze into mirrors, should never be left alone. However, Isobel was so adamant about her need for solitude that, despite my misgivings, I was soon as excited as Polly about going to London. Moreover, I didn't have any choice in the matter. Isobel wanted us out of her house and that was that. As it turned out, our fortnight in London was the happiest of my life.

When I first decided that Aunt Rose would approve of Peter – because of the way he ate his pear over dinner – I hadn't appreciated the tensions between him and Isobel. Now that I knew a little of what was going on, I found that instead of taking Isobel's side wholeheartedly, as I had taken my mother's, I couldn't help liking Peter.

Aunt Rose is an excellent judge of the masculine character. She appreciates it fully, a connoisseur indulging her passion. Unlike many of her contemporaries, who pray to

God for patience to withstand their marriages, complaining bitterly about the men in their lives, Aunt Rose delights in their strength, laughing at their foibles. She likes men. And as far as I know, her inclination to indulge them, occasionally teasing and sparring with them, has made her happy.

My aunt has never married. I don't believe she regrets being on her own; like Peter, she enjoys sampling what's on offer. She likes to taste without feeling obliged to sit down, over a lifetime, at the same table. So whenever I think of her, I'm reminded of Peter's appeal to women, the subtle manner in which he eats fruit: delicately, slowly, as if it were the most delicious food in the world. That's how he treated Polly and me in London.

The houseboat he rented at Chelsea Wharf was magnificent. Simple to the point of being spartan, the kitchen was tiny, opening out to the largest room, a broad expanse of dining-room and salon, chairs strategically placed to catch a glimpse of water. I'd never been on the Thames before but I soon got to know its character: on a clear morning, a seal surfacing; at midday, shimmering and bright; dark beneath a sullen sky; at night, soft as a lullaby caressing me to sleep.

I loved Peter's boat: its separation from the rest of the city, and the berth I slept in above Polly. I grew to love Peter's London as well. It was a world away from the streets of Lewisham I had walked with my mother, when she'd scanned the windows of newsagents looking for work and was careful of every penny we spent. Peter's London was completely different.

The best day of the whole summer holiday was when he took us to the Tate gallery, and in the evening a concert at Wembley. I remember it as a day he paid me particular attention by encouraging a trait he saw in me: sitting and staring, he called it; my habit of looking at pictures and people and dwelling on them.

As I recall, we were walking through the Tate with Polly when a particular watercolour caught my eye. Peter and I looked at it together for almost half an hour. The painting reminded me of the canvas in his study at Graylings. It had the same windswept quality, the same bleakness. It was called *Tench Pond in a Gale*, a murky pond surrounded by trees. Beside it was another painting by the same artist, Paul Nash: another watercolour of trees, though lighter in mood and fresher in tone with splashes of pink and yellow among graceful greens and greys. But it was the darker picture that held my attention. Noticing that Peter liked it as well, I asked him how he could sit and stare at the canvas in his study for hours on end.

He chuckled at my exaggeration and then he said: 'It was a gift from my father, Ajuba. He was a Church of England clergyman. Whenever I look at the picture, I'm reminded of the man he wanted me to be. You see, he left me it in his will but he gave it to me before he died. It was my reward for getting into Oxford.'

Polly, standing at the other side of him, asked: 'Will you give it to Theo when he gets into Oxford? Like Gramps did with you?'

'No, I want you to have it, kitten.'

Incredulous, Polly gave Peter a shove. 'Are you for real, Daddy?'

'You'd better believe it!'

'Really?'

When he nodded, Polly draped an arm around his waist, while Peter, his hand on my shoulder, encouraged me to look at *Tench Pond in a Gale* from another angle.

Sensing that the melancholy in the canvas was igniting

something similar in me, I said: 'But his pictures make you sad, Peter.'

'Of course, little one. Sadness isn't bad in itself. It's how you deal with it that counts. It reminds me of the mistakes I've made. It takes me back to when I was a boy.' He took a step closer to the picture in front of us, examining the brushstrokes carefully. I followed his example, curious to see what he could see.

'I grew up in Cornwall, on Bodmin Moor. And whenever I see a Paul Nash, I'm back there again, walking my dog in the rain. It makes me feel clean, unspoilt by the intervention of time, even though time's running out.'

I tried to understand what he meant. Looking at the watercolour, I felt the sensation of a cold wind on my face. I heard the faint cry of birds in the sky, and for a moment I glimpsed the England that the Derbys loved: rugged, unadorned, an elemental landscape.

When I had finished staring (Peter never rushed me; he moved at my pace, intrigued by what I saw) we wandered into the next room to see the paintings of a woman artist. She was a Polish exponent of Art Deco, Peter told us, an émigrée to France called Tamara de Lempicka who made a name for herself as a portrait painter. At the far end of the room was a canvas of a dark-haired woman, the Duchesse de la Salle, in jodhpurs and riding boots, a leg raised on a red staircase. Self-confident and powerful, her bearing reminded me of Miss Fielding. She seemed to be glaring at me, so I quickly turned away. Polly was transfixed by a self-portrait of the artist in a green Buggati. Beside it was a picture of the same blonde, or someone who looked like her, in a trailing blue scarf, and then another of a golden-haired sleeping child, her head cradled on an arm.

The child was the image of Polly the first time she slept in my bed, when her skin had seemed translucent, and we became friends. The woman in the green car and the blonde in blue were both Isobel, glamorously self-possessed, with a glint of steel behind the apparent frankness of her eyes. Noticing the resemblance between the grown woman and the child, Polly, with an openness I've never enjoyed with my own father, confronted what was uppermost in her mind.

'Do you like me, Daddy?' she asked, taking Peter's hand.

'What a question! Of course I like you. You're wonderful, kitten.'

'Wonderful like Isobel's wonderful?'

'Polly, you're nothing like your mother.'

'Do you love me more than you love Isobel?'

'I love you in a different way, kitten.'

'Different enough so's we can live together in London?'

The intensity of her questions was beginning to make passers-by stare at us. I'm sure Peter would have liked us to move on but Polly, absorbed by the portraits, refused to leave the room. We sat down on a bench opposite, so we could talk and look at the pictures at the same time. I think it was the bright lips of the woman in the painting, the tilt of her black beret above the seductively tied blue scarf, that reminded Polly of Isobel. The child beside her, fast asleep, was fragile as only a child can be.

Peter looked from the portrait that could have been his wife to the one that resembled Polly. When he turned to her, he held her hand: 'Sweetheart, I'd like you with me all the time, you know I would. Believe me, I'm working on it but –'

She interrupted him with the full force of her personality. 'It's my choice,' she said emphatically.

'It's what I want too,' Peter reassured her, 'but we've got to give your mother time.'

'Why? I want to live with you now.'

'I know you do, sweetheart. But let's talk about this later.' He was clearly embarrassed to be discussing custody of his daughter in a public place. But, much as I would refuse to be deflected from talking to my father when an opportunity arose, Polly's need to pin Peter down overrode any sensitivity she might have felt about his unease.

When? she asked. When would she be able to live with him again?

While I gazed at the canvas of the sleeping child, drawn to the warm radiance of her skin, Peter held Polly's hand. She laid her head on his arm as he explained why he had spent so much time in Paris. He was looking for another job. He was thinking of accepting an editorial post with the *Herald Tribune*. If his plans worked out, within a year or so he hoped that Polly would join him.

Somehow, he managed to assuage Polly's anxiety without realising that he was inflaming mine. I didn't want to lose my friend. I didn't want her to live abroad. With the consummate skill of a man adept with words, Peter persuaded Polly to see things his way. He explained that it would be easier for them to live together when Isobel was happier in herself; when she had settled down to a new life and found new interests.

'But what if she doesn't let up, Daddy? What if she doesn't get any better?'

'Believe me, kitten, she'll get better. I know your mother. I've known her for twenty years.'

Even though I loved them, the Venuses weren't my family. Yet I didn't want Polly to go and my affection for

her overwhelmed any sense of propriety, compe
speak out. I believed that if I knew what the pr
perhaps I could make it better. So in spite of mys
out: 'What has Isobel done wrong, Peter? Why
to leave her? Is it the menopause?'

Unable to escape the boldness of my questio
probing eyes, Peter sighed. Then, laughing at
said: 'Listen, both of you, Isobel's done nothing
fault is mine. I've treated her abominably and I
We simply can't go on like this.'

'But she wants you to stay,' I insisted. 'I kno
She cries all the time because she wants you ba
she, Polly?'

Polly nodded half-heartedly.

'I want you to understand,' he said, a hint of
igniting his blue eyes, 'that sometimes it's bette
to live apart, making new lives for themselves.
moved on.'

'Are you going to get a new wife?' I demande

Appreciating the power of two against one, P
in: 'Are you going to live with Maria and her m

'Whatever gave you that idea, kitten?'

'You mean, you're through with them already

'I made a mistake, OK?'

Polly touched his cheek. 'Hey, you needn't b
me, Daddy.' A grin spread over her face and she
going to have to look after you, aren't I, Daddy

'No, you're not; I'm going to look after you.'

'Let's both of us look after each other, OK? An
after Aj as well,' Polly added, including me in t

'It's a deal, Polly,' Peter said. He kissed her hand
as a courtier would his lady. Polly appeared

imagine she believed that she finally had her father all to herself.

That evening, Peter took us to Wembley Stadium for a Michael Jackson concert. It was then, I think, that I began to realise that, whether it involved people or paintings, the act of observing yet participating at the same time can be gratifying. While Michael, a hat on his head, a white spangled glove on his hand, moon-danced to 'Billie Jean', we leapt in the aisles, Polly and I, whooping with delight. And although he wasn't Michael Jackson's biggest fan, Peter demonstrated that our pleasure made the outing worthwhile. He got up and danced as well.

On our return to the boat, he produced presents for us both: a pearl necklace for Polly, a silver bangle for me. Souvenirs, he said, of our splendid fortnight together. We were his girls, his favourite girls. But knowing that Polly was extra special, for a moment I was jealous. I wanted Peter to be my father, and the largest part of him I wanted for myself: an uncomfortable feeling to have, when Polly was supposed to be my best friend.

The following morning, Polly found stains in her underpants and ran to tell her father that her period had started. He kissed her and hugged her and went out to buy sanitary towels for her, saying that now she was a woman she must pay particular attention to Isobel's counsel. I desperately wanted to be a woman too. But most of all, as he petted her and made much of her, I wanted to be Polly.

14

We drove back from London in the rain. Polly sat in the front beside Peter, touching his knee every now and again. The long, hot summer was coming to an end. On the journey I wondered what Isobel had been doing in our absence. Had she been able to think, as she wanted? Would she be pleased to have us back? I knew that Polly didn't want to return to her mother; as the car sped down the motorway, little by little, the familiar mask of sullen indifference hardened over her face.

Irrespective of biology and any affinity Peter believed she now shared with Isobel, Polly's sympathy was with her father. She abhorred what was happening between her parents but she intended to brazen it out. Her reward would be to live with Peter. I knew it was what she wanted. She was still wearing the necklace, and she kept fingering the pearls, as though counting a rosary to calm her nerves.

Unlike my friend, I wasn't annoyed with Isobel. I felt there was something of my mother in her, and I associated maternal love with feeling needed. I believed I loved Isobel and that she loved me. When I was with her, my longing receded. Isobel's unhappiness took me back to my mother. Their faces merged, they became one.

As Peter turned into the drive, the rain drumming on the

windscreen, the wipers beating back and forth, Graylings rose up dark and grotesque. There were no lights on, and for a moment I was seized with apprehension. What if, like my mother, Isobel had tried to hurt herself and, because I wasn't by her side, no one had found her in time? I twisted the silver bangle around my wrist, trying to contain my unease and growing sense of guilt, until, one after the other, the lights came on in a blaze of welcome. She must have been asleep, waking up when she heard the car coming up the drive.

Polly and I ran into the house, our heads covered by Peter's raincoat. The noise of the storm excited us, and while Peter retrieved our suitcases from the car boot, we dried ourselves on his coat.

Isobel was in the kitchen heating up soup. I sensed immediately that something fundamental had changed. She was no longer despondent. She was tense, expectant. She wouldn't let me close to her. There was no kiss of welcome, no finger on my cheek. It was as though an invisible cord between us had been severed and she was drifting away, preoccupied with an implacable force that had taken root inside her.

Dishing out our soup, she seemed pleased with herself, her mouth twitching in a grimace of a smile. She was watching and waiting in a cold silent place she had dug out for herself. But what was she waiting for?

I heard a door slam. A moment later Peter strode into the room, his face tight with fury, and seeing Isobel's cool, detached smile, I knew that she had done something bad.

'Where is it?' Peter shouted.

'What are you talking about?' Her face gave her away. She knew exactly what he was after.

'You know damn well what I'm talking about.'

'Oh. That picture of yours?' The smile spreading across

her face left her eyes unscathed. They were cold. 'Well, if you really want to know,' she said folding her arms, 'it's with your books, your music, the Kenzo shirts, your Armani –'

'What the fuck have you done, Isobel?'

'Temper, temper. You should try to see it as therapy, Peter. Expensive and painful, but worth every penny. And I'm a new woman now.' She spread her arms in a mockery of openness.

'Tell me what you've done with it!'

She laughed. 'You said I should talk to someone, didn't you? You said I should find myself a lawyer at the very least. "Find yourself a therapist," you said. So I invited Guy Fawkes a little early this year.'

'You didn't!'

'Yes, I jolly well did.'

He lunged at her, incensed. 'You bloody bitch!'

'Don't!' I shouted. I couldn't yet fathom what Isobel had done but the emotions she had ignited were terrifying. 'Please don't fight.'

Polly ran to try to pull Peter off Isobel. He had an arm around her mother's neck. 'Daddy, stop it! Daddy! You said it's people that matter. It's people, not things.'

Isobel kneed Peter in the groin and he doubled up in pain. I stumbled from the table, my face wet with tears. Then, seeing the raw hatred on Isobel's face, her rage overwhelmed me, draining my body of strength; and the house, opening itself up to me, revealed what Isobel had done. How I managed to see beyond my tears I don't know, but the memory the house foisted on my mind was searing in its intensity, hallucinatory in its power. I saw, but couldn't speak. I was a witness, yet I couldn't act. For what seemed an eternity, I was Isobel enraged.

Racing through the house, she had collected Peter's most prized possessions: his books, his maps, the rows upon rows of vinyl LPs that he'd accumulated over the years. I saw Isobel amassing his possessions with the unerring instinct of a woman who knows how to inflict retribution. She assembled his maps, and, grazing her fingers over their surface, appreciating their value and beauty, she ripped page after page, revelling in the violation of Peter's property. I saw her tossing his books on the study floor, and when she had selected the best of them, she took down the one possession that meant the most to Peter: his Paul Nash landscape.

I tried to scream. I tried to tell Isobel to stop, but the only noise that came out of my mouth was a frightened gasp. The past, replaying itself in my mind, brooked no intrusion. I was captive to what had happened. I watched Isobel pick up a pair of scissors from Peter's desk, and, lunging at the painting, she punctured the canvas. It was strong, but she was determined. She slashed it apart. And with every swipe at the picture, every puncture and laceration she made, pounding pain invaded my body and bound me tighter to Isobel, until her tears, falling between slashes of fury, became my own.

When she had finished, she threw what was left of the painting with Peter's other treasures on the floor. Then, almost as an afterthought, she ran upstairs, coming down again with the best of his suits, his shirts, his sweaters. She bundled everything into a wheelbarrow, rolling it down the incline of the hill to the bottom lawn. There, by Mr Furzey's compost heap, she unloaded Peter's belongings, doused them liberally with paraffin and dropped a single match on top of the pile. The fire caught immediately, cowling Isobel's face in flames.

I didn't want to see any more. Holding my throbbing head, I shook it, trying to break free, trying to rid myself of Isobel's anguish. I wanted my mother. I screamed, squeezing my eyes shut, but Mama didn't come to me. She didn't surface behind my eyelids as she usually did. Instead, I heard Malone and Leboeuf shouting: 'Get the hell out of here, kid!'

I opened my eyes. Peter and Isobel were still fighting. Waves of virulent hatred flowed between them, splashing over Polly and closing in on me. I backed away. The vile substance was lapping at my feet when the house shuddered awake. The house was heaving, its foundations swaying in a surreal dance it seemed only I could feel. The others weren't aware of the tremors, the floorboards screeching, splintering to swallow us whole.

'You'd better go, kid!'

I turned and ran for my life. I heard Polly following.

I fled from the house into the drive and the raging storm. Rain fell like stones on my head, and flashes of lightning lit up the path so that I felt disembodied, suspended between the present and the past, in the twilight world of a dream.

I have always hated thunderstorms, the heavens unleashed in fury, yet I felt safer outside, away from the Venuses. I ran stumbling against great swathes of rain towards the Gatehouse and Miss Edith, propelled by an inner fear I was unable to name. I couldn't fight it. Malone and Leboeuf were right. I had to get away from Graylings.

'Aj! Come back, Aj!' Polly was calling me. I turned to look at her. She was momentarily visible in a flash of light, huddled up wet, a changeling in the storm.

I ran on, struggling against the wind. It threw me over twice, and twice I got up with gravel stuck to my palms. The terror inside me was stronger than the elements. I battled against wind and rain, until finally I was at Miss Edith's door.

I shouted her name, I pounded the knocker. I yelled, 'They're fighting! They're fighting. Let me in. Let me in.'

After what seemed an age, the door opened and I fell inside. Miss Edith was brandishing her umbrella. She looked aghast, and then, because Polly must have arrived at the door as well, she exclaimed: 'What's happened to you both? Polly, come in at once.'

Miss Edith rubbed us down. She made us hot chocolate and wrapped us in a large eiderdown. In between the rub, the drink and the eiderdown, she tried to make sense of what I was telling her. Fear had rendered me incoherent. Eventually, Polly explained what had happened.

'She set fire to his painting,' she said. 'She burnt his favourite things, his Dylan LPs and everything, because he doesn't want her.'

Miss Edith was silent. She was chewing her bottom lip. 'I see,' she said tersely.

'And then Aj ran away and I came after her.'

I believe Polly felt responsible for me, but perhaps her parents' behaviour had frightened her as well. It was hard to tell; for it seemed, back then, that if the world were to fall apart, Polly would somehow survive.

'I see,' Miss Edith repeated.

She went into the hall and used the telephone. When she returned she said we were to spend the night at the Gatehouse. The Venuses were all right, but under the circumstances they thought it best we stay put.

Polly was silent. The facade of bored apathy, which I had come to know well, closed over her face again. 'Fine,' she mumbled. 'We'll stay here while they get their act together. Are you sure it's OK?'

Miss Edith assured us, a little wearily, that though she

rarely had guests staying the night, she didn't mind having us around.

I hadn't stopped trembling. I was still shaken by what I'd seen; however, I needed to hear the sound of my voice, to be sure that I was where I thought I was in order to feel safe again, so I asked: 'Do you mind having us around when we ask questions?'

Miss Edith gave a snort of laughter. 'Well, perhaps we'll call a truce on the questions, shall we?'

I looked at her carefully. A veil seemed to have lifted off her face, and her features were clearer, more transparent. She was familiar, but different somehow. Like Isobel, she was changing.

We agreed not to ask any more questions, and that night Polly and I slept in Miss Edith's guest-room, the dogs at our feet.

15

Peter returned to London the next day. It was clear that Isobel didn't want him around. She wasn't speaking to him; apart from a perfunctory 'hallo' to Polly and me when we cut ourselves slabs of bread for breakfast the following morning, she kept her own counsel. Even when Polly mentioned that her periods had started, Isobel didn't seem interested. Instead, I saw a glint of what might have been frustration darkening her eyes.

Peter didn't want to stay in his wife's house a moment longer than was necessary. He had apologised for his behaviour the night before when he picked us up from the Gatehouse. Thanking Miss Edith for looking after us, he explained that his temper had got the better of him. It wouldn't happen again because he was moving out. A removal van was coming later that day for what remained of his belongings. He would follow it home to London.

Polly placed her cheek against Peter's denim shirt. We were between Graylings and the Gatehouse, between our refuge and a house that filled me with a growing sense of foreboding. I'd witnessed enough the night before to know that Isobel's state of mind was precarious. Moreover, her presence frightened me. What I'd experienced through her – the deadly cocktail of desire and hatred that had leaked into my mouth with her breath – was almost more than I could bear. I was flailing, trying to keep both feet on the ground to prevent the quivering underneath seizing my ankles and dragging me down.

'Will I see you again soon, Daddy?'

'Sooner than you think, kitten,' Peter answered, cradling Polly's head.

A question hurtled out of my mouth before I could think: 'Can I go back to London with you, Peter? Please can I leave with you?'

After my experience of Isobel, the bleeding of her veins into mine, I knew I shouldn't remain in close proximity to her. I couldn't allow what had happened to occur again. I couldn't be in the house with Isobel without Peter.

'Yes, Daddy. Can we go back to London with you?'

Peter smiled at us in a way that only adults smile at children: firm in his belief that having thought the matter through, having weighed up the pros and cons, listing them carefully either side of a column on a clean sheet of paper, he was convinced of his case. 'Listen, girls, you have to stay here with Isobel,' he said. 'I have to go back to London to work and I need both of you to watch out for her.'

'Why do you ask us to do what you can't do, Daddy? You saw what happened to Aj last night. You saw how Isobel freaked her out. She doesn't like her any more.'

'That may be so,' Peter conceded. 'But don't forget I played a part in last night's spectacle as well. I'm sorry, but you've got to stay here for the rest of the holidays. You've only a fortnight left.'

He chuckled, trying to make light of our predicament, but Polly and I were not amused. She scowled, while I looked away. His hand behind my neck, Peter made me look at him:

'Will you keep an eye on Isobel for me, little one?'

I had been in a similar position before, so I understood how errant fathers, unable to take responsibility for their disintegrating wives, pass their burden on to their daughters. My father had asked me repeatedly to look after my mother, and now Peter was asking me to take care of Isobel. I nodded, disheartened at being manoeuvred into such an invidious position again. I would do my best, I mumbled, realising that as far as the adults around us were concerned, Polly and I would have to look out for each other. Peter was going to be no help whatsoever.

Indeed, throughout the course of the morning, his mood growing lighter, despondency giving way to sudden flashes of pleasure, Peter appeared to be as carefree as Polly and I had been on the last day of term. He may have lost his most treasured possessions but in a single, devastating act of revenge, Isobel had set him free; relieving him, I presume, of the burden of guilt he'd shouldered for years.

Helping him fold up the clothes Isobel had left unscathed – the oldest of his shirts, a couple of pairs of faded jeans and his underwear – I was aware that Peter kept smiling at himself. Watching the changing expressions of his face – amusement, sudden glimmers of surprise – I concluded that wading through the wreckage of his dressing-room was an enlightening experience. It looked as if a whirlwind had passed through it; a tornado with a virulent hatred of everything he stood for.

Looking around him once again, Peter shrugged off the havoc Isobel had wreaked on his clothes: the suits with a single trouser leg amputated, the Second World War bomber jacket spray-painted purple. 'Who'd have thought that behind the charade of a loving wife lurked a creature every bit as vicious and brutal as I am? Anyone with the nerve to pull a stunt like this is going to come up trumps in the end. Good luck to her!'

Polly, infected by Peter's good humour, translated her father's words to me: 'What Daddy means, Aj, is that you can take the girl out of the trailer park but you can't take the trailer park out of the girl; right, Daddy?'

'That's one way of putting it, kitten, though your mother's pedigree isn't what's normally thought of as trailer trash.'

Neither of them seemed to appreciate the seriousness of the situation. They didn't seem to realise that Isobel wasn't herself, that what Peter was doing was as bad, if not worse, than what Hansel and Gretel's father had done when their mother died. Having wanted Peter as my father only two nights previously, I decided that, along with woodcutters and international lawyers, foreign correspondents were lamentable parents.

'You mean a leopard never changes its spots?' I growled.

'You got it, kid. In the end, what's inside finds a way out. Isn't that so, Daddy?'

'Yes, Polly.'

We followed Peter into his study with cardboard boxes for his remaining books. All his music had gone, melted into globules of plastic on Isobel's bonfire. Peter picked up a discarded fragment of his painting and we followed his gaze to the gap on the wall. We started packing his books, while he continued staring at the blank space. He may have been able to shrug off the loss of his clothes; clothes could be replaced. I knew that his music was different: the Billie Holiday, Ella Fitzgerald and Maria Callas, the Dylan LPs he'd collected over the years, the coveted jazz labels he'd tracked down in America. And the picture . . . The picture was in a league of its own. Its destruction hurt him deeply. I could see that it would hurt him for a long time to come, just as Isobel had intended.

'Don't worry, Daddy. I'm going to paint a picture for your boat,' said Polly.

'And one of these days,' I added, 'I'm going to make something very beautiful for you.'

Peter thanked us for our kind intentions, our desire to soothe his pain with the promise of future gifts. 'She's going to survive,' he said again of Isobel. 'She's tough as nails when it comes down to it. She'll get through this, I know she will.'

I'm not sure if he was trying to reassure himself or us. As Peter stared at the empty space on the wall, his good humour, which had grated on me in his dressing-room upstairs, left him. The gravity of Isobel's revenge, the sheer audacity and power of her anger, seemed to hold him transfixed. He looked wretched; bereft of the life-line that had held him to his father.

'It's people that matter, not things,' he said, repeating his father's words. 'It's time to move on, children. It's time I started afresh.'

We spent the rest of the morning packing and labelling Peter's boxes. When the removal van arrived, we helped him carry his belongings outside. I was wondering how long it would have taken Isobel to burn every single item Peter possessed (too long, I decided), when she emerged from her subterranean life into the drive.

The stench of decaying violets no longer clung to Isobel's body. Her odour was sexual, confident, heavy with musk; and her face cleared of anger reminded me of what she'd looked like when I first met her. She seemed her old self again. I hoped she was over the worst. Having sustained her rage, directing it at Peter, she appeared calmer; secure in her claim over the man she'd once loved.

'Since you're leaving us, Peter,' she stated coldly, 'I'm assuming full responsibility for Polly. You'll see her only if I agree. And should you want to challenge me in any way, I'll meet you in court.'

Peter chose to ignore her. He wasn't prepared to inflame her displeasure again. He gave instructions to the driver of the removal van and then, kissing Polly and me goodbye, drove off in his Renault.

With Peter gone, I was left with the conundrum of how best to watch out for a woman whose presence troubled me. I'm not sure if I was more frightened of Isobel or myself. What I did know was that I didn't want to return to the emotional terrain she'd dragged me into, where my feelings were not my own, but hers. I resolved to observe Isobel from a distance, the better to protect myself.

While I taught Polly a Ghanaian game outside, a game of clapping and shouting and leaping, one foot in front of the other, I noticed Isobel sitting on a kitchen windowsill with a sketch pad on her knee. In her right hand she held a pencil, in her left an apple. She took a bite of the apple. She was eating again; a welcome sign of recovery. When she had finished the apple, she ate another. Then, after devouring a thick slice of toast, Isobel hastily turned a page and looked up at what we were doing. Gripping the pencil, concentrating on the task in hand, she began to draw us.

Polly, wearing the pearl necklace Peter had given her, seemed oblivious to her mother. She wanted to beat me at *ampae*. The pearls leapt up and down with Polly swinging in time to her laughter. They danced, winking provocatively.

Opening the window, Isobel called out: 'Darling, please give that necklace to me. It's going to fall apart if you treat it like that.'

Polly fingered the pearls. 'Peter said I should look after it.'

'The way you looked after Nana's necklace?'

'I'm older now. I'm a woman, Isobel, and I'm certainly not going to lose this necklace. I said as much to Peter.'

'If you were half the woman that you think you are, you'd know better! You shouldn't be playing in jewellery. Come on, darling, give it to me.'

Staring sullenly at her mother, Polly grabbed me by the hand, and then, racing across the lawn, we lost sight of Isobel.

Later that evening, Polly and I ambled home from walking Candy and Fudge to find Theo back from France. In our absence, Isobel had collected him from the station. His return appeared to have lifted her spirits. She was cooking again: a welcoming meal for her son.

He had brought back delicacies from the Continent: thick rolls of salami and varieties of cheese. He had also carted back several bottles of sparkling wine and fruit syrup to drink with them: blackberry, blackcurrant, strawberry and peach. He and Isobel had already started drinking, and when he offered me a taste of his glass I liked it immediately. It was like a potent fruit drop.

For Polly and me, he had brought Asterix annuals: to help us with our French, he said with a straight face. When Polly raised an eyebrow, he laughed, quickly producing a poster he had found in Paris of Bela Lugosi, the first Hollywood Dracula. Polly adored it. For me, Theo had bought a faded strip of kente cloth he'd come across in a flea market: woven prisms of blue, green and gold which, when new, must have been as vivid as the bottles of syrup on the table. I wound the strip around my wrist beside Peter's bangle.

Taking a sip of her drink, Isobel smiled at her daughter. 'Polly, you need a hair cut,' she said firmly.

Immediately, the warmth of Theo's homecoming was dissipated in the ensuing battle between mother and daughter. I backed away. The tension between them bound itself into a knot in my chest so that I couldn't breathe. I turned my back to them, hoping that if I didn't see the hostility on their faces, the tightness inside me would ease.

I held on to the windowsill where I had seen Isobel drawing that afternoon. In a corner was a ball of discarded paper. I teased it open, hoping to drown the crescendo of voices by concentrating on something new. But the knot tightened as the paper revealed a picture of Polly drawn by her mother: a drawing that made the poster of Dracula appear angelic.

The pearl necklace around Polly's neck appeared to glisten like tears on the crumpled white page. Above it, Polly's chin rose up proud and defiant, her eyes hard, angry jewels. The girl Isobel had depicted seemed possessed, brooding, with shadows beneath her eyes. The eyes themselves were dark with a corrosive glare directed hatefully at the viewer. I wanted to tear the sketch into tiny pieces or hide it where no one would ever see it. This wasn't Polly. It was a monster, a grotesque exaggeration created in malice. Young though I was, I recognised that the emotions behind the portrayal of my friend were unseemly; disturbing.

I looked over my shoulder. Mother and daughter were leaving the room, Polly having acknowledged that her hair was indeed getting too long, and Isobel agreeing not to cut too much off. Sensing my distress, Theo came over to me.

'What's the matter, little one?' he asked, using the diminutive Peter had given me. I showed him Isobel's drawing. Realising it was a sheet from the sketch pad on the windowsill, Theo picked it up, flipping through it.

'There's one of you here!' he exclaimed, showing me.

I glanced at the sketch. 'That's not me. That's my mother.'

'Then you must look like your mother.'

Did I look like that? Did my eyes have the accusing sadness of someone badly hurt, like this woman on the page? 'I don't look like that. I'm not unhappy.'

'You are sometimes. Everyone's unhappy sometimes. Have you heard from your mother lately?'

I shook my head. I didn't want to talk about my mother. I wanted to talk about Isobel, so I showed him the picture of Polly again. He screwed it up, tossing it into a bin with a lunge of his long arm.

France had turned Theo a golden colour: a soft brown that gave his skin a peachy sheen. His hair was like the sun and his eyes shone. I didn't know it then, but Sylvie had been good to him. Perhaps that's why he was good to me. He said: 'You shouldn't let Polly and Isobel get to you. They were like this before you came along, you know. They've always been like this.'

'Why don't they like each other?'

'God knows. Sometimes that's the way it is between people. But it doesn't mean they don't care for each other. They just don't get on.' He looked at me intently, and, opening the pad, he started sketching.

'What you've got to remember, little one, is that when Isobel and Polly are having a go at each other, it's not your fault. You shouldn't let the buggers get you down, kid.'

'Buggers?' I asked.

He chose to disregard me, saying: 'The first rule of survival in this house is: ignore them. And never, ever interfere. If you do, they'll go for you like a pair of piranhas. Don't say I didn't warn you.'

He showed me the sketch he'd drawn. It was a cartoon of me, a grin plastered on my face. 'Is this one more like it?' he asked.

I smiled in reply, and I could see he was glad he'd made me feel better. Then I remembered what Isobel had done in his absence, and I told Theo about Peter's painting, his books and music and his clothes. That changed everything. He was horrified. So much so, that he was gone in a couple of days. He claimed he wanted to swot for his Oxbridge exams at the home of a friend who lived near his school.

He needn't have lied. We realised he didn't want to be at Graylings. As it turned out, Isobel didn't want to hear about Sylvie; and for his part, Theo didn't want to be subjected to his mother's contempt for his father. So Theo left as soon as he could. I wish I could have followed him. Failing that, I wish I had heeded his advice.

16

One night, about a week before the end of the holidays, I was lying on my bed listening to Polly and Isobel quarrel again over Peter's pearls, when I came across a story in *True Murder* that I recognised. It was an article about the Ellbergs, Polly's neighbours in Washington. She had told us that Mr Ellberg had murdered his family on the Fourth of July: his family and their dog, a red setter named Frisbee. Polly had said Jacinth Ellberg had been her best friend. But according to the magazine, the Ellbergs hadn't lived in Washington. They'd lived in Chicago, in a house by a lake. And there wasn't a Jacinth; there was a Jacob, a ten-year-old boy shot through the head with a bullet from his father's gun.

I closed the magazine quickly. Polly had lied. In order to claim she had touched a dead body? I curled up in bed with Miss Fielding's shawl, sucking its fringe of tassels to help me think. If I'd been Polly I would have changed their names, so no one would ever know that I'd lied. But why had she pretended to know the Ellbergs when she couldn't have done? As far as I knew, she had visited New York and Boston, but never Chicago. And the Ellbergs had had a son, not a daughter. If Polly had lied about Jacinth, what else had she lied about?

'I'm not going to go,' Isobel was saying, 'until you take that necklace off.'

Since Peter's departure, they'd quarrelled constantly about Peter's gift to Polly. It was as if the onset of puberty in her daughter had inflamed Isobel's sensitivity, bringing the rivalry between them to the fore. But now the rivalry was laced with venom. The argument always began in the same way. Isobel would insist that Polly remove the pearls before going to sleep, and Polly would refuse. She said she was never going to take them off, which wasn't true, because she removed them for her bath. Isobel stood over her daughter, trying to persuade her to give her the necklace for safekeeping, while Polly stubbornly held her ground.

'I'm not going to go,' Isobel repeated, 'till you take that necklace off. If I asked Ajuba, she'd do as she was told. I know she would, because she's sensible.'

'Leave her out of this,' Polly retorted.

That night, determined to break her daughter's defiance once and for all, Isobel sat down on Polly's bed, folding her arms. 'I'm waiting, Polly.'

It was going to be a long evening for all of us unless she conceded to her mother's request. After twenty minutes' silence, Polly slowly unfastened the necklace, dropping it in its velvet case.

'Satisfied?' she asked.

Isobel gave a slow smile. 'Thank you, darling. You deserve a kiss for that.'

Polly turned away, so Isobel kissed me goodnight instead, her lips as cold as marble.

Even after all these years, I find it hard to describe what happened that night. Although there were only three of us in the house, I became convinced that there were others among us. What I lived through was agonisingly real at the time.

Teasing a tassel of Miss Fielding's shawl, using it as a comforter, I heard the house stretching itself and yawning. I heard its breathing, its sighs. And at midnight, counting the chimes of the grandfather clock, I sensed ghosts from the past treading the floorboards outside. There were two of them, one with a slow dragging step, the other firmer, quicker. They walked up the corridor towards the rose room. I heard their cries and whispers. Or was it Mrs Venus again? Gathering the shawl around me, I pulled a pillow over my face.

While Polly lay sleeping, I yearned for my mother's arms to cradle me once again. I fondled the shawl, my fingers following the pattern of embroidered roses: Miss Fielding's roses. They writhed beneath my fingers. Tossing from side to side, I wondered when I would see my mother again. When would I hear her laughter? I wondered how I could possibly have sensed her presence in Isobel. I thought of Isobel in the rose garden, a maggot in my mango. I thought of her tears, her face merging with my mother's, her incandescent rage. And then I remembered the babies in Miss Fielding's trunk.

I found myself gasping for air. Why had Polly lied? Why had she lied to me, her best friend? Of all her friends I would have kept her secret. All the questions I wanted answered became tangled up with thoughts of my mother and Isobel, and the horror of Miss Fielding's trunk, so that by the time the bedroom door swung open, I was in a state of acute distress.

But I saw her. Believe me, I did. I saw Isobel step in the room and walk over to Polly's bed. I glimpsed an expression on her face that has never left me. Her eyes bright with anger, Isobel stared at her daughter. She wanted obedience and Polly's resistance had infuriated her. I saw her holding her daughter's necklace and, opening her mouth wide, drop the pearls inside, swallowing them completely.

I shut my eyes. Only after hearing the rustle of Isobel's nightdress as she closed the door did I open them again.

Then it seemed that the room itself was alive. I heard a groan and a baby crying, a jug emptied of water, hands washed and the muffled voices of women talking. And then a scream of terror, and a sobbing I shall never forget. A woman was heartbroken, her lips wet with the bitter salt taste of surrender. The tighter I clung to the shawl, the more vivid my waking dream became. Then, gasping for breath again, for control of my senses, I flung the shawl away. Leaping out of bed, I ran over to Polly.

She seemed impervious to any sound in this world or the next.

'Polly,' I called, shaking her. She half-opened one eye. The woman had stopped crying, and so had the baby. 'They've stopped,' I said.

'What?'

'Didn't you hear them?'

'Hear what?' Making a space for me in her bed, Polly allowed me to get in.

'I heard a baby and a woman crying,' I told her. 'And I saw things.'

'Sure,' she said turning over. 'Freddy Kruger lives.'

She was on the verge of falling asleep again when I decided to ask her about Jacinth. I didn't want to be the only one awake. I didn't want the shadows to reappear.

'Polly, why did you lie about Jacinth?'

She was immediately alert. 'Who says I lied?'

'*True Murder* says there wasn't a Jacinth. She was Jacob

Ellberg from Chicago, and you've never been to Chicago.' I was beginning to feel better, talking about facts recorded in print for the world to see.

'So I'm a liar, am I?' In the darkness I could feel Polly's eyes cutting into me.

'You could have told me. I wouldn't have said anything.'

'Aj, why don't you go sleep in your own bed?' She might as well have suggested that I buy a one-way ticket to hell. I was too frightened to sleep on my own.

'I won't tell, Polly,' I pleaded. 'I promise I won't tell.'

'Well, shut up then!' With that, she turned over and pretended to sleep.

In the morning, when she discovered her necklace gone, I told her what I had seen.

Isobel was at the dressing-table mirror when Polly ran into her bedroom. I hesitated by the door. Standing behind her, Polly scowled at her mother's reflection. 'Where is it?' she demanded, holding the empty necklace case in her hand.

Isobel smiled. She knew her daughter well. She must have been waiting for Polly's entrance. I heard her say in her clear, distinctive voice: 'How many times do I have to tell you, Polly? You should knock before you come in here.'

'I want it back!'

'I told you –' Isobel began in an all-knowing tone.

'I haven't lost it. You've stolen it.' Polly flung the velvet case at her mother's feet. 'You always want what I've got,' she cried, 'but you can't have it. He gave it to me, not to you. And it's you he's leaving. He's not leaving me.'

'Polly, please calm down.' Isobel swung round to face her daughter.

'You can't take him from me!' Polly shouted.

'I'm not trying to. Let's try and discuss this sensibly, shall we?'

But Polly was in no mood for discussion. Something vital was at stake, something to do with her father. She retorted: 'Daddy says I'm wonderful!'

Turning to the mirror again, Isobel started brushing her hair with quick strokes. Her voice remained steady. 'Of course you're wonderful,' she affirmed. Catching Polly's eye in the looking-glass, she continued smoothly: 'Have you asked Ajuba about your necklace?'

Polly hesitated. She stood very still. 'Peter says I'm nothing like you.'

'Ajuba may have borrowed it, you know, darling. I'd ask her if I were you.'

Incredulous at her mother's suggestion, Polly stared at her wide-eyed. 'No wonder he hates you. Peter's right. You're a bitch. You're a bloody, fucking bitch!'

Turning quickly, Isobel struck her daughter. I ran back to our bedroom, hearing Polly close behind me. Isobel, immediately sorry, ran after Polly. But Polly bolted the door.

I sat quietly on the firm wooden bed beside hers. When I saw Polly's face, I was glad that in a few days' time we'd be back at school again. She held a hand against her cheek and wept with fractured sobs that seemed to tear her apart. I couldn't keep the sympathy out of my eyes. She greeted it with anger.

'She says you took it.'

'I didn't take them. I didn't take them!' I cried.

'Promise?' Did she really doubt me? A hint of cunning crept into her eyes.

I crossed my heart, saying the words: 'Cross my heart and hope to die!'

'You've got to promise something else,' she said in a tone suggesting that if I dared cross her, I'd live to regret it. 'I want you to promise not to tell about Jacinth.'

There it was. She didn't trust me. She didn't believe I could be loyal of my own volition, unless she had something against me: the necklace she knew I hadn't taken.

'I promise not to tell about Jacinth,' I agreed.

'So we're best friends again?'

'Sure,' I said, remembering Theo's advice. 'Of course we're best friends.'

I was a fly caught between mother and daughter. They had me in their web.

17

Polly and I spent the last day of the holiday with Miss Edith at the Gatehouse. Her home, filled with curios and memorabilia of a bygone age, had become a haven from the endless manoeuvring of Graylings. I still wanted to solve the mystery of the babies in Miss Fielding's trunk, but Polly's interest in the case had waned. Apparently, Miss Fielding's coffin wasn't going to be dug up after all, so Polly decided, unilaterally, that playing detectives was childish. She no longer wanted Beth around, and she said she couldn't understand why I continued poring over the notes of our interviews, when it was so obviously a waste of time.

Though I didn't yet realise it, our agreement not to question Miss Edith about her life with Miss Fielding paid dividends. The former companion, released from the onslaught of our investigation, became almost protective of us.

It was the beginning of September, and though there was a hint of autumn in the air, it was still warm enough to play outside. We were sitting at a card table in the patio garden, learning how to gamble with Miss Edith. She had already taught us how to play poker, which Polly was exceptionally good at, and we'd just finished a set of Racing Demon, which I had won.

Miss Edith shuffled the pack to begin another game. Although arthritis restricted her flexibility, she was still adept at handling cards. She was about to teach us how to play Gin Rummy when Polly yawned and asked: 'Did people divorce when you were young?'

Without waiting for an answer, I said: 'They didn't, did they? Not in the Olden Days.'

Miss Edith laid out the cards for a solitary game of Patience. 'We were brought up to stick together,' Miss Edith explained, turning over a card. 'Which means that in my day there were some very miserable people around.'

'Everybody divorces nowadays. They divorce even in Ghana. Don't they, Aj?'

I nodded. I watched Miss Edith turn over a series of cards ending with the Queen of Hearts.

'Not everybody divorces,' Miss Edith replied.

'Everybody divorces more or less.' Regret had given way to exaggeration in Polly's voice; pain was visible in her eyes. She wanted Peter at home again.

I think Miss Edith felt sorry for us, Polly especially. 'I like to think of it this way,' she began. 'Being unhappy is one of the hazards of loving someone, because we usually want things to stay the same. But they change. You can't stop them from changing. So you can only hope for the best.'

Miss Edith turned over the Jack of Hearts, and, placing it beneath the Queen of Clubs, she flipped over the next card. It was the Queen of Spades.

'And while you're hoping for the best,' she continued, 'you have to pray that love, being what it is, doesn't lock you up and throw the keys away.'

Despite our stint as the crime-busting trio of Venus, Benson and Bradshaw, neither Polly nor I had the experience, as yet, to understand what Miss Edith was talking about. However, an image of Rapunzel locked up in her tower caught in my mind. 'You mean like in a fairytale?' I asked.

'Exactly. Like in a fairytale,' Miss Edith confirmed.

'If only it had been like that, Ajuba,' Miss Edith reflected, when she thought me old enough to hear her account of events. I was eighteen, a suitable age, in her opinion, to be told the elemental facts of her life: the story of her friendship with Olivia Fielding. Miss Edith was in her eighties by then, and I'd cycled from the Bradshaws' farm to the Gatehouse to say goodbye.

I had finished my secondary school education at Sherborne Girls', which I attended with Beth. I was about to start a foundation course at the Slade and I must have appeared nervous of the transition from boarding school to college. My relations with my father's new family, which never fully recovered from my anger towards Nina, had reached a tentative state of accommodation. At best, Nina tolerated me. It is the lot of stepmothers, I suspect, to experience the worst of other people's children, and after what had transpired, Nina wasn't able to forgive me. I can't say I blame her. There are some deeds, apparently, which are beyond rehabilitation.

When I arrived at the Gatehouse I probably seemed a little fragile. Miss Edith, believing that my obsession with the past would be my undoing, derailing me once again, decided to take me in hand. In a gesture of generosity that I appreciate to this day, she managed to persuade me that what happened to Polly was not my fault, but rather a coincidence: a collision of random events.

'You see, it's never quite like what they say in fairytales, is it, dear? People grow tired of each other; they feel the urge to try out new things. But in the end, I stuck to Olivia like a limpet. And somehow we survived my adventure in the Lakes.'

The two of them had gone to the Lake District on holiday. They had quarrelled. Edith had lingered. She had tried to sever contact with Miss Fielding but failed. And when Olivia had welcomed her back to Graylings, she had taken her over completely. But not without a struggle.

Miss Edith recalled an argument over breakfast seven months after their reunion. Olivia had handed her a letter and, recognising the writing, Edith had looked away, leaving it unopened. This, apparently, had been the third and final letter from the mystery man we had seen in the photo seven years ago. His name, said Miss Edith, was Arthur Grey. The arrival of the other two had caused dissension.

'Olivia jumped to conclusions as she always did,' Miss Edith said. 'She assumed I was still in touch with him, that I'd told him everything, which, of course, I hadn't. We had decided not to tell anyone, Ajuba. She made me promise not to, and at the time it seemed for the best. You have no idea what people would have said back then.'

Miss Edith turned away, shaking her head. When she was able to look at me again, a bleak smile played on her lips. 'I thought she was going to help me, Ajuba. She'd sent the Bramleys and Mr Furzey away, and we were on our own. Then that letter arrived and she was furious. She made me open it in front of her and read it out loud. We were to have no more secrets from each other, Olivia said. We were to be as one. I should have known better,' Miss Edith confessed. 'I should have walked away, but I left it too late. And in the end, I couldn't. I failed miserably.'

We were sitting in Miss Edith's patio garden, which was now overgrown with clematis and honeysuckle, tendrils of summer jasmine clambering over the french windows. The air was heavy with the overpowering stench of rioting climbers in bloom. Miss Edith stroked a Persian cat on her lap, a gift from Beth and me when the last of her boxers died.

'You never failed me,' I said.

I took her hand, rubbing her gnarled fingers until her regret seemed to subside and I tasted the sweetness of her nursery-pudding smile. It was the smile that had reassured me as a child that whatever calamities befell us – the unsolved mysteries of life and death, and the cloud of shame that hovered over her after the inquest on the babies in the trunk – Miss Edith was my friend. Somehow, the smile of a wayward English woman had managed to convince me that I too was loved.

Wiping tears from my eyes as I began to take leave of her, I sensed Polly's shadow settling between us. Perhaps Polly, overhearing us, understood that after all these years our journey had come to an end and I was letting her go. Perhaps Polly was setting me free.

'Are you thinking of her?' Miss Edith enquired, as she always does when my tears fall unbidden.

I nodded, believing that she had sensed Polly as well.

'Do you remember the weeks after Peter went, dear? The two of you spent every single day with me. The poor child was lost without her father around. I'm sure Isobel did her best but with a child like Polly, a daughter love-struck with her father, she just couldn't cope. No one could. Not even you. And you were her best friend, Ajuba.'

I nodded again, incapable of speech. I didn't need reminding that after failing my mother when my father left, in the end I failed Polly as well.

18

When I think of my old school, I remember it with fondness. It was clean and orderly and the Derbys had created a safe, happy atmosphere. I remember the shadows of the front hall, the old wooden furnishings smelling faintly of polish, suggesting stability and longevity. It was a place that, although conscious of pain and respectful of it, was somehow able to absorb it. At school I slept easily in my bed, and the knot of anxiety deep in my chest was soothed by wind and rain lashing the leaded windows of Exe.

At the start of the autumn term, Polly was adamant that our investigation of Miss Edith over the summer holidays had drawn a blank, and that being Crimebusters was 'so passé, so last term', that we should throw away our badges and think of something else to do. We were gathered around her bed after Lights Out, our *True Murder* scrapbook in the middle and Maria pouring sherbet into our palms. She had ingratiated her way back into the gang with gifts, though Polly was still disdainful of her. Some of the sherbet spilt on the scrapbook and Polly shook it out. Maria apologised, offering her some more.

'I hate sherbet,' Polly replied.

'I've got some chocolate, if you want.'

'Forget it.' Then, speaking to Beth and me, Polly continued: 'So we drop the case, right?'

I didn't agree. I was aware that something fundamental was at stake. Moreover, as a dedicated follower of Malone and Leboeuf, I believed that a true detective never gives up. 'A case is never lost,' they wrote in their column. 'It unravels at its own pace. Remember, a time will surely come when facts fall into place. Persistence, the Third Principle of Detection, is the key to success.' So I stated categorically to the rest of the gang: 'We can't drop the case. We haven't found the murderer yet.'

Beth pulled a face. 'We want to play something else, Aj.'

'Yeah, we've got to move on,' Polly reiterated.

'This isn't a game,' I reminded them.

Beth pulled another face. 'It is too!'

I looked from one to the other, saying firmly: 'Polly, you said it's not a game! That's what you said, isn't it?'

She was taken aback. Apart from the time I'd kicked her on the shins, Polly wasn't used to me challenging her. But the way I saw things, I had to. The babies in Miss Fielding's trunk were a clue to the weight crushing my chest. The babies were faces in the mirror, and they were telling me something I needed to comprehend but wasn't yet able to, even with the assistance of Malone and Leboeuf.

'What about Jacinth?' I reminded them.

'What about her?'

I could see Polly had taken my question the wrong way. She thought I was playing her game of blackmail to get my own back on her, which wasn't my intention.

'Well, she was murdered, wasn't she?'

'Sure she was.' Polly's face was grim.

'Well, the babies were murdered too,' I muttered, folding my arms defiantly.

'So?'

'So it could happen to anybody. Anybody at all. We can't drop the case until we find out what happened.'

Closing the scrapbook, Polly tossed it over to me. 'OK, hotshot. You want to solve the case? Then you solve it.'

It hadn't been my intention to shoulder the responsibility on my own, but Polly and Beth didn't want to play any more, and as Maria was merely a hanger on, I didn't have much choice in the matter. In any case, I was a keeper of secrets, so I was used to perusing thoughts I was unable to reveal. I hadn't told anyone about the faces in my mother's mirror, and I wasn't going to tell anyone about Jacinth. But what about Mrs Venus? Should I tell about her?

As the school timetable sucked me into its routine, I did my work but with half my mind on Mrs Venus. I no longer called her Isobel. When she came to mind, I remembered the contents of Miss Fielding's trunk: the ghosts in Graylings and the babies in the attic. And somewhere in the middle of it all was my mother. My father's periodic calls, which resumed at the start of the new term, brought me little relief. Our halting, brief conversations, in which I told him what he wanted to hear, were no longer enough. I wanted to know where my mother was. Someone had to answer my questions before the pain in my chest broke me apart. 'What should I do, Mama? Who should I tell?' I asked, as the weight I was carrying grew heavier and heavier.

I talked to Malone and Leboeuf about my predicament. They told me to take things one step at a time: to separate the various elements, the main players in the drama, so I could see the case as a whole. Then, murmuring in my ear, they asked me to consider the facts. If the police weren't going to dig up Miss Fielding's coffin after all, where did that leave Miss Edith? 'All you need, kid, is one solid piece of evidence,' they advised me. 'The missing piece from the jigsaw . . .' I listened to them, only to discover that the ache inside me, burrowing through my chest, was forcing its way to my throat to voice the unspeakable.

While I struggled with my burden, Polly professed indifference to the loss of her pearl necklace. However, she used her conviction that Isobel had taken it to persuade Peter that she should spend alternate weekends with him on his houseboat. He promised to discuss the matter with Isobel. And when she agreed, Polly decided the pearls were a fair exchange for her father.

One damp, autumn Saturday while Polly was in London, Miss Edith invited me to the Gatehouse for tea. I took the opportunity to look through her photographs again. I had already done her shopping for her, but because I was too young to purchase alcohol on her behalf, she had left me alone to go and stock up on sherry. She was gone five minutes before I dared look around; and then it took some time to locate the boxes containing her albums. When I found them, in a cupboard filled with musty coats and umbrellas beneath the staircase, I rooted inside, searching for the picture of the man from the Lakes: the man with his arm around Miss Edith. I couldn't find it; almost all the photographs were of Miss Fielding. There were sheaves of photographs of her, and in the few that I flipped through which included Miss Edith, she was invariably in attendance on her mistress: in the background, slightly out of focus. Then suddenly, just as I was about to give up and was certain that Miss Edith would be home soon, I had it in my hand. Tucked in the back of an album of holiday snaps, in a battered, brown envelope, was the photograph I was looking for. On the back, in Miss Edith's writing, was the name of the man and the location. Arthur Grey, Windermere, 1954. With the photograph were three letters.

They were written in an old-fashioned hand, in ink so badly faded that the script looked as delicate as a broken spider's web. I read what I could quickly, scarcely understanding the text and the emotions within it. It was only when I heard Candy and Fudge barking at the door that I stuffed them back in the envelope and shoved the boxes in place. Having read what had been written so many years previously, I felt strangely emboldened, and somehow, later that afternoon, I managed to express what I was feeling to Miss Edith.

She was settling down to a cup of tea and chocolate éclairs and invited me to join her. I had already taken the dogs for a walk and she was surprised when I offered to clear her patio of leaves. Taking a mouthful of éclair, she said: 'You haven't become a Brownie, have you, Ajuba?'

'What if I have?' I hadn't of course, but I wanted to see what she would say. I took a large bite from the pastry that she passed to me.

'Well, it's not exactly Polly's cup of tea, is it?'

'Polly and I aren't Siamese twins, you know.'

She looked at me closely. 'Have you two fallen out?'

'Not exactly, but I'm worried about her.' I had finished my éclair and was licking remnants of cream from my fingers while I tried to phrase the question that I wanted to ask. At last I had it. 'Why do adults hate children?'

'Whatever gave you that idea?'

'I'm not talking about you. I mean the others. Sometimes adults kill children. They do, don't they?'

She had gone pale. She put down what she was eating to

give me her full attention. She conceded, reluctantly, that very occasionally adults transgressed the bounds of decency. But this happened rarely, she said; extremely rarely.

'It happened to the babies in Miss Fielding's trunk, didn't it? She hurt them, and she still makes you cry.'

'What on earth are you talking about, child?' She was sitting very straight on the sofa and she was looking at me sternly. She wanted me to shut up. But I couldn't. Not now. I had to know what had happened.

'I hear you in Polly's room, Miss Edith. In the rose room. You're crying. You can't stop crying.'

Her hazel eyes were suddenly fierce and a tic at the side of her mouth set her bottom lip trembling. 'If this is your idea of a joke, Ajuba, I don't think very much of it.'

I wasn't joking. I was in earnest. I ran over to her, grabbing her gnarled fingers. 'I heard you, Miss Edith. I promise I did. You couldn't stop. Because she killed them, didn't she? Then she hid them.'

The effort of my deliberations with Malone and Leboeuf was hitting home. And the letters had confirmed my suspicions. Day after day, I had picked over the contents of my waking dream, separating my emotions from the sounds I had heard, scraping my terror away from the bones till I pieced together the elements of a scene. A child had been born in the rose room and the child had been murdered. And she had had a twin.

Miss Edith placed her hand over her left arm to stop her body shaking. She was rocking back and forth, as she had done in the summer rain. But this time, she struggled to control her emotions.

'Listen, Ajuba,' she said in a whisper. 'Sometimes, when it's dark, we imagine all sorts of strange things. Sometimes –'

I interrupted her. I *hadn't* imagined it. It had happened. She couldn't fob me off as Isobel had done. Isobel had said I was dreaming when I'd seen her in the rose room. She said I was dreaming or imagining things. I wanted the truth. I was determined to find out one way or the other. I was convinced that the babies belonged to Miss Edith. The man in the photograph had given us a clue, but we had ignored him, casting Miss Edith as the villain of the piece, when in fact she had been its victim.

'Why did she do it?' I asked. 'Why?' Then I remembered what Miss Edith had told us after our game of Racing Demon. 'Did Miss Fielding lock you up and throw the key away? Did she want you to herself?'

Miss Edith brushed a tear from her cheek.

'Isobel cries too,' I told her. 'At least she used to. But she's not like you. She's like your friend, the Queen of Hearts. Isobel hates us too.'

'Olivia loved children!' Miss Edith exclaimed.

'Polly says you've got to hate someone to kill them.' I had to tell her about the expression I had seen on Isobel's face. 'Miss Edith, I saw Mrs Venus eating Polly's pearls.'

She looked horrified as I enacted the scene I had witnessed: Isobel stuffing Polly's necklace in her mouth.

'I think she's going to hurt her,' I whispered. 'What should I do, Miss Edith?'

The old woman's fingers clutched mine in a commanding grip. 'You're wrong about Olivia,' she insisted, her face so close to mine that I could count the wrinkles around her eyes. 'She was like Othello,' she said vehemently. 'She loved not wisely but too well. Ajuba, listen to me. I want you to do something for me.'

I thought she was about to ask me not to tell anyone

about our discussion. I was wrong. She wanted me to talk to someone at school about Polly. She wanted me to talk to Mrs Derby.

'But *you* didn't tell anyone,' I reminded her.

She sighed and stroked my hand gently. 'Believe me, Ajuba, there was nothing to tell.'

19

Later that afternoon I waited for Mrs Derby outside the drawing-room. She had brought me back to school and was parking her car. The drawing-room was where the Derbys relaxed between lessons and after meals. In the holidays it was where they invited me to watch television with them, the place where we ate supper on our laps. It was where they entertained parents, and, every once in a while, admonished the most persistent of the school's miscreants. So to us, it was a hallowed place scented with wood smoke. There were photographs of Major Derby's old regiment displayed on the mantelpiece, a faded Axminster carpet on the floor and, either side of the fireplace, two stone lions glared at each other.

Not surprisingly, when Mrs Derby ushered me in I was trembling. I had never before sought the Derbys' confidence, and the enormity of what I was about to say made me nervous.

'Sit down, Ajuba.'

I remained standing, a hand on the sofa. Sarah Derby attempted to reassure me with a smile as she sat down. Nervous though I was, I looked straight at her.

'What can I do for you?' she asked.

'I've got something to tell you, Mrs Derby.'

'About your holidays?'

I knew Isobel had been to see the headmistress several

times since bringing Polly and me back to school. I assumed she had told Mrs Derby what she'd implied to Polly: that I had taken the pearl necklace. So I said: 'I didn't take it.'

'What didn't you take?'

'Isobel says I took Polly's pearls, but I didn't, Mrs Derby. I didn't.'

'No one's accusing you of anything, Ajuba,' she said gently. She was peering at me through metal-rimmed glasses that made her eyes look bigger than they were.

'I saw Isobel taking them, and I saw a picture she drew of Polly. She hates her, Mrs Derby. She hates her.'

'What makes you think that?'

As best as I could, I explained what had happened over the summer holidays: the Venuses' separation, the burning of Peter's possessions, Isobel's distress, her visit to the rose room that awful night. As I spoke, Sarah Derby gazed at me calmly, prompting me with sympathetic nods and enquiries. She encouraged me in the telling of my tale, so that, gaining confidence, I told her things I hadn't meant to. I told her about our investigation of the babies in Miss Fielding's trunk. That I had heard one of the babies crying and I'd tasted Miss Edith's tears. Before that, Isobel's crying had kept me awake. When I had come full circle, I repeated the statement I began with: 'So she hates her, Mrs Derby. Isobel hates her.'

'Nobody hates Polly, Ajuba.' She straightened her glasses. Then, seeing that I was deeply concerned for my friend, she chose her words carefully: 'Look, Ajuba, divorce is very distressing. That's the way it is. It's painful for Polly, and it's painful for Mrs Venus too.' She paused and looked at me earnestly. 'Was it dreadful when your parents divorced?'

'What have my parents got to do with this?'

Very quietly she replied: 'They divorced, didn't they? Divorce isn't anything to be ashamed of, Ajuba.'

I didn't realise that I was ashamed. Her questions puzzled me, and when she asked me if Isobel reminded me of anyone, I sensed danger immediately.

'My mother doesn't steal!' I protested. 'She doesn't!'

'But Isobel does remind you of her, doesn't she?'

'No! She's nothing like my mother. Mama believes in the power of God, Mrs Derby, and with God everything is possible!' I cried, quoting my mother's favourite Adinkra symbol: *Gye Nyame*, the power of the moon and the sun in one: the symbol she wore as earrings and on a chain around her neck. 'Mama doesn't steal!'

With infinite care, Mrs Derby touched my arm. She stroked it with a forefinger and asked: 'Do you want to talk about what happened to your mother, Ajuba?'

'Nothing happened to her. She's getting better, and she'd write to me if she could, but she's not very well at the moment.'

I wanted to tell her that my mother was with Aunt Lila, and that because even Aunt Lila didn't know where I was, none of them could write to me. But the expression on Mrs Derby's face took my voice away. What had I done wrong? What had I said that I shouldn't have said?

Mrs Derby held on to my hand: 'Ajuba, I want you to try and tell me what happened to your mother.'

'She's at home,' I insisted. 'Aunt Lila's looking after her.'

'Ajuba, you know that isn't true.'

The moment she said those words, the air rushed out of me as if she had bludgeoned my chest with her fist. I couldn't catch my breath. Tiny ants of fear, scrabbling beneath my skin, ignited my senses. Her face grew large as she brought it close to mine. I saw the hairs on her chin, grains of powder on her nose. How could she tell such a blatant lie? I knew that what I was saying was true because of the evidence of my eyes. It had to be true. Mama had told me time and time again: through God everything is possible. And one day in the distant future, Pa, the most errant and irresponsible of fathers, would return to us and we would be a family again.

'Ajuba, your mother's dead.'

I tore my hand away, clenching it into a fist. 'She didn't die. She didn't die. She opened her eyes. I woke her up!'

'My dear, your mother died in hospital.'

'But I saw her open her eyes. And the ambulance took her away.'

'Didn't your father tell you?'

'He said . . . he said . . .' Pa had said that I was never going to see my mother again, and that I should forgive her, even though what she had done was dreadful; an affront to everything he stood for. But Mama had told me to turn my back on my father, and not to believe his lies. Gradually, the possibility came to me that perhaps Pa hadn't been lying after all. What if he had told me the truth?

My resistance weakening, I felt tears trickling down my face, welling in salty pools around my mouth. I remembered Miss Edith's tears, the bitter taste of surrender. I wiped my face with a sleeve, struggling to suppress my feelings, but I couldn't stop crying, and for a moment I was in the rose room again. Did I see Miss Edith? Or was the person I saw crying me? I heard a child sobbing. What was happening to me?

From a distance I was aware of Mrs Derby holding me in an awkward embrace. My body stiffened but, with my tears persisting, I slowly gave way to her sympathy.

*

Mrs Derby kept me for the rest of the evening, bringing in a tray for our supper. Banishing Major Derby from the drawing-room and yet another repeat of *Dad's Army* on television, she gave me her undivided attention. Between my disbelief and my tears, the fractured sobs of bewilderment that threatened to rend me apart, she pieced together my account of Mama's nervous breakdown: our flight to London, Mama's attempt at suicide, and how I managed to raise the alarm. And then, when Pa told me that I would never see her again, I explained to Mrs Derby as best as I could the many reasons Mama had given me not to believe a word he said. My mother had warned me that one day my father would try and steal me from her. If he did, he would try to deceive me by poisoning my mind, so I should block my ears to whatever he said. Mama had promised that wherever she was, she would always love me, and before long we would find each other again.

'Are you sure Mama died?' I asked again, still unable to grasp the finality of the words. I was hoping that a mistake had been made, and that my mother was with Aunt Lila. She wouldn't have wanted me to grow up without her. I needed my mother alive.

'I'm afraid she did,' Mrs Derby confirmed. 'I would never lie to you, Ajuba, I promise. I am telling the truth.'

'Cross your heart and hope to die?'

She did what I asked of her, and when I started crying again, she drew me into her arms. Despite her scent of lavender and the accommodating flatness of her chest, her arms – reminding me of arms that had held me since birth – made me push Mrs Derby away. Mama smelt of jasmine and traces of lemon and nutmeg.

'If she really died,' I argued, 'then why wouldn't Pa let me see her?'

'I don't know what was in your father's mind, Ajuba, so I can't speak for him, but many people don't think it's appropriate for a child to see a dead body. It can be upsetting and very painful indeed.'

'Is that why they wouldn't let Maria see her father when he died in Angola?'

Sarah Derby nodded.

I still couldn't believe her. It wasn't possible. Mama wouldn't abandon me. I was certain that if I tried hard enough, one day I would track her down. All I had to do was believe and it would happen. I wouldn't fail her again. I attempted to bolster my conviction with memories of my mother's love for me, but, seeing unwavering compassion on Mrs Derby's face, my confidence faltered. Furious at my father and at my own inability to distinguish truth from lies, I kept trying to make Mrs Derby see things my way, in the hope that she would say the words I wanted to hear: Mama was alive. She was with Aunt Lila.

'But I asked to see her, Mrs Derby. I wanted to see her so I would know if he was telling the truth.'

My mother used to say that the truth would open my eyes and set me free. It had done no such thing. It was crushing every hope I had for tomorrow.

'If I had known, if I had seen her, then I would have said goodbye to her. How can she be gone, Mrs Derby, if I didn't say goodbye?'

'You're beginning to say goodbye to her now,' Mrs Derby assured me. 'I know it's not going to be easy, but you're a very brave girl, Ajuba.'

I was in her arms again, clinging to her scent of lavender as I swayed back and forth. Struggling to comprehend the horror of what she said Mama had done, I tried to bite through the palm of my hand. I needed to see my blood, to taste it on my tongue to make sure I was alive. If, after all this time, Mama no longer existed, how could I be sure that I was real? I tried desperately to puncture the flesh, but Mrs Derby wouldn't let me. She held me, comforting me, while I wept in her arms.

20

That night I slept in Polly's bed. Even though she was in London, I couldn't bear to be in my own bed alone with my grief. I needed to feel close to Polly, hugging her duvet while I remembered my mother: her face that last morning in Lewisham as I waited for the ambulance. I had held her hand and stared into her eyes. She hadn't wanted to stay with me, and no matter how good I was, how much I loved her and cared for her, I was simply not enough. I wept into Polly's pillow, clinging to traces of orange and cinnamon from her hair.

The following night, when she returned to school, I crept in beside her as soon as the lights were out, holding on to her as if my life depended on the rise and fall of her breathing. Without realising it, Polly kept me afloat in uncharted waters. And when I felt the tentacles of octopuses dragging me down by the ankles, it was Polly who unwittingly brushed them away. Yet I couldn't tell her what I was going through.

Strangely, as I absorbed Mrs Derby's revelation, my mother's presence crystallised around me. Surfacing from behind my eyelids, she stepped into the open. I felt her touch on my hand while I struggled to accept she was gone. Smelling her scent on my breath, catching a glimpse of her shadow in the doorway of Exe, I followed her into the corridor outside. But she wasn't there. She had left me stranded; alone in a place where I was deemed deluded, over-imaginative, in need of help. 'Cranky,' Polly called me. I suppose I was all those things. Yet there was truth in what I had seen at Graylings. My misfortune is that no one believed me.

My deepest regret, after my conversation with Mrs Derby, was that I hadn't allowed her closer, sooner. Had I done so, and had she known me better, perhaps she would have taken my concern for Polly seriously. What's more, the focus of Mrs Derby's attention shifted to me and she became preoccupied with my problems rather than Polly. For that I can never forgive myself.

That's why I had to see Aunt Lila in London last September. I needed someone of my blood, from my part of the world, to tell my story to. When she had heard everything, Aunt Lila told me that she believes I have a special gift, a way of seeing the world that goes beneath the surface to a reality that is too bright for most people to grasp. It is an ability that, if used in the wrong way, can lead to madness. It had that effect on my mother and my uncle, who summoned up the sea goddess from the lagoon.

But Aunt Lila appears to have confidence in me. She told me last summer that, having come this far, she sees no reason why I shouldn't stay the course. 'After all,' she said, 'you're over the worst now. You spent your childhood among strangers who didn't understand you. And no matter what you may think, Ajuba, you are *not* your mother. You are much stronger than Grace ever was.'

Yet if I'm honest with myself, it's the fear of madness that keeps me from mirrors.

After her weekend in London, Polly assumed that my

unhappiness at school was connected with my father. Halfway through a call from Rome, he had informed me that he was about to marry Nina.

'Come on, Aj. Hurry up!'

Polly was calling me. She was dragging me upstairs. I lay down, stiff and cold on my narrow bed.

'Lighten up, Aj. Snap out of it. If Peter married again, I would understand. I'd have to. Anyways, Nina's not so bad.'

'She's not my mother.' I wanted Mama. I wanted Mama.

'Aj, it's going to be fine. You'll see.'

Where was Mama now that she was gone? Where do people travel when they die?

'Aj, I hate it when you're like this! You've got to snap out of it. Nina is awesome, kiddo. You'll get to like her.'

I buried my face in my pillow.

I didn't know it then, but my stepmother, Pa's new wife, was already pregnant with the son my father had always wanted. The following week, Pa called me again. The excitement in his voice made him sound younger, and for a moment I wasn't sure who I was talking to. His usual ponderous tone was warm, almost tender, when he told me that in the new year he would be moving with Nina to London. He said it was his dearest wish that we should celebrate the start of the year as a family for the first time. He had been headhunted for a job at the Commonwealth Secretariat. I believe my father knew he had neglected me. However, he rejected Mrs Derby's suggestion that I see a child therapist. He hoped that having regular contact with me would resolve my problems; and most important of all, Pa had convinced himself that life with Nina would turn things around for both of us.

His good intentions notwithstanding, when I most needed the support of an adult, it was Mrs Derby who stood by me. Within a few days I was in the drawing-room again, explaining as best I could that although Polly had invited me home for the weekend and I was happy to spend the daylight hours with her, I didn't want to spend another night under Isobel's roof. Appreciating how deeply I felt, Mrs Derby made sure that I got my way.

Somehow, despite my reservations and night terrors, Polly had managed to coax me back to Graylings. Isobel was much better, she assured me. OK, she wasn't a full dollar yet, but then she never had been. She had always been inclined, to use Polly's words, to 'hum a little off key'. The thing to remember, Polly insisted, was that Isobel was no longer freaking out.

'She's found herself a shrink,' she told me. 'A geek called Robert she dumps on twice a week. And she's getting better, Aj. She's really getting better. Peter seems to thinks so as well. Do you know what a shrink is?'

We had spent the morning playing in the autumn sunshine, a game we made up as we went along: Genghis Khan laying waste to the world, which entailed running through woodland, a stick in hand, attacking everything in our path. Of course, Polly was Genghis Khan, and I was one of her rampaging hordes assisting in the subjugation of the civilised world. But there are only so many ways to enact conquest, rape and pillage; having exhausted our limited repertoire, we were lying beneath our beds in the rose room, shining torches in each other's faces.

We weren't pretending to read now. We were simply looking at one another. I was hiding from Isobel and Polly was humouring me. I replied that I didn't know what a shrink was, so she proceeded to enlighten me.

'They're guys you go to when you're too stupid to figure things out for yourself. They help you sort out your head when you're totally, totally messed up. Like when you do things like Isobel did to Peter.'

'You mean when you go mad?'

'Yeah. Like when you're so fucked up, it's awesome.'

'We call them psychiatrists in Ghana,' I explained.

My mother had seen a psychiatrist. He had given her medicine to clear her head. It had made her sleep a lot. I used to watch over her while she slept.

'Is Isobel taking medicine for the mess in her head?' I asked.

'No way! I promise, she's a whole heap better, Aj. OK, I'm not saying she's a bundle of laughs. She's never been that. But she's not on my case all the time. She's too busy figuring out her feelings.'

'Oh?'

'You better believe it, kiddo. She lets me eat what I want now and she's even talking to Peter. Is that wholesome or what? Hallo? I mean, it's so much easier for a pre-teenager if the folks who brought her to Planet Earth talk to each other. Right?'

'Right.'

'I mean, life sucks enough already without them fucking me up as well. And she's taken up karate, Aj. Which is kind of cool, don't you think?'

'Kind of.'

She must have heard a note of caution creeping into my voice. Setting her bravado aside, she expressed a niggling suspicion, a blot on the picture she was describing of a reconstituted, rational Isobel. Polly's concern was to do with the drama unravelling in Peter's old study. Isobel was reclaiming the one room that had truly belonged to him. And it was her mother's compulsion to enter the study day after day and what she was doing inside it that perplexed my friend. It was why Polly wanted me back at Graylings. She had invited me home to check it out.

I wanted to find out what was going on, but with the memory of Isobel's fury still bright in my mind, I refused to leave our sanctuary unless there was another adult in the house. So when Belinda Bradshaw arrived for an afternoon visit, we finally ventured out of the rose room. Isobel had instructed us not to disturb her while she was in the study. In fact, she had said that she didn't want anyone there under any circumstances. But now that she was entertaining, I was as curious as Polly to investigate what she was up to.

To get to the study unobserved, we had to creep through the kitchen. Isobel had lit a fire and the two women were relaxing on a sofa drinking coffee and consuming what seemed to be the remnants of a large bottle of Spanish brandy. Outside, it had turned damp and blustery, thin sticks of wisteria tapping the windowpanes. Perhaps the brandy opened a confessional streak in Mrs Bradshaw; I heard her saying to Isobel: 'Charlie would leave me if he could. He'd leave me if he wasn't so lazy and the farm wasn't mine. All it would take is some bimbo with enough dosh, and he'd be off. Mark my words.' She added a splash of brandy to her coffee. 'Men!' she scoffed. 'Bloody, bloody men!'

Polly raised an eyebrow, amused by the opprobrium Peter's departure had provoked in Isobel's closest friend. Then, opening the study door quietly, she watched my face as I took in the transformation before me.

'What do you think, Aj?'

I didn't know what to think. I was astounded by what I

saw hanging on the walls, leaning against them, on the bookshelves, spread out on the floor. Isobel had turned Peter's study into the space she had planned for the attic. She had converted it into a studio. When I thought about it, it made perfect sense: the light was from the north, the space generous. She was reshaping with the ferocity of her imagination the one room that Peter had possessed.

She must have spent every day sketching her children. On a trestle table were scores of pen-and-ink drawings, and beside them photographs she had used to help her etch out their features: Theo as a baby; Theo as a boy, compliant and easy; Polly a defiant toddler of two, and then a smiling six-year-old. Peter, Isobel had left alone, presumably because there was enough of him to contend with in Polly.

'You see why I had to show you, Aj? It's kind of weird finding out after all this time that Isobel, of all people, paints. Hallo? Mommy dearest an artist? I think not.'

We were rifling through Isobel's paintings and sketches, tracking her artistic progress together. Stacked in a corner was a series she had done in oil. Discarding her brush, she must have painted them with a soft piece of wood, playing with it to create an impressionist haze of colour: the curve of Polly's cheek, her questioning gaze. All her most recent pictures were of Polly. The studio was cluttered with them, and despite my friend's indifference to almost everything else her mother did, she was naturally intrigued by Isobel's new passion. It revealed a side of her mother new to us; a side that was usually kept hidden. We didn't need anyone to tell us that Isobel was obsessed. She had painted her daughter again and again.

'Is this creepy or what?' Polly asked, leading me to another set of canvases. Experimenting with style, Isobel had distorted her daughter's features, giving them the attributes of birds and animals. She had painted her with arms transformed into the giant wings of an eagle; as a cat, her face obscured by fur; then Polly became a crow, a hedgehog, a deer.

I remember that the pictures made me uncomfortable, but I couldn't put my finger on exactly what it was about them that I found disturbing. They were flamboyant explorations of Polly's character: her streak of rebelliousness, which made her clash with her mother; an ingrained wildness that Isobel was unable to contain. She captured the essential Polly, transforming her into an exotic freak of nature. I could tell that Polly was flattered, even though the cumulative effect of the images was unsettling. They sprang out at you, each stroke so vivid in detail, so bright in execution that they lacerated the eye.

Bewildered yet fascinated, Polly and I were intent on deciphering the tantalising code in each of Isobel's paintings. It was as if we had stumbled on her diary and might find a way of understanding the secret language of her soul. We were on our hands and knees, our backs to the door, the canvas of Polly as an eagle in front of us, when the voice I dreaded hearing interrupted our deliberations. It was Isobel.

'I see Polly's brought you into our secret, little one.'

We hadn't heard her entering the studio. Alarmed that she had discovered us doing exactly what she had forbidden, I was about to apologise when Polly said, 'Isobel, my mouth isn't like this!' She was pointing to the beak her mother had given her in the eagle painting. 'And why've you given me cat's eyes in this one? And I'm certainly not like this, Mommy dearest!' Polly went through the canvases, Isobel squatting down beside us. 'And, hallo? Polly an antelope? I think not.'

Enchanted and perplexed though she was by her mother's

obsession, Polly had a strong sense of how she wanted to be seen, and with a spark of defiance gathering in her eyes, she ended her criticism of Isobel's oeuvre with a calculated provocation: 'Bet you can't paint me for real, Isobel. You know, like with regular eyes, regular nose and real hair. Just me, no animals anywhere. Bet you can't paint me for Peter.'

To my surprise, Isobel accepted the challenge. Perhaps Belinda and the Spanish brandy had put her in a good mood. Immediately mother and daughter embarked on their first project together: a project for Peter. Isobel was going to paint a portrait of Polly as a gift they could give him together.

'What do you think I should wear, Isobel?'

Polly never asked her mother's opinion on anything; at least she had not in my presence as far as I could recall, and certainly not about what to wear: a contentious subject at the best of times. I think her question surprised Isobel too, who paused setting up her easel and looked at her daughter intently before replying: 'Something blue, I think. Something that brings out your eye-colour. Your eyes are just like your father's.'

The easel up and Polly clothed, Isobel set to work. Still unsure if her mother could meet her conditions, Polly said once again: 'You won't make me look weird, will you? You'll make me look like a regular person, like me. Promise?'

Isobel promised to do her best.

I spent the rest of the afternoon watching them: Polly seated in a chair, Isobel standing in front of her; sketching at first and then, having established a composition that suited the blueprint in her mind, forging ahead.

She worked quickly, completely absorbed, so that when Polly started asking questions, she was silent, focused on a world of her own creation. The depth of her abstraction reminded me of how my mother had been sometimes. In spite of my determination to remain attentive, on guard, I felt tears clouding my eyes. Mama had often seemed to drift irretrievably from me, far from the shore where I was standing, drowning in her own world. Yet I would rather have had her alive, like Isobel, than cold in her grave.

'Perhaps we should give him this for Christmas,' Polly was saying. 'Do you think he'll come home for Christmas, Isobel?'

Her mother didn't reply. She was poised, daubing paint on canvas with an intensity that was strangely compelling. She hadn't heard a word Polly had said. At least she appeared not to. So Polly tried again.

'Mommy, do you think he'll come for Christmas or stay on his boat?'

Again, there was no reply.

'Isobel, if I ask him and you ask him too, we might persuade him to come home. Just for a few days over the holidays, anyways.'

Isobel sighed. 'I wouldn't hold your breath, darling. After what happened, he might not want to come here again. I'm sorry, Polly.'

'But you will ask him? And whatever happens, you'll try and have my picture painted by Christmas. Just in case he comes.'

'I'll do my best, darling.'

On my next visit, a fortnight later, they were still hard at work on the portrait. Mother and daughter behaved like friends, casual friends perhaps, but friends all the same. I have to admit that, observing Polly with her mother, I began to doubt my apprehension, which had reignited – despite Mrs Derby's reassurances – on seeing Isobel's paintings. For the first time since I had known them, they were laughing together. Polly wore a polo-neck jumper the colour of her eyes, and her hair, brushed furiously that morning, was carefully arranged. She was sitting very still, and her face, bright and alert, revealed a glimmer of mischief. It was the gaze with which she always approached Peter, and, capturing it, Isobel added her own insights into their daughter.

There was boldness in the eyes and behind them a suggestion of vulnerability. True to her word, Isobel depicted her daughter with a tenderness lacking in her previous pictures. There were no animals or birds in sight: no beaks, or claws, or feathers, or paws. Just Polly, incorrigible; resplendent. Sensing the warmth radiating from the half-finished portrait, I let my anxieties slide.

I had believed that Isobel hated Polly, that she wanted to harm her. I was wrong, I decided, in much the same way as I'd been wrong in my first impressions of the Venuses. Grieving for my mother had humbled me, and I began to think that perhaps I hadn't seen what I'd believed was real after all: Isobel taking and eating the pearls. And even if I had seen her, at the time I'd believed my mother was alive, when in fact she was dead. I no longer trusted myself and my ability to distinguish what was real from what was imagined. Grief, having silenced my voice, was making me question my existence.

Hearing Polly and Isobel laughing, I suddenly remembered what Theo had told me. They might not get on, but they cared for each other. Their laughter slit my heart open as I remembered that once I had laughed with my own mother. On her good days.

I was never going to hear her voice again, or trace the outline of her lips with my thumb. Or experience those moments of intimacy when, putting on my gold earrings,

Mama dabbed powder on my face and left a trace of perfume behind my ears. Gazing at me she would say: 'Ajuba, do you know who's the most wonderful girl in the world?' 'Who, Mama?' 'You, my daughter. My beautiful daughter.' I would never hear her laughter again.

I allowed my grief to wash over me. It no longer frightened me as it had done at the beginning. It was gentler now. And with Isobel's shout of laughter still ringing in my ears, I felt the radiance of Polly's smile turning towards me. She winked, and little by little, what was left of my apprehension dissipated, and I joined in the laughter myself.

21

One afternoon late that November, when the portrait of my friend was almost finished, Polly and I walked down a muddy bridlepath to a copse of trees at the edge of the estate. We were collecting fir cones for Christmas decorations. It was going to be a special Christmas according to Polly, because if she got her way, Peter would return home. It was going to be the last Christmas the Venuses would celebrate as a family, before Isobel and Peter went their separate ways.

Not surprisingly, despite Polly's persistent entreaties, Peter was reluctant to return to the scene of Isobel's revenge. He said he would think about it. A few days later, when Isobel called him saying their daughter desperately wanted a family Christmas, and wouldn't he join them, Peter repeated his statement: he was considering their invitation. Isobel, claiming that she wanted nothing more than to give Polly a Christmas to remember, assured him that there was nothing to worry about. They could use the opportunity to discuss their daughter's future. It wouldn't hurt to come home for a few days. Unwilling to set aside his reservations completely, Peter promised to let them know what he'd decided a week before the holidays began.

I was invited for Christmas Day as well, and, anticipating that Peter would be with us, Polly and I had decided to put on a show. What we called a show was in fact a rendition of two songs the Venuses loved: an old favourite of Isobel's, 'Living Doll', and Roy Orbison's 'Love Hurts', which Peter adored and used to play at his impromptu parties. That is when he still had a record collection.

I had heard the Cliff Richard song for the first time on Peter's houseboat, the radio tuned to Capital Gold. It was the only song that Isobel liked that Polly admitted to enjoying. I believe there was a strong streak of sentimentality mixed up with Polly's love of the macabre, for she adored Bryan Adams' 'Everything I do', as well as most of Cliff Richard's early songs, and this one we were going to sing as a duet. It was a song for best friends who, having found in each other a perfect Living Doll, are at peace. The Roy Orbison ballad was a sad song about the pain love inflicts on those who experience its power. Sung in the smooth tenor voice of the man in dark glasses with the huge black quiff, it captured precisely my melancholy mood.

All the same, I had enjoyed our rehearsal that morning, the companionship of dancing and singing together as I choreographed our moves. I had taught Polly to dance Aunt Rose style, hips swivelling and body shaking in celebration of sacred joy. Memorising our steps, synchronising them to the words of the songs, Polly and I moved in unison with audacious glee. The Cliff Richard lyrics reminded me of Rapunzel in her tower and Miss Edith and Miss Fielding. It made me want to tell Polly about my discussion with Miss Edith over the chocolate éclairs. We still hadn't solved the mystery of the babies' bones but not for want of trying on my part. The inquest was going to come to a close in February after further interviews. Detective Inspector Roberts had questioned Miss Edith several times but no arrest had been made, so, assuming the old woman was in the clear, I told Polly about my conversation with her.

'She said I was wrong about Miss Fielding,' I explained, picking up a fir cone. 'Then she said the Queen of Hearts loved not wisely but too much.'

'Meaning what?' Polly exclaimed.

'I don't know. She said Miss Fielding was like someone called Othello.'

'Who the hell's she?'

I didn't know the answer to that question either; all I knew was that Othello was the name of someone in a Shakespeare play. And because I knew the story of Romeo and Juliet, I assumed that Othello had died for love as well.

'I bet you Peter knows who she is,' Polly said.

It was a crisp November day with an east wind so vicious it was like a knife against my cheek. The copse, littered with discarded fir cones, was covered in a thin blanket of pine needles.

'Perhaps Othello was like my mother,' I wondered out loud.

'How come?'

'Well, I think that maybe she loved my father too much, because in the end she couldn't live without him. When he left us, she killed herself.'

'You're kidding me, right?'

I shook my head, and for once Polly was lost for words. She stared at me with a mixture of surprise and awe. I thought she wanted to know more: a detailed description at the very least, a blow-by-blow account of how the deed was done. But I didn't have the stomach to say anything else. I was cold; I was shivering. I took a hand from the pocket of the grey duffel coat I was wearing, and, after pulling down the knitted hat on my head so that it covered my eyebrows, placed it against my face to contain my misery.

'It happened over a year ago,' I added reluctantly. 'She was very unhappy.'

'I'm sorry,' Polly replied. Then, probably because she didn't know what else to say, she took my hand, warming it against her cheek. She stroked it, then, feeling the chill in it, she brought both my hands to her mouth, blowing over them as she rubbed them together.

'Why didn't you tell me, Aj? Why couldn't you tell me?'

I was crying. I didn't know how to answer her. Instead of wanting to know the details of my mother's suicide, Polly wanted to comfort me; to reassure me. Somehow, through her enquiring gaze and the stillness that followed it, she seemed to assimilate what I was feeling, easing the sting of my tears with her touch.

A sudden glint of red distracted us. To our right, in an open field beyond the copse, was a vixen grooming herself. A shaft of autumn sunlight gleamed on the animal's fur as, licking her paws, she wiped her face clean, staring at us coolly. We watched her for ten precious minutes, her lustrous yellow eyes taking us in as we stood motionless, my hands warming in Polly's, my tears ceasing. When the fox had finished, she turned her back to us and trotted into the undergrowth.

Polly and I smiled at each other, enraptured by what we'd seen. Arm in arm, we started walking back to the house, our Wellington boots leaving a trail of footprints in the mud.

'Is that why you've been sad lately, remembering your mother?' Polly asked eventually.

I nodded.

'Do you want to talk about it?'

It was the sort of question Peter would have asked. I suppose she thought it fitting for the occasion to use words and expressions he would use. He was one of the most understanding adults we knew.

I shook my head and Polly appeared relieved. I was discovering that proximity to violent death isn't as fascinating close up as most people imagine it will be. My revelation had taken the wind out of her. For all her bravado in claiming to have touched Jacinth's dead body, Polly preferred reading about death in the pages of *True Murder* to tackling it head on. Like most of us, she enjoyed it packaged in neat parcels to puzzle over and unravel. To have it touch someone she cared for was quite another matter.

For the rest of the day, Polly was solicitous towards me. She watched me as we sat cross-legged in front of a log fire painting the fir cones gold. Flecks of paint splattered our fingernails and cheeks. Engrossed in the task, the fire illuminating the colours of our skin, I was aware of Polly's intermittent gaze. Eventually I said to her: 'I'm still the same, Polly.'

'No, you're not,' she answered. 'You're different; like I was different when I started my periods. But you're still my best friend, aren't you?'

'Of course. Are you still my best friend?'

'Always.' She put down her fir cone and, inching closer to me, she put her hands on my knees. 'Whatever happens, Aj, promise you'll always be my best friend.'

I promised that I would. To mark the occasion, Polly decided we should become blood sisters. She found one of Isobel's needles and pricked my forefinger. Then she drew blood from her own, mingling it with mine. To ensure that we were bound, one to the other, with the exclusivity of twins, she licked my finger clean, while I licked hers. We would be as one for eternity, we promised. We would never divorce. We were blood sisters, each other's living dolls. Then, because we understood the importance of ritual when making a never-ending pact, we sang the Roy Orbison song we had memorised. And singing it, I realised that the man with the quiff was right. Love hurts.

22

He was coming home. Peter was coming home for Christmas, and Isobel, as jubilant as Polly and me, was trying to contain her excitement. With the precision of politicians preparing for an election, Polly and Isobel laid plans for the four days of Peter's holiday. Of course, I joined in as well, and we spent hours decorating the house with baubles and tinsel. There were Christmas cards on the walls and on mantelpieces; and in the entrance hall a tree, laden with gold and silver fir cones, sparkled with blood-red candles at the tips of its branches. Together, the Venus women were intent on pleasing Peter. But while Polly's aim was to have a good time with her father – she had no idea when she would be seeing him again after he moved to Paris – I sensed that Isobel's excitement was tinged with longing.

I'm told by Mrs Bradshaw that Isobel laughed at Robert, her counsellor, when he had tried to warn her of her emotional susceptibility. The past was the past, she asserted; she was thinking of her future; she had no intention of re-entering hell. Anyway, Peter was only coming home for a few days. What harm could that do? 'He's such an old woman,' she confided to Belinda Bradshaw, indignant at Robert's lack of trust in her emotional stability. 'I've never felt better. I'm over the worst now, and Polly and I are good friends. I'm a new woman.'

Belinda accepted what she said. I would have done as well had I been in her position. Physically, Isobel was radiant, glowing with inner vitality. And there was about her a sense of direction, a new sense of purpose, which Polly and I responded to. Isobel, no longer despondent, was excellent company. She made us laugh, mimicking the rude noises Polly and I practised when we were in the bath together. Her talent was such that she held us spellbound while she was icing the Christmas cake, as she pretended to emit a series of stupendously loud farts. I begged her to make the noises again and again and she happily complied, a mischievous smile on her face, while Polly, gasping, shrieked in disgust. Apparently, pre-teens weren't even supposed to pretend to fart in public. Not when adults were around at any rate. I was delighted, none the less. Isobel could burp on demand as well. She was kind enough to teach me how to do the same trick, demonstrating that, just like with singing, it was a question of breath control. 'Control is everything, Ajuba,' she insisted. 'Everything.'

As Christmas loomed closer, Peter casually informed Polly and Isobel of the day he would be coming home with Theo by car. I noticed that Isobel was immersing herself in the business of festivity with the same energy she'd deployed in decorating her home. Her standards were exacting, her organisation meticulous. Like a Prussian general involved in military manoeuvres, she made lists and work plans, allocating her time with tactical zeal. She chose an organic turkey from a neighbouring farm, she made delicious mince pies, dainty sausage rolls; she stocked the house with drinks and liqueurs, chocolates, Turkish delight, Brazil nuts, hazelnuts, walnuts. She even bought chestnuts for roasting on the fire, and, for Christmas stockings, succulent, bright clementines. Such was her excitement that I'm convinced that with every food purchase she made, every present she bought, she made a wish that this Christmas it would all come right; they would be happy together; and somehow, they would be a family again.

I had seen the same excitement on my mother's face. I had felt the same burning desire through Mama: that with Christmas and the coming year she could somehow recreate the good times we'd enjoyed at Kuku Hill, when it seemed the whole of Accra devoured the cakes she had baked for New Year. Pa had never succumbed to Mama's determination to rebuild the past on a new foundation. But perhaps Peter would, I reasoned. With Polly and Isobel working together, he might succumb to anything. After all, he'd agreed to return, despite the destruction of the painting he loved most in the world.

Peter arrived on the 23rd with bad news. Theo would not be home for Christmas Day. Peter had refrained from calling Isobel to forewarn her of the exact hour of his arrival, knowing what a stickler she was for time and detail. He hadn't wanted her to fuss over what was, after all, a mere four-day holiday. I suppose he hoped that a relaxed homecoming would underline the casualness of his visit as well as giving him the advantage of surprise.

After the initial mayhem of his return, Polly and I helping him in with his parcels, Isobel embraced him warmly. Momentarily flustered by Theo's absence, she had quickly regained her poise, no doubt rearranging meals, juggling cheeses, puddings, the consumption of Christmas delicacies in her head. Peter explained Theo's delay: he had gone to Paris as soon as his exams had finished, where, released from academic constraint, he was indulging in a frenzy of adolescent romance. He claimed to be in love, and in his enthusiasm for Sylvie had missed his return flight to London. He promised to be home for Boxing Day.

I felt a stab of jealousy at the thought of Theo spending Christmas with Sylvie. I had already decided that I was going to marry him when I grew up. He gave me sound advice and was kind to me. I hoped Theo would have me, even if my breasts didn't ripen into the voluptuous mounds on Sylvie's chest. I was tired of being a Benson. I wanted to be a Venus, in name at the very least.

'Drat the boy,' Isobel said, laughing. 'I think he's avoiding me!'

Peter appeared surprised at the note of self-irony in her voice. He must have anticipated anger, complaints about the disruption of her plans followed by a family conference. Should they have the turkey on Boxing Day instead? Should they open their Christmas presents later? Isobel was always punctilious about performing rituals. But if such details crossed her mind, she kept them to herself.

Instead, she seemed as happy and relaxed as if an old friend was visiting her home. Peter was visibly relieved. He remained reassured over lunch and throughout much of the afternoon. While Isobel drove into Axminster for a final shopping expedition, Peter walked with Polly and me in the grounds.

The improvements Isobel had embarked on that summer were complete: a brick terrace swept out from the back of the house, and outside the kitchen door a herb garden of rosemary, sage and varieties of mint imprisoned in pots recommended the culinary skill of the mistress of the house.

I remembered walking the grounds with Isobel on the first day of the summer holidays, when she'd described her plans to me. At the time, I'd wondered if the Venuses would survive their marriage: if Peter would return and make Isobel happy again. Walking around the estate, my arm linked to Peter's, I could see he was impressed by what Isobel had achieved. And with Polly and me giving him a blow-by-blow account of what had happened and when – I knew the details better than Polly did for I'd listened closely to everything Isobel had told me that summer – I watched Peter marvelling at Isobel's single-mindedness. He had never been interested in the house and its grounds, yet making the rounds with us on that cold December afternoon, the gardener Mr Furzey doffing his cap as he finished spreading gravel on a path, Peter seemed charmed by what he saw and full of admiration for Isobel.

I became aware of a change in all of them the longer they spent in each other's company. I sensed growing exhilaration and eagerness when Isobel, returning from her shopping trip, started conspiring with Polly. To say that the Venus women ganged up on Peter would be untrue. They ensnared him in a web of complicity by exchanging smiles while teasing him about the present they were giving him for Christmas. They had bolted the door of his former study to prevent him guessing what the present might be; and when Peter innocently asked if he could look at some of Isobel's paintings, the two of them laughed. There were whispers, winks and raised eyebrows, so that the atmosphere, thickening with intrigue, aroused Peter's senses. Before long, I noticed him looking at Isobel with renewed interest. Like a cat cleaning himself by the fire, watching every movement at the far end of a room, he observed her; appraised her; deliberating whether he should step closer or not.

As far as I was concerned, I wanted them to be a family

again. The Venuses possessed an alchemy that stirred whenever they were together. It radiated from them, warming outsiders, drawing us in. Bereft of my mother, I was ravenous for love, yet a part of me remained alert to Isobel. Despite her new-found ability to make me laugh, having absorbed the pain of her distress that summer, I couldn't forget it. I half-hoped that Peter's return would make Isobel and the house safe once again.

'How are you?' Peter asked eventually. 'How are you getting on, Isobel?' He was looking at her with new eyes. In my mother's words, his eyes were opening and he was seeing her clearly for the first time in a long while. Isobel was slicing chunks of crystallised ginger to flavour the rhubarb crumble she was making for dinner.

'I'm very well,' Isobel replied. 'Getting back to painting has helped enormously. And there's Robert of course. My therapist,' she added with a smile, noting a flicker of interest on Peter's face. 'I do get lonely at times but I'm learning how to live with myself.'

'Same here. I've missed you, Isobel.'

She admitted that she had missed him as well. He seemed surprised at her openness, the ease with which she stated her feelings without complaint or recrimination. They fell silent and in their silence I felt the tension rise between them as Peter, stepping closer, sniffed Isobel out. I could tell he was aroused by her, because the blue in his eyes flashed turquoise and his body odour changed; exuding the heavy scent of musk.

'A woman is her own watchdog,' Aunt Rose had once told me. 'Even a one-eyed woman can find someone to love her. As far as men are concerned, Ajuba, there's no such thing as an ugly woman.' Isobel's watchdog, a black mastiff with ferocious teeth, was sitting poised at her feet. And

Isobel was still beautiful, despite the lines on her forehead and the grey hair she had acquired that summer. She had aged, but maturity became her. She had the look of a woman who, weathering a terrible storm, has learnt how to survive. There was a toughness about her, a hardy resilience bred of experience. 'Control is everything,' she had said to me. Unlike Maria's mother, Isobel appeared to know what she was doing.

Polly, oblivious of what was happening between her parents, was sorting out two packs of cards for a game of Racing Demon. I remember thinking at the time that if Peter wanted Isobel again, and if she were to have him back, he wouldn't make Polly move to Paris when he settled there. She could stay at school and we would remain friends. I can't say for certain exactly what I wanted for the Venuses. I know that I craved their affection, but the shape their love would take left me confused.

I started wondering what Malone and Leboeuf would make of my dilemma. I had not heard from them since I'd discovered that my mother was dead, most probably because they no longer considered me a competent detective. They had written in *True Murder* that a detective should be clear-sighted at all times and I had deluded myself. But to my surprise, just by thinking about them, I began to hear them whispering in my ear. Magnanimously ignoring my short-comings, they murmured: 'Listen, kid. Don't get your hopes up. As you know already, adults are by nature unreliable.'

Nodding in agreement, I placed my hand on Peter's knee. 'Would you like to play with us?' I asked.

'Yes, Daddy. Why don't you join in?'

Though I could see that his interests lay elsewhere, Peter graciously accepted our offer, and Polly dealt his cards. He prepared his hand while Polly and I waited for him. When he was ready, and I'd said, 'Go!' our fingers flew over the table, piling cards up in the centre. Peter fumbled. He kept turning around every now and again to look at what Isobel was doing. Every time Isobel sensed his interest, she smiled, enticing him closer. She was a model of self-control, seductive yet evasive.

Perhaps I should have told Polly what was happening before she saw it herself. Perhaps I should have drawn her attention to the game her parents were playing. Maybe, if we had sat them down and talked to them seriously, they might have considered their intentions in a sober, rational manner. Yet I believe that if I had spoken to Polly earlier, she would merely have shrugged, saying: 'Lighten up, Aj. I've been living with these guys for almost thirteen years and they still don't get it. I've learnt to ignore them because they always do what they want to in the end.'

I wasn't able to talk to Polly, but when Peter turned for another peek at Isobel, I said to my friend, 'Adults, huh?'

Polly raised an eyebrow, winning the set of Racing Demon.

On tenterhooks with the scenario Isobel had set in motion, and agitated as to how its outcome might affect me, I tried to distract Peter with a question I had been considering since my conversation with Miss Edith: 'Who's Othello?'

'Yeah, who is she?' Polly seconded.

'Othello,' Peter sighed, 'is Shakespeare's Noble Moor. He was a soldier from North Africa who married a woman from Venice called Desdemona.'

'How come he loved not wisely but too well?'

'Well, he's the hero of one of Shakespeare's tragedies, Ajuba.'

'And what exactly is a tragedy?'

'A play with a sad ending. You see, Othello doubted his wife's love, and murdered her in a jealous rage.'

I was trying to hold Peter with the force of my eyes but he kept turning to Isobel. They were speaking a secret language, a silent language of shining eyes and soft glances. I was no closer to understanding the meaning of Miss Edith's statement, so I demanded to know why Othello had murdered his wife.

'Iago led him to it,' Isobel replied, placing a bowl of nuts on the kitchen table. Polly wolfed down a handful, while Isobel's watchdog, though still alert, began wagging his tail. To my alarm, he seemed to want to lick Peter's hand.

Aware of my incomprehension, Peter explained gently: 'Someone Othello thought was a friend lied to him, Ajuba, feeding his insecurities. And then, believing Desdemona had betrayed him, Othello strangled her.'

'Just because of sex?' I spat out in disgust.

'It was much more than just sex, little one. It was jealousy and love combined. In the end, the poor fellow lost control. He murdered his wife and then killed himself.'

'He wasn't very clear-sighted then, was he?' I retorted.

Placing a hand casually on Peter's shoulder, Isobel said, smiling at him: 'Beware the green-eyed monster.'

Their secret language, instead of enlightening me, left me perplexed. Struggling to understand Miss Edith's words, it came to me that perhaps if Shakespeare had listened to Roy Orbison, he'd have written a sad song instead of an impenetrable play. 'You mean Othello murdered her because love hurt him so much?' I enquired of Peter.

'Exactly, Ajuba.'

By five o'clock, Polly, overjoyed by the prospect of Christmas Eve the next day, was too excited to notice anything amiss. She was in her element, vivacious and affectionate with her father. Every now and then she ran to the Christmas tree, examining the presents awaiting Christmas morning. Imagining Peter's delight at her portrait, gift-wrapped at the side of the tree, she ran her finger down the length of its frame.

'Do you think he'll like it?' she asked me.

'Of course he'll like it, Polly. It's just like you.'

'But it's not as cool as his Paul Nash, is it? It's not half as gloomy or depressing. It doesn't make you want to cry, does it, Aj?'

'That's why he'll like it.'

'Are you sure? You know how much he likes gnashing his teeth when he stares at things.'

'Of course he'll like it. Isobel's good. She's much better at painting than Rolf Harris is, and this is the best picture she's done yet. Peter will love it.'

We sauntered back into the kitchen. Peter, leaning against the mantelpiece, was still staring at Isobel. As far as I could see, he wasn't gnashing his teeth. He seemed dazed by an emotion I'd never seen on his face before. Like Isobel, he was sipping a glass of white wine. The web Isobel had spun with Polly's help held him spellbound. I thought at first that what I saw on his face was the look of love: his features had softened and his eyes shone with tenderness. If only it had been a look of love, an expression of faith in Isobel and their future together. I know now that what I saw was a haze of bewildered desire. I felt the strength of the tug between them. I tasted the potent brew of chemistry and charisma that sizzled whenever they were together. I imagine that having lassoed Peter once again, Isobel was trying to decide what to do with him. I saw her watchdog, its tail wafting gently, beginning to doze by the Aga. I crossed my fingers, hoping that Isobel knew what she was doing. Young as I was, I understood, thanks to Aunt Rose, that when a woman's watchdog falls asleep, she opens herself up to pleasure and pain in equal measure.

Polly, seeing with my eyes, was suddenly aware of the current crackling between her parents. She moaned, exasperated: 'There they go again,' she said to me. 'If I wasn't a pre-teenager, I'd have divorced them long ago.'

'Are you going to be all right?' I asked her.

Malone and Leboeuf were telling me that it was time to split. It was time to exchange the uncertainty of Graylings for the calm sobriety of school.

'Sure. I'll be fine. This is always happening, Aj. I'm used to them now.'

'Adults are so pathetic!' I exclaimed. 'They just don't get it, do they?'

'You got it, kid. They can't learn because they think they know it all already. And they never listen. Not on this planet, anyway.'

'Do you think they're still going to get divorced?'

'Sure. Peter's made up his mind. He doesn't want her – not like before, at any rate.'

I didn't really know if what Peter and Isobel were doing was sensible or not. I didn't much care, as long as Polly could stay in England and she remained my friend.

'Best friends?' I enquired.

'Always,' Polly replied.

Peter took me back to the Derbys that evening, although by seven o'clock on Christmas Eve, I was back at Graylings again with a group of carol singers from Sunday School.

When we had sung the final chorus of 'The Holly and the Ivy', I shook the box of donations I was carrying. Polly, in a red dressing-gown Isobel had bought her for winter, waved at me from an upstairs window, shouting my name. I waved back. A minute later, Isobel was at the window, a protective hand on Polly's shoulder. And when Peter joined them, I wanted to be with them. As soon as the carols were over, Polly ran downstairs and opened the front door to me.

She led me into the house, and while the other singers trampled in behind, she grabbed my arms and drew me to her heart. Her blanket of golden hair fell against my face and I felt the pulse of her breath as she warmed my body with hers. 'Let's go upstairs and rehearse our songs,' she whispered in my ear.

'In a while,' I said. I wanted to see what her parents were up to. I wanted to see if they were behaving themselves and if Isobel's watchdog was wide awake.

Isobel was warming mince pies for us and Peter was pouring out glasses of ginger wine. Although they were separated and Peter was supposed to be a guest in Isobel's house, the season's festivities seemed to make them a couple again. Peter behaved as the man of the house might, refilling glasses, passing plates. And when the food was almost finished, a glance at Isobel produced another tray of mince pies from the Aga.

Isobel's mastiff had disappeared, yet the intense excitement between Peter and Isobel was palpable. It was as if only they knew how to elicit the full magic of Christmas, replenishing it with generosity and glee.

For my part, I recognised their exuberance as similar to my feelings for Polly. I was convinced that we would always be best friends. My mother might have abandoned me, but

Polly would be my friend for ever. Tugging at my shoulder, Polly dragged me upstairs for a final rehearsal of the show we were going to perform the next day.

We were perfecting the dance steps for 'Living Doll', which we were going to sing back to back and then facing each other, when I heard Mrs Derby shouting my name. She called me a second time, bringing our rehearsal to a halt.

'Why don't you sleep over?' Polly suggested. 'Peter's staying, so you needn't be scared of Isobel any more.'

I was already through the bedroom door. 'I'll think about staying tomorrow night,' I said in the corridor.

I ran downstairs, Polly following me. As I slipped on my gloves and coat, struggling to put on my shoes without undoing the laces, Polly demanded of Mrs Derby: 'Why can't Ajuba stay? Then you won't have to bring her tomorrow.'

Polly looked at her father for support. Peter smiled at Sarah Derby and Sarah at me. I shook my head.

'I'll bring her tomorrow,' Mrs Derby said firmly. 'It's no trouble, believe me.'

'But she could stay now. I want you to stay, Aj.'

'That's enough Polly,' Peter said, drawing his daughter into his arms. 'We'll see Ajuba tomorrow.'

He waved goodbye to Sarah Derby, who was holding my hand. I waved back, mouthing, 'Best friends?' to Polly.

'Always!' she yelled.

23

'Are you sure, Ajuba?'

It was Christmas Day and Mrs Derby was driving me back to Graylings. I had expressed the desire to spend the night with the Venuses as Mrs Derby, turning left through the open gates, drove past the Gatehouse. Now I nodded. Having Peter back made all the difference, I'd decided. I would feel safe with him under the same roof.

'Well, if you're sure, it's OK by me,' Mrs Derby replied.

I was excited. On my lap was a small duffel bag stuffed with pyjamas and a change of clothes. My presents were already under the tree: a scarf I had knitted for Peter, a basket woven for Isobel, a collection of horror stories for Polly, and for Theo a red woollen hat I had spent hours over: retrieving dropped stitches, and then dropping them all over again. Scarves, I had decided, were much easier to knit than hats.

The Derbys' Rover came to a shuddering halt and Sarah Derby got out.

'You don't have to come in, Mrs Derby,' I said, wanting to get rid of her so that Christmas with the Venuses could begin in typical high spirits. I wanted to dance to that Van Morrison song again, yelling out all the *sha-la-la*'s in the chorus. I wouldn't feel comfortable dancing with Mrs Derby around.

It was no bother coming in with me, she replied. She wanted to thank the Venuses for their hospitality the night before. They had donated generously to the WWF, and generosity of spirit was not a trait Sarah Derby treated lightly. She believed a special thank you was in order, as well as the season's greetings.

She followed me to the front door and I rang the doorbell. Usually I went straight inside, announcing my arrival with a shout before running up to Polly's bedroom. That Christmas morning, because Mrs Derby was with me, I stared patiently at the circle of holly on the door waiting for it to draw back as Polly or Peter, whoever came first to lift the heavy latch, welcomed me inside.

It was a Christmas Day of unusual brightness, a surprisingly mild morning after a frosty night, and for once my hands weren't encased in gloves. I slipped my fingers into my pockets, sticking them through the holes in the lining of my coat. Thankful that the chilblains on my toes were no longer itching, I stood on one foot, scraping a tickle at the back of my leg with the other. The winter sun bouncing off the windows of the house gave it a look of cleanliness that whetted my enthusiasm. Inside was the tall Christmas tree I had decorated with Polly and beneath it were the presents we had fingered longingly, day after day. I looked up at Mrs Derby, and, taking her nod for assent, turned the front-door handle.

As always the house was warm. Isobel hated the cold. Dumping my bag on the floor, I walked to the Christmas tree. The presents were still unopened as Polly had said they would be when I arrived. We were going to open them after brunch, Peter handing them out to us, one after the other.

Smiling at the eagerness on my face as my eyes wandered

over the gifts, Sarah Derby asked: 'Are some of those for you? Good for you, Ajuba!' she chuckled, acknowledging my nod. 'Where is everybody?'

The house was very quiet but I wasn't perturbed. 'Upstairs,' I replied, knowing that the Venuses were late risers. 'They never go to church. I'll go and tell them you're here.'

I ran up the stairs, calling Polly. No one replied. Undeterred, I ran into her bedroom.

She was stretched out on the bed, hiding beneath her dressing-gown, her face covered with a pillow.

'Merry Christmas, lazybones. Polly?'

When she didn't reply, I assumed she was playing True Murder. 'Oh, you're supposed to be dead, are you? Well, you can't fool me.'

I leapt on the bed, pulling the pillow from Polly's face. Then I screamed. I screamed, and in that instant my world stopped, as I tumbled into a gaping abyss that gulped me down.

'Wake up!' I cried, hitting her. 'Polly wake up!'

She didn't wake up. She was rigid and cold, lost in some distant arctic tundra. Her hands, half-clenched, were motionless, her feet frozen; her hair, its riot of curls spilling on linen, seemed as incongruous as blossoms of laburnum on snow. It was the first colour I registered: her hair, then her dressing-gown, scarlet and gold. And above us, leering in a parody of evil, the Bela Lugosi poster Theo had brought from Paris, which at the time had made us laugh uproariously.

The echo of our laughter receded. The scene, bruising the retinas of my eyes, revealed everything in an instant. On the floor between our beds, a pile of *True Murder*, a Walkman on top. On the chest of drawers, a glass, dregs of milk at the bottom; beside it Polly's Mickey Mouse alarm clock and, discarded on my bed, the clothes she had worn the day before, a symphony of pink angora and corduroy. Staring down at her body, the zebras of the savannah in her favourite picture had stopped grazing. Alert to danger, scanning the horizon, they were moving, whinnying, as vultures circled the darkening sky, glided and swooped down. It was then that it started. The zebras stampeded, their hooves flinging dust in my face, filling the room with the scream of birds and a rushing, thunderous wind as the past and the present folded together and the floorboards of the rose room – the room I had slept in so often – split asunder. I didn't want to see, but I had no choice, for the house, searing its memory of past events into my mind, demanded a witness.

'No!' I screamed. 'Not again, not again.' I didn't want to feel such murderous rage again. I pleaded, but the house, disregarding my protests, dragged me to a place where I saw Isobel, sodden with alcohol, disembodied, a receptacle empty of everything but pain.

What had Peter done to her? What had he done to her?

I watch petrified as, suspended in time, drained of reason, Isobel opens a bathroom cabinet. Emptying a bottle of painkillers, she clenches them in her fist, pouring a glass of water. Carrying the load into her bedroom, she relinquishes the tablets, lying down on the bed.

'No, Isobel,' I beg her. 'Please don't. Stay with me. I'll look after you, I promise. I'll look after you and make you happy again.'

For a moment, I think that Isobel can see me. She pauses, looking straight at me as the house, pregnant with emotions that have lain dormant for years, clamours to speak to us. The house, swaying, grows dim as at gloaming, when dusk deepens into night and time trembles. I cling to Isobel's hand, terrified of what is to come, while the past, cradling the house in a sigh, relives its story.

Where is Peter? Where has he gone? If he were here, he could prevent this happening. I try to call his name out loud but my voice has gone.

The house is slowly opening up. A shape emerges by the dressing-table mirror. I begin to make out a face that resembles mine: the face Isobel drew that summer. It is dark as molasses dripping over a Benin bronze. It inches closer to Isobel.

'Mama? Is that you, Mama?'

If it is my mother, she doesn't hear me. She is talking to Isobel, saying: 'Your daughter, think of your daughter.' And Isobel, overwhelmed by a void Peter has breached within her, stumbles into the rose room.

I run after her, begging her to stop, clutching at her clothes to halt her progress. But I can't stop her. There is no substance here to cling to, no logic to twist to turn events around. My will is as nothing to what is unfolding before my eyes.

I see a rose washbasin in the room I am standing in – Polly's room. Miss Edith's room. Olivia Fielding is pouring hot water into the basin and washing her hands. I hear Miss Edith's screams, and I see the first of them, a boy, born dead, in Miss Fielding's arms. A moment later there is the lusty wail of the second. A girl, Miss Fielding says, carrying her to the washbasin. Then the crying stops. Life is snuffed out as easily as drowning a farmyard kitten.

And then I am with Isobel again in the same room, flames cowling her face as she glares at her sleeping child. She is standing by Polly's bed as she did that night in the summer. Beside her is Miss Fielding, a Spanish shawl flung over a shoulder.

The house is confiding its secrets, revealing itself one last time as it urges Isobel on. The woman standing sentinel nods and, picking up a pillow from my bed, Isobel falls on Polly.

The pillow stifles her breathing, silences her screams. Though Polly struggles and kicks, with Isobel's arms embracing her, death is delivered as a final gift to my friend. Polly will never feel the pain of a woman discarded, contemptible even to herself.

The struggle over, Isobel covers her with the dressing-gown. In the tussle it has fallen to the floor.

She returns to her room and downs the pills. Then she remembers. Opening the drawer of her bedside table, she pulls out a string of pearls. Isobel kisses the cold stones, trailing them between her fingers: a gift from a father to his daughter.

Far better never to have been born than to witness horror such as this.

'No!' I screamed. 'Wake up, Polly! Wake up!'

I had woken my mother in Lewisham, so I could do it again. I would give Polly my life; my breath.

I heard someone rushing up the stairs and suddenly felt myself being pulled away. I had been hitting her body, shaking her in a futile attempt to revive her.

'Oh my God!'

'She's playing, Mrs Derby,' I cried, unable to accept what my eyes had seen. 'She's playing True Murder. Tell her to stop, Mrs Derby. Polly, wake up. Wake up!' I shrieked.

Mrs Derby dragged me yelling and kicking from the room. As she shut the door, and leaned against it, I heard a high-pitched wail that came again and again. It was the cry of a trapped animal yelping in terror, a creature in acute distress.

Mrs Derby held me tightly. And when I realised that the

screams were coming from me, I felt Mrs Derby's tears on my cheek. She was crying too. 'Ajuba . . . I'm so sorry, Ajuba,' she kept saying. 'I'm so sorry.'

Suddenly the noise stopped and I was still. I was carried downstairs, and when I started shaking, Mrs Derby wrapped me in a blanket.

I can't remember what happened next. My memory is clouded with patches of darkness, suggesting that I lost consciousness. What I do remember is that over the next few days I wouldn't allow Mrs Derby out of my sight; and that on Christmas Day itself, I had held onto her hand, a capsized child clinging to the wreckage of my childhood.

I was clutching Mrs Derby when she called the police. Later on, emerging from a spell of darkness, I recognised the muffled sound of adults discussing disaster. They were whispering; murmuring. I expect they had found Isobel's body. People were walking up and down the staircase, talking in hushed tones. Then a man's voice said rather loudly, 'Poor little bugger,' and taking my arm, Archie Whittaker the school doctor, stuck a needle in it. There was dandruff around the collar of his jacket; I remember thinking that it looked like a sprinkling of dirty snow.

24

I woke up late the next morning. Mrs Derby was sitting beside me still holding my hand. I shut my eyes. I didn't want to wake up. Yet I didn't want to sleep either, because I saw them in my dreams. All of them: my mother and Isobel and standing between them, Polly. In front of them was the vixen we'd seen in November. Polly was stroking it and she was calling me. It was all a game, she said. True Murder was easy. And now that we were blood sisters we were inseparable; best friends.

I tried to reach her, but I couldn't. My feet were stuck to the ground. Later on, in another dream, my fingers stretching to brush hers, I almost touched her before she disappeared. They all kept disappearing: my mother, Isobel and Polly. Running after them I tried desperately to catch up.

Such were my days and nights. Waking or sleeping, my world was peopled by shadows. It was as if, walking indoors on a bright summer's day, I could see no one around me. At night, blinking in the radiance of my dreams, the pain in my eyes rendered forms indistinguishable. They shimmied, they blurred. Everyone around me whispered in low voices and I heard my father speaking. As soon as he had heard what had happened, he travelled from Rome to see me. I recognised his shoes, but when I looked to where his voice was coming from, I failed to register his face. He held my hand while I clung to Mrs Derby, unable to decipher words. I was dislocated; adrift.

As the days followed, one after the other, my vision gradually cleared. Waking with each morning, I began to realise that the sounds, the murmurs I thought I heard, and the stares that made me turn around, only for them to disappear again, were not imagined. People did look at me strangely; they did whisper.

Little by little, I began to comprehend what was happening. It dawned on me that when people looked at me, they saw Polly: I was her best friend and for as long as I lived, she would live as well. Seeing me, people were reminded of what had happened; what Isobel had done to her daughter. This was as it should be, I reasoned, for Polly and I were blood sisters.

While I grappled with my new place at school, and yearned for Polly to revive me by flowing through my veins once again, the adult world was trying to piece together what had happened. Three weeks after the Christmas break, there was an inquest into the Venus tragedy at which a coroner, giving his verdict, reflected the opinion of the local community. He said that the dreadful events that had taken place would never be forgotten. At the time of her death, the alcohol level in Isobel's blood had been dangerously high. She had died through a combination of alcohol and an overdose of painkillers. Traces of semen were found in her body, indicating that she'd had 'relations' with Peter Venus, a fact he confirmed. Then, after an argument – during which she forced him to leave the house – while the balance of her mind was disturbed, Isobel Venus had murdered her daughter before taking her own life.

Everyone was horrified by what she had done. Yet at the same time they pitied rather than condemned her. They said that for a mother to commit such an atrocity, despair must have driven her mad. As far as I am aware, no one but Belinda Bradshaw said a word about Peter's role in the affair. No matter what anyone thought at the time, they didn't dare implicate Peter. It was clear from the phone records that after evicting Peter at midnight on Christmas Eve, Isobel was lucid enough to try to contact Belinda. Unfortunately, the Bradshaws were on their knees at midnight mass and Robert, Isobel's therapist, was with a friend in Morocco.

Mrs Derby told me that after the inquest, Peter Venus had tried to see me at school. He was distraught, incapable of conversing coherently with a child. Thinking that I was not in a fit state to see him, and that his grief would exacerbate my own, the Derbys encouraged Peter to talk to them.

'He was devastated, Ajuba. He was all over the place, talking about Polly one moment and in the next breath berating Isobel and himself. He said things he wouldn't normally have said. He desperately needed someone to talk to, my dear, so Philip and I spent an evening drinking with him.'

Straightening her metal-rimmed glasses, which she still wears to this day, Sarah Derby filled in the gaps of what I'd failed to understand as a child, providing me with information that even Theo doesn't know.

'As I anticipated, Peter wanted to talk about the last time he was with Isobel. It turned out that she'd wanted more from him than he was prepared to give, so she chucked him out of the house. He reproached himself for everything that happened. He felt so guilty that I had to speak out. I told him I shared some of the blame. You'd warned me that

Isobel was unwell and might harm Polly. I stupidly misconstrued what you said, my dear. I let you and Polly down terribly.'

In the circumstances, I imagine everyone remembered when they had last seen Isobel and what, if anything, they might have done to alleviate her pain. At school I heard teachers saying how well she had looked before the end of term, and how elegant she'd always been. People remembered the clothes they had last seen her wearing; I heard them talk of her beauty, her kindness. I suspect that each of them, remembering, remarked privately how well she had deceived them. They had no inkling of the depth of her anguish; no suspicion of it at all. And though they absolved themselves of responsibility, I'm sure they couldn't help wondering what they could have done to help.

A general feeling of helplessness pervaded all our sensibilities, and I'm told that people were, for the most part, sympathetic towards Theo and Peter Venus. Having survived the tragedy, they had to brave the curse of living with it for the rest of their lives.

I cut out the report of the inquest from the local newspaper, pasting it in our *True Murder* scrapbook. Beth, Maria and I, the remaining Crimebusters, had decided that sticking the article in place would be a fitting memorial to Polly. We had also preserved a portrait of the Venuses from the front page of the newspaper.

We closed the book together, promising never to forget Polly. We promised despite knowing that, had we been able to, we would have tried to forget. Her death was so traumatic that, privately, I think each of us wanted to destroy the book, to bury it in a deep hole where it would never be found again: as I had wanted to do with the remains we found in Miss Fielding's trunk. Collectively, however, we swore to remember.

After Polly's murder, Beth hardly spoke to any of us. When, occasionally, she did talk to me, she prefaced her sentences with shrill neighing sounds. Animals, she said, were better than humans; until the human race improved, she was going to be a horse. She kept it up for six months. Grief affects people in different ways.

Beth told me later that her parents' quarrelling aggravated her distress, and that her escape into a world peopled by four-legged creatures had as much to do with that as the Venus tragedy. That's how everyone eventually described what Isobel had done: the Venus tragedy.

According to Beth, her mother's reaction to the news was violent. Belinda Bradshaw had considered herself a close friend of Isobel, and after her initial disbelief and tears, her anger was incandescent. 'Bloody, bloody men!' Belinda had cursed, glaring at Beth's father. 'It was his fault. That bloody man was to blame.'

'Hell hath no fury . . .' Charlie Bradshaw began, then, seeing the rage on his wife's face, he got up and slipped out of the room.

'Mummy says Isobel flipped because of Peter,' Beth relayed to us in Exe. We were preparing for Polly's funeral the next day. The whole school was going. Afterwards my father and Nina were taking me to London for a short break. I wasn't looking forward to any of it.

'You can't blame Peter for what Isobel did,' I replied, instantly protective of Polly's father. I still have the silver bangle he gave me; and once in a while I meet up with him in a disreputable after-hours Soho drinking club he belongs to.

Maria agreed with me; Peter wasn't to blame. But because

it was Maria who had made us aware of problems in the Venus marriage by her revelation that her mother was having an affair with Peter, Beth let rip at her.

'I suppose your mother wants him back in her bed,' she said sarcastically.

'Get yourself a brain, Bradshaw,' Maria sneered. 'If everyone went about murdering because their husbands left them, there'd hardly be any children left in the world. We'd all be dead, wouldn't we?'

Maria was polishing her outdoor shoes for the church service, and as she exhaled on them before rubbing them vigorously, I saw tears in her eyes.

The logic of her argument was an unsettling one. And even though Beth, who until then had always been optimistic, interjected that grown-ups didn't usually go around murdering children, the knowledge remained that we were acutely vulnerable in a world controlled by adults.

'Do you think dying hurts?' For some reason, Maria addressed her question to me.

'I don't think so,' I replied, though of course I was ignorant of the truth. But the thought that Polly might have died painfully, fighting for breath, was too horrifying to contemplate.

I found myself wondering what would have happened if I had spent the night at Graylings, as Polly had asked me to. Would Isobel have murdered me too? Or would she have allowed Polly to live, killing only herself? I wouldn't have minded that. I wanted Polly alive again. I hadn't been completely at ease with Isobel for a long time. She was too like my mother.

For the hundredth time, Maria exclaimed, 'How could she do it? How could she kill Polly?'

It was the question on everyone's lips. But for Beth and me, perhaps hardened by our exposure to *True Murder* and a summer spent puzzling over the contents of Miss Fielding's trunk, the Venus tragedy, although shocking, was not extraordinary. It was as if our discovery of the babies in the attic had been a warning of a greater calamity to follow; as if Polly, with her obsession with death, had spent her months at school preparing for a murder, not knowing it was to be her own.

I said as much to Beth after Lights Out. Maria had moved into Polly's bed, and at night Beth and I slept together.

'We asked the wrong questions,' I whispered to her. 'You see, the babies were a warning, Beth. But we were too close to see. We didn't hear what they were telling us.'

She whinnied and then said: 'Dead babies don't talk.'

'They do if you listen hard enough. They were trying to tell us that what happened to them was going to happen to one of us . . . to Polly.'

'As if.' Beth lay trembling beside me.

I was no longer frightened of what had happened. My discovery of Polly's body had pushed me beyond fear into a knowledge of darkness that had permeated the marrow of my bones. I thought nothing could ever frighten me again. I had reached a stage of acute sensitivity in which other people's thoughts and emotions merged with mine, and Malone and Leboeuf were with me constantly, ensuring my safety. I thought nothing could touch me again. I had forgotten about the faces in my mother's mirror.

At last, Beth asked a question that I realised she'd wanted to ask for ages. When her trembling ceased, she said: 'What did she look like dead, Aj?'

I closed my eyes and thought for a moment, and as Polly's

dead face surfaced behind my eyelids, I described it. 'She looked as if she'd seen something horrible and was furious that she couldn't tell us about it.'

I would never forget that face, or the pressure of Beth's hand on mine as she asked me a final question.

'Aj, do you think Polly's trying to tell us what she saw?'

I told her that I thought she was. After all, Polly and I were blood sisters. We were inseparable, even in death.

25

Although Maria Richardson and many of the adults present wept freely at the funeral, Beth and I remained calm. It seemed to us that our endless discussions of the summer term, our macabre meetings in the Glory Hole and Polly's relentless questioning of us had been a rehearsal. We each believed – as Mrs Derby shepherded us into a small village church with a star-spangled ceiling and Mrs Venus's coffin appeared, followed by Polly's – that we now understood the lessons of the summer: we inhabited a brutal, dangerous world and would never be safe. But while we were young, we were less safe than the others – the adults.

We stood side by side, bound together by our love for each other and our bond with Polly. Beth's friendship with Polly was coming to an end, but my own feelings for Polly were entering a new phase. We had tied ourselves to each other through the exchange of blood. Perhaps the call of grief had infected my mind, but it seemed to me that Polly's presence in my life was stronger in death than it had been before. Watching her coffin moving down the aisle to the altar, I smelt a trace of orange cinnamon on my breath: Polly's scent. And turning around to see people staring at me, I caught a glimpse of gold and scarlet. How else could

I explain Peter Venus's inconsolable grief, which intensified on seeing me in the congregation?

'Trust your gut,' Malone and Leboeuf had told me. So I knew. I knew, instinctively, that I would see Polly again. I was learning to live without my mother, but Polly was life itself.

My father and Nina arrived late and squeezed down the pew to sit beside me. Nina attempted to take my hand but I refused to touch her. I would never like her and I wasn't going to start pretending now.

My father and Nina had come to take me away for a short holiday. Their arrival in London, precipitated by a call from Mrs Derby, had apparently steeled Pa's resolve to remove me from school. He believed that having me living with them, in daily contact with Nina's affection, would revive my well-being, dispelling the accumulation of misfortune I had accrued over the years. He blamed my ability to attract disaster on Mama's excessive hysteria and my bad luck at meeting the Venuses. Pa had somehow managed to expunge his own part in my story, reinventing himself as a benevolent benefactor in a more stable future.

Thankfully, on one point at least, Nina and I agreed: I should remain at school. Though sympathetic towards me, my stepmother was heavily pregnant and absorbed, as most mothers-to-be are, by her child. The truth was that I wasn't a priority to her. I've been led to understand that very gently, very persuasively, Nina wore Pa down with arguments suggesting that remaining at school in Devon would be in my best interest. She was right. I was determined to remain close to Mrs Derby and Miss Edith. I believed they held the key to my sanity. I knew that until I could understand what had happened to Polly and the babies in Miss Fielding's trunk, I would never be at ease with myself. And I liked Mrs Derby much more than I did Nina.

Nevertheless, counting the thoughts streaming through Nina's head at Polly's funeral, absorbing her mood of impending maternal bliss, I was aware that she was moved by the ceremony and that she found my calm detachment throughout disturbing. What did she expect? Tears? I had shed all my tears long ago. I was exhausted by other people's thoughts, their inner voices reverberating in my mind. I wanted to go to sleep for a long time. I wanted to be with Polly.

When the coffins were carried from the village church into the steady drizzle of a grey January afternoon, Peter and Theo, weeping openly, followed. Nina and Pa, his protective hand on my shoulder, led me to the graveside with other well wishers. Many of them were wiping tears from their eyes, and as the vicar intoned the final words of the burial rite and the coffins were lowered, Nina started crying as well. She found Theo and Peter's grief overwhelming. It was certainly distressing, but I had seen far worse, having witnessed Polly's murder and discovered her body, and their tears left me numb. I wanted Polly. I wanted my best friend alive again. Half-supporting each other, Peter and Theo threw earth on the coffins, followed by a single white rose from each of them.

Then Peter walked towards us and stopped in front of me. Trying to hold his emotion in check, he cried: 'Forgive me, Ajuba. Please forgive me.'

I wanted Polly. I wanted her so badly that had I been alone I would have crawled into her coffin with her.

Expressing his condolences, Pa led Peter away. I suppose they had a lot to talk about. After all, both of them had had wives who had killed themselves rather than live without them. Mama, however, had forgotten to take me with her.

The funeral was over and the mourners were going their separate ways when Nina approached the Derbys. She was giving them a date on which I would return to school when Miss Edith, in a black astrakhan coat, drew Mrs Derby aside. The Bradshaws had stopped at the church gate. It seemed they were waiting for Miss Edith to join them.

'Did the child talk to you?' Miss Edith enquired. 'I told her that she should.'

The events of the past weeks had aged Miss Edith. Her lips were blue with cold and, walking with a stick, she made her way very carefully along the shining cobbled path, slippery with drizzle. Sarah Derby took her by the arm, guiding her to the Bradshaws. 'Yes, she did,' she replied. 'But I didn't believe her.'

'I didn't *want* to believe her.' Miss Edith stopped a few yards from Belinda Bradshaw, observing her impatience to be gone. She smiled. Belinda had offered her a lift so she would have to wait for her.

Intensifying her grip on Sarah Derby's arm, Miss Edith asked: 'Do you think she's going to be all right?'

In the moments before the question was answered, they both looked over at me. They were concerned with what I was experiencing behind my calm demeanour. They didn't realise that standing to one side I could hear their thoughts trickling to the rhythm of their voices. They had no idea how deeply I absorbed the sensations passing between them. *But there's nothing wrong with me*, I wanted to tell her. I had never been more lucid. It was then, I think, that I realised how much Miss Edith liked me and I grasped that with time and persistence on my part, and help from Malone and

Leboeuf, one day I would understand how Polly's murder was linked to Miss Fielding's trunk.

'Will she be all right?' Miss Edith repeated.

'I think so,' Sarah Derby answered at last. 'I certainly hope so.'

The two women parted, looking at me once again. I turned, catching a glimpse of scarlet and gold. They had caught sight of Polly standing behind me. I smiled, knowing that soon I would see Polly as well.

26

It is after Polly's funeral and I am staring out of a hotel window near Victoria station. Outside it is raining hard, and the rain, solidified by sleet, drums against the windows and runs down like angry snakes. It reminds me of torrential downpours in Accra, when Tawiah, running from room to room, would cover the mirrors of our house on Kuku Hill with my mother's cloths. To keep us safe, she would say. To keep the spirits of our enemies away from our reflections. I wonder what Tawiah is doing now and if it's raining in Ghana, whose mirrors she is covering today.

It's unusual for it to rain so heavily in England, though the greyness of the pavements and the buildings outside, made greyer still by the weather, is not so unusual. Perhaps Mama was right. Perhaps the end of the world is coming and one day very soon we'll meet in heaven. If heaven exists, that is. I don't really care. Nothing is as it was before. Yet I can't help wondering if my mango tree is still alive. And if it is, is it bearing fruit? Or has a colony of fruit bats devoured it as my mother foresaw?

For three days I've been sleeping in a small room adjoining Pa and Nina's larger one. During that time I've tramped through innumerable strange houses in south London with Nina. We've gone from Clapham to Tooting, Putney Bridge to Chelsea, and none of the houses or apartments we've visited are as nice as Graylings. I've kept my opinion to myself but I suspect my indifference has shown. I am bored; deeply bored with the stultifying tenor of Nina's thoughts and feelings. All she can think about is the baby in her womb and the house she wants to live in: its size and the shapes and colours of the rooms. In this regard, she is as demanding as Isobel. She knows what she wants and refuses to settle for anything less.

Poor Pa. I wonder if he realised what he was getting into when he married a Senegalese Executive Administrator: a term that I've discovered is a glorified title for a secretary. Executive Administrator indeed! Mama was a qualified nurse. She spoke English much better than Nina does. And she read books. I've never seen Nina reading a book. She flips through magazines, glancing at models parading in clothes she can no longer wear. I know Nina doesn't read, because she can't spell very well, and she hasn't a clue about African capitals. Only last night I asked her what the capital of Morocco was. She couldn't tell me. She didn't know the capital of Algeria either. Or Tunisia.

Nina: the new Mrs Benson who wants me to call her Mama. I would rather slice out my tongue. I am my mother's daughter. None the less, I'm trying my best to behave, to make the world a better place by passing through it. I'm biting my tongue, attempting to say the right things. Yet I know that I'm letting Pa down. I can't help myself. Take last night, for instance.

The four of us were having dinner downstairs: me, Pa, Nina and the infant inside her, the son Pa wants so badly. He hasn't even been born and yet already he has their cloying, doting attention.

The child started kicking and Nina, a glass of water in her hand, quickly put it down. She closed her eyes. Before a single word passed between them, Pa stretched out his hand, found the place where Nina hurt and rubbed it. His son must have reciprocated his touch. Pa laughed, saying to Nina: 'Little me.'

'And a bit of me too,' she replied. 'Don't forget that, Michael.'

I coughed. Nina put a hand on my arm. I shrugged, pulling away while Pa, trying to draw me into their circle, grinned. 'You're going to have a little brother soon, Ajuba.'

Nina tweaked my ear. I wish she'd stop touching me, fondling me, putting pomade in my hair, saying how nice it is and how pretty I am. I wish she'd stop trying to be my friend.

'Are you looking forward to meeting your brother?' Pa persisted, folding Nina's hand in his, rubbing it against his thigh.

I didn't know what to say, but when I spoke, I knew I'd stumbled on the words Mama would have chosen: the words that hurt stepmothers and errant fathers the most. Smiling at Pa, I said to Nina: 'I don't suppose anyone's told you, but I had another little brother once, Nina. And a little sister. A long time ago before my Pa met you. Babies can die before they're born. And sometimes they die soon afterwards because witches kill them. It makes mothers go crazy. Isn't that so, Pa?'

They didn't smile again after that. They couldn't, because Pa got annoyed and said something about calling the new Mrs Benson 'Auntie Nina' if I couldn't call her 'Mama' as they'd asked me to. He said that in our culture we don't address adults by their Christian names. It's considered rude.

'Is it the same in your culture, Nina?' I enquired.

'Ajuba!'

'Go easy on her, Michael. Give her time. That's all she needs. Lots of love and time.'

Jeez, she makes me want to puke! I wonder if it's raining as much in Devon as it is in London. I wish I was back at school. I'd feel safer at school away from Nina. I'm counting the days till I go back. But before I go, there's something I have to do. I've got to do it. I've got to.

It's simple really, looking into a mirror – if you're not me, that is. But I've got to do it. Just a moment ago, as I watched Nina putting on lipstick at her looking-glass, she beckoned. I turned and ran. She doesn't know that I don't like mirrors. She doesn't know how much they frighten me.

There's a mirror in this room where I'm sleeping. It's in a dark corner attached to a dressing-table. Once I've bolted the door, I'm going to look at it. I don't want Nina coming in and interfering while I'm doing what I've got to do. Though the size she is, I'm surprised she can still walk.

Locking the door, I turn towards the mirror. I'm convinced Mama and Tawiah were wrong about mirrors. The way I see it, it isn't your enemies who come to you through them, but your friends. Why else would they want to talk to you?

Why can't I look at the glass? Why am I staring at pads of hotel stationery instead? After all that I've seen, why am I still such a coward?

I will look. By dint of sheer willpower, I force my gaze upward to a point on the right side of the glass. My own reflection in the centre is of no interest to me. I look at the empty space on the right, determined to see what I want to see; willing it to happen.

Slowly, like a figure forming in mist, she surfaces, and

I touch the cool mahogany of the dressing-table to stop myself reaching out. If I move towards her, I know she will disappear.

The glass clears, revealing the face of a pale, angry child, her eyes flashing blue in a stormy sky. She wears the sweater she wore in Isobel's portrait for Peter, but there is little mischief in her expression today. It is sullen, vengeful, more defiant in death than in life.

'Polly?'

'You took a long time! I thought you'd never look.'

'Are you OK?'

She gives a little shrug, nodding. 'What's with you and mirrors, anyway?'

'They frighten me.'

'You've got problems, kiddo,' she laughs derisively.

'Are you really all right, Polly?'

She gleams with anger. 'Hallo? My bitch of a mother murders me, and she wants to know if I'm all right! Jeez, Aj, give me a break. I thought you, of all people on this planet, would know what I'm feeling.'

'But I do, Polly, I do!'

There is an awkward silence while she gauges the extent of my sympathy. Then I ask the question I've wanted to ask for a long time: 'Does dying hurt as much as loving does?'

'No way!' The child in the mirror starts inspecting the split ends of her hair. Looking up for a moment she says, 'A little, maybe, but not much. It was over quickly.'

'That's what I told Maria. She's sleeping in your bed now, Polly.'

She continues inspecting her hair. Her disdain for Maria Richardson hasn't diminished. Discarding a golden curl with an impatient flick, she looks at me with the cool, disinterested gaze of the vixen we saw in November. 'Aj, you know I miss you, don't you?'

'I know. I miss you too, Polly.'

'And you know that what happened to me could happen to you. You know that, don't you, Aj?'

I shake my head vigorously. 'I'm different to you, Polly. You were special.'

'When it happens you'll wise up. No one's special. And, believe me, it's happening all the time, Aj, like in *True Murder.* People hating each other, doing each other over. Shooting and strangling and knifing each other, beating the shit out of each other. It's fucking *gross*, kid.'

'Gross,' I echo.

'I mean, take Nina.'

A knocking sounds on the locked door.

'She wouldn't hurt me,' I whisper.

The child in the mirror laughs. 'She's not even your real mother. Look what your real mother did. And what Isobel did to me.'

'Nina wouldn't hurt me. She's trying to be nice to me.'

The knocking is getting louder as Nina twists the handle, trying to enter the room. I close my ears to my stepmother's anxious calls. I want to talk to Polly.

'She's mad at you,' hisses the angry child. 'Wait till she gets her hands on you. Listen, you've got to be prepared for everything. You've got to be able to defend yourself, Aj.'

Sensing my uncertainty, the girl imprisoned in the looking-glass becomes belligerent. 'Are you my best friend or not?' she demands.

'You'll always be my best friend, Polly. You know that.'

'Then do as I say. Do it now.'

I pick up a thin steel comb from the dressing-table.

I finger the sharp tip of its handle as Nina rattles the door, calling me.

'Go for it, kid!'

On the verge of opening up, I turn once again to the mirror. 'I will see you again, won't I, Polly?'

'Sure you will. Wherever you look for me, you'll see me. Whenever you want me, I'll be there. I'm your best friend, aren't I?'

'Always?'

'For ever.'

I smile, turning to open the door. At last my eyes have opened and I have seen what my mother saw in her mirror. The steel comb in my hand feels as cold and sharp as one of Isobel's kitchen knives as I slowly open the door to Nina and her unborn child.

LIMERICK
COUNTY LIBRARY

Acknowledgements

My thanks go to Ellah Allfrey at Jonathan Cape and my agent, Clare Conville. My thanks also to friends and colleagues whose encouragement and generosity contributed to the development of this book: Amina Mama, Abena Busia, Harvey Klinger, Cam Provis, Asmaa Pirzada, Annie Paul, Wendy Hollway, Fenella Greenfield, Juliet Annan and Margaret Busby. Finally, a big thank you to my family, and to my editor at Conville and Walsh, Matthew Hamilton, who helped transform an obsession in to an exhilarating voyage of discovery.

www.vintage-books.co.uk